FRANCES-MARIE COKE

WHEN BANANA STAINS FADE

A JAMAICAN FAMILY SAGA OF ADVERSITY AND REDEMPTION

Black Rose Writing | Texas

This is a work of fiction. Names, characters, businesses, places, events, and incidents are either the products of the author's imagination or used in a fictitious manner. Any resemblance to actual persons, living or dead, or actual events is purely coincidental.

ISBN: 978-1-68513-396-2
PUBLISHED BY BLACK ROSE WRITING
www.blackrosewriting.com

Printed in the United States of America
Suggested Retail Price (SRP) $21.95

When Banana Stains Fade is printed in Garamond Premier Pro

*As a planet-friendly publisher, Black Rose Writing does its best to eliminate unnecessary waste to reduce paper usage and energy costs, while never compromising the reading experience. As a result, the final word count vs. page count may not meet common expectations.

Dedication

To the resilient, courageous "Jamaican Family," which despite being described as irreparably broken, remains the backbone of a country still recovering from the violence of its colonial history, and reconciling its enchantment and fortitude with pervasive consequences of poverty, inequity, and violence.

PRAISE FOR
WHEN BANANA STAINS FADE

"Stunning! The first thing that hooked me was the language—lyrical and evocative. This is an engaging and gripping multi-generational story with a strong sense of place, time, and culture. It is everything you want historical fiction to be, to do— immerse you in unfamiliar places and times, put you at the center of the action, and surround you with visual details you can also hear and feel. There are harrowing scenes that clutch the heart, a cast of characters who stay with you, and in the end, there is hope."

–**Karen E. Osborne, author of** *True Grace,*
Tangled Lies **and** *Reckonings*

"*When Banana Stains Fade* will draw its readers into the compelling drama of over four generations of a Jamaican family, told through the lifeline of its women. This saga traces the family fortunes through the journey of a stain – a designation as omen and curse born of fear and ignorance. It travels down a long legacy of self-inflicted pain, rural and urban, from mother to daughter in the grim aftermath of slavery as history's original sin. Her well-drawn characters are victims in these shadows who fight, often blindly, for enlightenment. In a narrative that is hard to put down, Frances-Marie Coke traces both a family's story and the modern history of her island Jamaica, her message ultimately uplifting: "But her glorious little island prevails."

–**Rachel Manley, Author and winner of 1997 Governor General's Award for**
Literature in Canada for *Drumblair: Memories of a Jamaican Childhood*

"Using as her backdrop a rich tapestry of the sweetness, sorrow, pain and pleasures of life in an island community interwoven with social class and skin colour dynamics, Coke has skillfully crafted an intricate saga using sheer poetry to capture the epic narrative of one Jamaican family. This is a must-read! Fiction yes, but with a truth that resonates."

–**R. Degazon-Johnson Ph.D., author of** *Anusha's Gathering*

"Once I started reading *When Banana Stains Fade*, I was completely immersed in this captivating and completely engrossing story. Coke's novel powerfully addresses the story of women who battle extreme abuse, oppression, loneliness, and pain, reflecting ugly truths about their society that force them to accept the value of silence over words.

Without missing a beat, the many unexpected events that follow generations will keep readers consumed all the way to the end, turning page after page to find out "What next?" Among the best novels I've read recently, *When Banana Stains Fade* is a must-read that twists and turns through the battles each character fights for identity, equality, and choice.

Congratulations to the author for creating a roller-coaster of emotion through unexpected events that follow generations!"

–Debra Ehrhardt, actress and playwright, *Jamaica Farewell* **and** *Look What Fell out the Mango Tree*

"This is a brilliantly authentic Jamaican story, but also a story about everything, to be enjoyed by everyone. You become so invested in the fate of this inter-generational family, as they move from country to town, from Jamaica to "foreign," from the 50s to the 2000s, that you can hardly bear to put the book down. Coke's characters stay with you as you appreciate the women, the children, and the men. She does not allow you to take sides, even when you think you should. Her rich, thoughtful description of events that are inherently unpleasant - even dying, reminiscent of Toni Morrison's *Sula* - is sheer genius.

The action and scenery call for a movie, and no need for a sequel as the denouement is totally satisfying. The famed Jamaican resilience and hopefulness will not allow those banana stains to last forever - they absolutely must fade. Coke's incursion into fiction with this first novel leaves you seriously wanting more. This is modern Jamaican storytelling at its best."

–Elaine Douglas-Harrison, Ph.D. author of the soon-to-be published sociology thesis *When Wives Migrate and Leave Husbands Behind: A Jamaican Marriage Pattern*

"Adjectives that come to mind after reading *When Banana Stains Fade* include insightful, captivating, and culturally savvy! Adding to the authenticity of her story, Coke's coherent blending of the island's Creole with standard English evokes feelings of familiarity and nostalgia."

–Jacqueline Bertram, Educator and Veteran teacher of language and Literature

"This engaging historical family saga describes the unmooring of love, societal brutality, and loss of Faith in God, but when the emotional hurricanes are at fever pitch hope comes like a cooling zephyr to the homestead of Idlewild, a speck of a village in rural Jamaica. *When Banana Stains Fade* is an exquisite read that will resonate long after the book is gently set down on the nightstand."

–Lana M. Ho-Shing, author of *The Alabaster Box*

Acknowledgements

I firmly believe that no writer completes a piece of work without help; it may come from persons who are not even aware of contributing to a story that is not yet conceived, or is well on its way. They helped by sharing an insight, an experience, a feeling from deep in their hearts. I am grateful to all who planted a seed in my head that has come to fruition in this novel. Without a doubt, the strongest seeds were planted during my formative years among my own family members, notably my parents Richard and Dorothy, my sisters, and my two grandmothers—one of the seaside and one of the riverside—who among others, shaped my views of my Jamaican world. Deep appreciation to them all, for contributing to my early sense of self and family.

To those who contributed in other specific ways, I express gratitude. I thank Reagan Rothe for believing sufficiently in my story to add me to the growing list of authors published by Black Rose Writing (BRW). To the BRW team for their various contributions to the final product, notably David King for his work on the book design and cover.

A big thank-you to my friends, past students, and book club members who responded without hesitation to my requests for feedback at various stages of the process: Jackie, Karen, Jeff, Stephen, Rachel, Orett, Mark, Berl, Kay, Wyvolyn, Lana Mae, and all those who after reading *The Spirit of Clovelly Park* urged me to keep on writing.

To members of the 2021 "The Art of The Story" fiction workshop, who gave such encouraging feedback about the early chapters and particularly the workshop leader Bob Jenks who walked with me to the end of the final draft, providing expert guidance all the way through.

To everyone else who made a contribution but whom I have unintentionally omitted here, I am no less grateful.

WHEN BANANA STAINS FADE

PART ONE

CHAPTER 1
THE LANDING

Kingston, 2002

One ill-fated decision, three missing years, and at last, Zarah sets her sights homeward. Though she knows coming home will reignite old hurts, her inner voice whispers of possibility. Perhaps she can make amends for the past and usher her family onto a new road, with reconciliation at its end. Her stomach tightens with familiar fear and doubt, mingling with the remorse and longing that rise in her every time she thinks of the family she abandoned so long ago, carried away on the wings of her worst judgments. *Lord, you brought me this close; give me regret, but not doubt and fear.*

Air Jamaica Flight JM16 lurches and swoops as if the pilot has gone blind. The seatbelt warnings light up again. Paper cups swerve and keel over. Zarah's right hand returns to the metal bar under the seat where she had clenched her fingers, draining the blood from her knuckles. Left thumb and forefinger cling to the Saint Christopher medal hanging from the silver necklace her grandmother Naomi had pressed into her palm on her seventh birthday, her message a mere whisper, "Listen good, little girl: Dis is the patron saint of travel. Keep it safe and wear it when yuh travel far." Zarah has cherished her gift more than ever on the last lap of this journey that has been not only the longest, but the one for which it seems she may pay forever. The captain's voice brings her back, "All is well again; please get ready for our descent into Kingston, Jamaica. The time is 4:05." Zarah's sigh merges with two hundred and fifty-one others that break the brief silence.

Brilliant and brazen, the sun is in its finest moment. The Blue Mountains break through the landscape, sporting their seventy shades of green. Glimpses of the island's hills and valleys, its multiple rivers and raging red poinciana trees—even the rusty zinc roofs, bullet-ridden fences, and garbage-cluttered gullies—stir a long-forgotten joy inside her. The stubborn scars from her ugly New York years—murky gray skies, the slushy snow, and the unrelenting cold sealed inside her after winter—battle her effort to absorb her comforting surroundings. But her glorious little island prevails.

A short distance below, the airport revives memories of her last night—the night she walked away from a life that had threatened to suffocate her under the weight of conflict and disappointment. The early months in New York had brought ample proof of how grave her mistake had been, but the readiness and courage to seek home and healing had been slow in coming. Now, she hovers above home, after a narrow escape from becoming the wrong person. Her face against the window, she twists her neck to get a better view of the cobalt waters receding as the aircraft steadies, thuds, and rumbles along the runway. *Please, Jesus, help me manage what is ahead, so things can work for us.*

For weeks, almost identical words had dominated the prayers of her parents Esther and Bradley, who despite their divorce, had always come together to get through the endless years of conflict over Zarah's determination to be with Damien, a boy whom no one except their daughter considered right for her. The one who had badgered God most was Esther's mother, Naomi, or "Grams," as Zarah had called her ever since she could first say the word. With Zarah's arrival at hand, none of the three harbored any illusions about the difficulties they would face welcoming home a daughter and granddaughter whose steady withdrawal from them had culminated with that final callous stride out of their lives. No word from her in three years; not until the peculiar visit five weeks ago, when Donovan McIntosh presented himself at Esther's office door. "I know you know nothing about me, Mrs. Thomas," the earnest young man had said. "I hope that will change sometime. For now, please just hear me out."

"I don't understand; Donovan, you said?"

"Yes, but not a name you would know. I've been Zarah's friend for a few months, and I'm here to ask for something that may be difficult for you; she needs your help—"

"Something happened to her? Is she okay?" Esther's blood pressure surged as she showed the young man inside.

"Things are improving, but Zarah needs to be with you ... with her family. Please help her come home, and the quicker the better. She explained what she could in this."

Barely able to whisper her thanks, Esther took the plain envelope, bracing herself for the words Donovan and Zarah had struggled for hours to put on paper. Incurable mother that she was, Esther resisted rummaging for the story behind the missing years, focusing instead on her daughter's plea for help. The message reopened all the wounds everyone had plastered over to survive the terrible years of silence, but Donovan's urgency convinced Esther.

That evening, with Bradley and Naomi next to the phone, she had called Zarah, her knees buckling from the agony in her daughter's voice. They had kept their tremulous words to the minimum and urged her to get ready to come home. *Even if that wretched boy is out of her life, how much will all these years of trouble with him cost her... and us?*

What will Zarah be like, and how difficult will it be to rebuild their severed bridges? With no answer in view, Esther, Bradley, and Naomi teeter on the narrow ledge between fear and relief, anticipation and dread, hope and resignation. Waiting is all they have.

***

Esther's white Corolla whizzed along the Norman Manley Highway. Her fingers clutched the steering wheel, and a thousand questions raced through her thoughts, bouncing into Naomi's warnings, "Remember, give her time before yuh question her." For days, the tears that had dried up as Esther settled into life without her daughter had slipped out in sullen pairs.

The clock drew her eyes to the dashboard again, but she pressed her fingers against her lips; *calm down; keep it together.* With a minute to spare, the blast of a horn jolted her back into her lane, inches from the peril of the green Fiat speeding past her passenger door. *That blasted phone!* She threw her handbag with its maddening sound behind the seat and fixed her eyes ahead until the enormous sign came into view.

WELCOME TO
THE NORMAN MANLEY INTERNATIONAL AIRPORT
JAMAICA-40 INDEPENDENCE, AUGUST 6, 2002

Smartly dressed as always, this time in avocado-green linen pants, a light beige cotton shirt, and platform sandals, Esther stepped from her car. Aware of the throb in her temples, she grabbed her water bottle, sipped, and swallowed the blood pressure tablet she had neglected all day. *That wretched phone again?* "Bradley?"

"Yes, everything awright?"

"I'm at the airport ... rushing to check the flight now."

Her ex-husband's voice was nervous and weary. "Been trying to get yuh all day to remind—"

"I've been up and down, and I tell you all the while I don't answer this phone unless I can pull off the road. It rang before, and I couldn't even get it from my handbag."

"Sorry; I just needed to talk. This is a hard day, Esther, but try an' stay calm; remember the blood pressure; plus, I wanted to tell yuh I would pick her up or meet yuh out there."

"It will settle down. But what you mean you would pick her up? You didn't think I had to come myself? How it would look if I didn't meet my own daughter?"

"So, I couldn't say the same thing? I'm only her father. Anyway, it don't matter now. Miss Naomi said I could come and check the computer I set up for Zarah, so I'm here."

"But—"

"But what? I shouldn't be here when Zarah come home?"

"I'm tired; do whatever you think is best. I have to see if the flight landed."

Esther and Bradley had settled into an uneasy harmony over the years of trouble, albeit a harmony interrupted by insistent noises from the past. The tension always simmered below the surface, but neither could risk attempts to unearth and resolve it. News of Zarah's unexpected return had brought them together, but their uncertainty about what might come home with her had sparked extra levels of anxiety.

CHAPTER 2
"YES, I'M HOME."

Passengers trickled from the crowded immigration hall, gathering around Carousel 3 as the luggage began its leisurely spin, and their muffled chatter about the turbulence and rough landing grew louder. In the background, Bob Marley's "Three Little Birds" promised "every little thing will be awright," perking Zarah's spirits–until the doubt took over. *Will I ever enjoy birds, or music, or anything again?*

Almost two hours later, the first few arrivals streamed out into the fading Kingston sun. Esther's shoulders were losing their certainty. She drew closer to the display to be sure she had not misread the arrival notices. *Lord, please let her be on the flight, and please help us do what is right if she is.* She wiped the gathering beads of sweat from her forehead and craned her neck over a few shoulders, peering between heads, eager to make out the face she longed to see but feared seeing.

There it was: the vaguely familiar gait of her dancer. Esther swallowed her disbelief as the gaunt young woman dragged an oversized duffel bag, halting along the passageway as if unsure where she was. "Zarah, I'm over here."

Zarah twisted her head from side to side, eager to spot the face behind the tentative voice. As soon as her mother's face emerged from the crowd, she mimed the words, "Hi, Mum" and looked away, first quickening, then slowing her pace, waving every few seconds, as if in disbelief that anyone had turned up to meet her. Mother watched daughter's tentative steps and wondered where her purposeful stride had gone–the strong elegant back, the youthful certainty that once lit up her face.

Esther was already on the move, throwing her words into the air toward her almost unrecognizable daughter. "Wait here while I get the car; look out for a grumpy white Corolla." Glad for the respite to help her process what Zarah looked like, Esther allowed her mind to go back to her friend, who had beseeched her not to look shocked or disappointed, no matter how different her daughter might appear.

Thumping rhythms of reggae and dancehall soared through car windows, as motley drivers pulled up, greeting passengers, reversing into unlikely spaces, and screeching to sudden halts. Zarah picked her way through the crowd, her thoughts fixed on what she would say to Esther when they stood side by side for the first time in three years. In a garish outfit sporting Jamaica's black, green, and gold, an energetic plus-size woman loaded three bulging suitcases, and several oversized cardboard boxes onto the back of a pickup truck. The man behind her pressed down on his horn, forcing his way through the narrow space and scattering everyone in his path.

"Cut out the noise in the people airport, blasted red-Ibo idiot!" a short blubbery man in a purple track suit retorted, shuffling boxes and bags stuffed with trappings of American life. Brass dangled around his neck, everything glistening in sweat. Zarah managed a smile. *Yes. I'm definitely home.*

Esther maneuvered the Corolla into a tight spot, brushed off the passenger seat one more time, pulled up, and jumped past the engine's hum with a quick glance at the luggage.

"That's all?"

"Yes, I don't have … I just brought a few things," Zarah said, a trace of embarrassment behind her words. They reached for each other in a short-lived hug, exchanged awkward glances, and heaved the luggage into the trunk. Esther looked Zarah up and down in disbelief and swallowed her slew of insistent questions.

A long look passed between mother and daughter as they fumbled with their seat belts before Esther floored the gas pedal, her gaze straight ahead. Fearful of what she might see in her mother's eyes, Zarah stole a sideways glance across the space.

CHAPTER 3
ONE UNCOMPLICATED HUG

The clutter of the airport behind, and the Norman Manley Highway ahead, Zarah cracked the unnerving stillness.

"Mummy ... I just want to say ... thanks for letting me come, and for meeting me."

"Letting you come? This is home."

"Still, I'm grateful; I couldn't explain enough in my letter, but I really appreciate you and Daddy for helping me get here. It was hard to say much on the phone, and I didn't thank you enough; I know after everything, you didn't have to let me come—"

"Please, Zarah; let's leave all that for now." They did so until a small voice ventured into the vehicle's half-light.

"So, how are you keeping? What about Grams and Dadd—"

"Grams is well and your father is fine. He would have come for you, but anyway, he may be at the house." *If only I had agreed to make him come; things wouldn't be so tense.*

Afraid that any word, any tone, any elevation of an eyebrow could send the wrong message, each woman swallowed the multiple emotions that threatened to part her lips. Esther navigated the potholes through Windward Road to Mountain View Avenue. Zarah closed her eyes, letting her head fall on the headrest. *At least if I act exhausted, she won't notice how afraid I am, and the questions won't start just yet.* Who could say what words they should have spoken, what gestures shared, what looks exchanged in the small dark space mother and daughter occupied in the thirty-minute drive?

Esther struggled for breath, concealing her confusion at the person next to her, at the tangled paths that had brought them to this eerie stillness. She longed for the simplicity of the old days. It had been comforting to stride through them with Bradley, the husband who had loved her for so long, the father who had been there at every step with their only child. That was before the unraveling, before she set foot on that perilous road that refused to end. *How did I ever get myself into that one reckless episode that brought nothing but chaos into our lives?* How many times had she faced the same question since those fateful three evenings she stole from her real life years ago to catch up with her old flame Patrick? A mere few hours; enough to destroy her marriage and unleash a series of events that brooked no interruption—until Zarah's disappearance.

Now, here they were, close enough to touch across the Corolla's suffocating quietness where each drew into herself. Esther grappled with her daughter's appearance while Zarah remained locked in a lost-and-almost-found box with no keys. Uncertain where to begin, they settled for the wordless ride through the dying sunset to a house Zarah had never seen.

"Almost there," Esther soon announced, relieved to end the apprehension, if even for a few brief moments.

"It's hard to believe you're living in Mona; I passed this place so often to and from campus. Daddy's?" She pointed to the car she had not seen before, pondering how much else would be new.

"Yes, he changed the old one a few months ago. It was on the last cylinder," Esther said with a nervous chuckle. The memory of the family's first car brought smiles to both faces as they recalled the remnant of a former life.

"By the way, you have ... enough space?"

"Of course; your room is ready." Zarah's eyes fell on the long scar along her mother's forearm. She recalled how at six years old she had almost fallen from the veranda step, when Esther rushed to reach her, tripped over an overturned flower pot, and rammed her arm into a sharp bamboo stake.

How she longed to run her fingers along the scar and tell her mother again how sorry she was for the pain she'd caused then–but even more for all the heartache her own ill-judged decisions had rained upon the family.

***

Bradley and Naomi stood together at the front door as the car pulled into the driveway. Naomi still mourned the end of her daughter's marriage to this man. He had been a perfect remedy for the somber young woman that Esther became after finishing high school and starting a drab working life that offered few options. Despite the years of trouble in the family, the bond between Bradley and his "second mother" had never weakened. Uncertainty looming, each drew comfort from the other.

Esther made a beeline toward the car–a safe place to conceal her anxiety and catch her breath. *Thank God he's here.* Bradley and Zarah hurried to each other, a look without a name on each face. She fell into him, and he held her in a long, tight embrace. The corners of Esther's mouth twitched as she eyed them with quiet longing and a trace of annoyance. *How come it's so easy for him after what Zarah did?* She turned her back and fumbled with the bag, but Bradley rushed over and grabbed it. Naomi and Zarah shared the only uncomplicated hug of the evening.

"Zarah, thank God yuh reach home safe! Come here, let mi look at yuh good," Naomi said, withdrawing a few inches for a long look before nesting her granddaughter's head into her shoulders. A whisper brushed against Naomi's ears.

"You smell like home, Grams."

All three sat at the kitchen table while Zarah looked from corner to corner. Just enough furniture adorned the living room–every piece handpicked and set in the right place, with every shade and texture perfectly matched. Each shelf contained a few familiar ornaments and photographs in elegant frames. *Well, one thing hasn't changed; it's all still in straight lines.* Eager to see if there was a picture of her, she leaned in, and her eyes misted: One ... two ... three ... her parents' favorite pictures of her growing up stretched across an entire shelf just as they had done in their only other home at Duhaney Park.

"It's lovely."

"Glad yuh like it," Esther said.

Naomi led Zarah by the shoulder, "Come, stew peas and rice waiting for yuh; it better still be yuh favorite."

"Of course, I still love stew peas, Grams, but I'm not hungry; I promise to eat two servings tomorrow." Her voice was flat, her eyes following the looks her parents and grandmother exchanged. *They will look at each other like that every time I say or do anything from now on.*

Busy with drinks, Naomi paused behind Esther, her fingers closed on her daughter's shoulders in a gesture of support.

"Where can I put this?" Zarah asked, pointing to the luggage, hoping to find a space to exhale. Her mother gestured toward the corridor.

"Second door on the right."

Bradley released the breath he had held too long and walked away with his daughter and her one bag.

"Mama, yuh see her condition? Look how thin and pale she is, like she didn't eat one good meal all these years. How we can find out what happened? I need to know where she was, and why we didn't hear a word all this time."

"She's here," Naomi said. "We have to leave everything else alone for now. Try and mek her feel the only important thing is dat she come home. Remember, we talk about it over and over; leave out the questioning for now."

Both turned to Bradley as he came into the kitchen, Zarah close behind. "Please, everybody," she said, stepping ahead of him. "I need a minute to see if I can get out a few things before I lose my nerve." His nerve already lost, Bradley assured his daughter it could all stay until another time; they could hear little by little. Unsure whether she could manage what they were about to hear, Esther echoed his thoughts. She shot a grateful look at her ex-husband, hoping his words would protect them all from too much knowledge and too little understanding.

"Give her a minute; she can do it," Naomi said, as if Zarah were a little girl again, learning to walk.

"Thanks, Grams," Zarah said, her anxiety rising, her feet shuffling as she turned to face her parents.

"It's hard to know where to start; so much happened. I knew you would figure out I went to be with ... him. It was wrong to leave like that, but the war had gone far enough; I feared what might be next." Her words wobbled, and her heartbeat sped up as it had done on that trip she invented to get away from Jamaica. Could she ever share all that had happened? Pacing the floor, she started, waited, and started again. In her pauses, they held their breath, fearful that whatever was to come would be worse than anything they had imagined.

At breakneck speed, random pieces of the story tumbled out. Esther could not hold back another minute. "My God, Zarah! How long you lived like that? How you could stand being in a place that sounds like Standpipe Lane?"

"It was worse."

"But we know people in Queens; we have relatives there; yuh couldn't find somebody who could tell us you were in trouble?" This time it was Bradley, the tremor in his voice underlining his disbelief.

"I convinced myself it would get better, but every day it got worse. Shame made me vow to remain silent about what my life was like. I felt none of you would want me around, and you would be right. It was disgusting, and it was my own fault for choosing it." Zarah could not go on. Against the support of the window, Esther stared into the darkness, clasping and unclasping her fingers. But her simmering bitterness exploded, and the long-buried disappointment and anger escaped.

"Yes, you did choose ... over and over, and then you walked out on your family and went after that piece of—"

"Esther, this may not be the best time—"

"Daddy, wait; she has a right ... all of you are right to be upset. Perhaps I shouldn't have asked to co—" The resignation in her voice hinted she was about to give up the effort to explain. Bradley moved closer to his ex, feeling what she felt, but terrified of what would happen if they reverted to the old days of constant arguments. Esther shoved his hand away and was about to tackle Zarah again.

"Wait please, Mummy, we all know what I did was ... I don't even know what to call it; and we may never get over it. But I'm begging you to believe this one thing at least: I truly regret what I did. I didn't set out to hurt you, but I was tired of the fight. It was destroying everybody, especially you. I was desperate for a change, and leaving felt like the only way; I figured in a few months, I could explain and make it up to all of you."

Naomi inched closer to Esther, but her daughter stepped away. "So what we were supposed to do in the meantime? Forget we had a daughter and granddaughter? Forget about all the love we poured down the drain; everything we invested in your care and the best upbringing we could manage?" The words cut like a shining knife through the dimness, across to Zarah's feet, her mother's rage spattering everywhere.

Bewildered and exhausted, Zarah racked her brain for the plans she had made with Donovan to deal with whatever might happen when she faced them for the first time. She clawed at the air for the phrases she rattled out on her laptop on the flight home. The words she had practiced struggled to come out, but her lips refused to listen to her brain. Fear weighed down her tongue, and even when she formed the words that seemed right in her head, no sound came. The image of her mother, and her familiar rant, resurrected the angry teenager of the past, slamming her room door, bringing the usual end to their old arguments. Taking refuge in the response that had always been enough, she wrenched herself away from her father, who had drawn closer throughout Esther's outburst.

"I don't know why I thought coming back could work," Zarah said. "I understand if you all can't get over what I did, and I guess everybody was better off without me." With that, she escaped to the perfect room, earmarked for the perfect girl for whom they had waited all those years. But she was no longer that girl; this door was not hers to slam. Without a sound, it closed.

***

"She can't talk anymore right now," Bradley said.

"Neither me; and I can't listen anymore," Esther said. "And the truth is I'm not sure about any of this. God knows I tried to stifle how I feel, but it's too hard."

They watched each other in silence, as a familiar fear crept into their eyes. It was the dread that had enveloped them years before, when Zarah first glared at them with the eyes of a teenager who had lost her trust in them and in the world.

CHAPTER 4
HURRICANE WINDS

Kingston, 1988

At the center of a small predictable world, with Bradley and Esther as her bookends, and Naomi's lap as her sanctuary, Zarah had grown up certain of her right to be there. The ground beneath her feet never tilted; and not once did they break their unspoken promise to take care of her. Her father lived at her side, filling her life with music, safety, and laughter. Whether Zarah was at her parents' humble Duhaney Park home, or at the side of the house her grandmother rented at Ulster Road, she could count on her "grams" to caress her to sleep with warm tales of country women plaiting miles of straw under the light of moonbeams, little girls reaching for peenie-wallies, in their ears, the words of "Yes, Jesus Loves me." Esther showered her with attention, coaxing her every thought and gesture into words, hammering the importance of truthfulness into her head. "No matter what, Zarah; nothing can be too bad to tell me or Daddy." To be "a good girl and do your best" was all the three ever asked of her, and in return, despite their hardships, their reassurances never ended, "you will always be okay."

Before Zarah had arrived on the scene, Esther had taken to heart her early stumble of an unexpected pregnancy outside of marriage, but once she became Mrs. Bradley Thomas, she set her sights firmly on making life better for her family. The child filled up their lives, and by the time she reached thirteen, their dreams, though modest, were well on their way. Esther was a supervisor in the Ministry of Education—one of thousands of ambitious Jamaicans who worked their way from poor rural origins into the up-and-coming lower middle class swelling the outskirts of Kingston. Bradley progressed into the senior technician rank at the phone company and looked set for a secure future. He bore no resemblance to the common stories about wild and irresponsible Jamaican men.

Every month, they set aside enough from their wages to cover "two hands" in the office partner, the old-time "community bank" Naomi had inveigled Esther to join from the first time she earned a paycheck. Naomi taught her to sew, and as she progressed at work, the outfits she wore always topped the agenda for daily office chatter. She had little money to spend on clothes, but her taste and money management were impeccable.

Zarah had just the basics, but her shoes shone from generous doses of Nugget polish, and her clothes sparkled after Esther's rigorous hand washing and ironing. Her parents pinched their pennies to provide her with the necessities for school and dance classes, where she excelled from the start. Though they rented a modest house in Duhaney Park, Esther decked it out like her own little castle, with Zarah's room a tiny fairy-tale kingdom. Bradley made steady payments into his workplace credit union, and every month they eyed the balance in their special "no more rent" fund. They celebrated their anniversary with the first mortgage on the same tiny house, delighted to become the first in both families to stop paying rent. An incredulous Naomi smiled when Bradley said, "... is really the credit union own it, but we don't mind."

That same year, Zarah celebrated her teenager status with a party for four friends, and there was no happier girl in Jamaica.

"It was the best party ever! You rock, Mummy and Daddy! Thank you soooo much! Daddy's music and old-time games, cake and ice cream and cheese crunchies ... my friends said it was totally cool." Bradley leaned against the creaking door, watching his two girls and smiling as if a red Honda Acura with his name had arrived at his gate.

"She's right, Esther. You are the best."

"Thanks, guys; you know I couldn't do less for our girl—our government scholar, winner of so many seventh-grade prizes, and now a teenager." Bradley lifted Zarah in the air, and all three did a little jig.

***

Days after the party, Esther was busy clearing paper from her handbag when the business card fell to the floor: *Patrick Prendergast. Sales Agent.* Her old flame, from what seemed like a century before, had pressed it into her hand when they surprised each other as she rushed in and out of shops, on the hunt for cheap party supplies.

"Esther? Is really you? Girl, you look better than ever."

"Of course, it's me; but how come you're here? I thought you were in Fort Lauderdale." Patrick was full of excitement as always, but being preoccupied with her to-do list, Esther hurried him through his barrage of words about his exploits overseas.

"Oh, he's just a guy I used to know," Esther told her friend, who had seen the quick exchange.

A week later, Esther fingered the letters of his name, reliving memories of the brief but torrid relationship they had shared, the storms it created with Naomi, and the suddenness with which it ended when she found herself pregnant with Bradley's baby. About to tuck the card in her address book, she glimpsed the message on the back: *I'm here for a couple weeks; call me.* It faded from her mind, but as her routine returned, his face flashed before her, a nagging reminder of his suave talk, his smooth dance moves, his wild plans for the future. *We are big people carrying on with life; so what's the harm? I'll call and hear what he has to say; it will be nice to chat about old times.*

***

Even as the sunset threw its orange glow across the Kingston sky, Esther saw no harm in having a nice dinner with an old friend. Between the taxi and the hotel, she smiled to herself. *Bradley will have a good laugh when I tell him about this.*

High above New Kingston, on the top floor of the Pegasus Hotel, Patrick and Esther punctuated the sumptuous meal with safe details about their lives. The second Wray & Nephew rum cream added a special ring to her laughter at his endless jokes. Across from her, he downed a third glass of vodka and eased his chair closer to her in the soft light of the far corner. Pride all over her face, Esther updated him about the diplomas she had gained, and her promotions at work, reminders of her ambition and her many goals from years before, when neither of them had much.

"You were always a go-getter, so listen to me: I can't count how many good jobs you could ... you and your husband could get in Fort Lauderdale. People from Jamaica with your experience and job training get great opportunities over there and believe me, they live better than here!" His enthusiasm stirred vivid recollections of the reasons she had found him so attractive back then.

A part of her longed for the life he described: roads without potholes, high-rise office complexes and fancy malls, big houses without grilles to keep out thieves and murderers. Life with Bradley had been a struggle from the start, but the light that Zarah had brought always distracted Esther from the dullness of their own relationship. Caught up in making ends meet, they had never been to dinner in a hotel, and she could not recall the last time they had shared an evening out. *It's so hard in Jamaica; every day the dollar going down and prices going up; everywhere is dirty; this place getting worse and more dangerous every day.*

She had always been the one in her marriage whose eyes roamed outside of their limitations, on the lookout for more opportunities, more adventures, more achievements. Bradley's eyes had already seen all he wanted, and he was at peace with where they had reached; Esther wished he would want more out of life. Patrick's presence had her wondering for a quick minute what life would be like with a husband who had his ... spirit. On her wrist, Bradley's inexpensive Christmas present caught her eye, and she reached for her purse. "This was nice, but I have to go."

When Patrick helped her up, and his hand lingered in hers, she did not move. When he drew her close to him, she let the Brut cologne fill up her senses, rekindling the twinge she felt the first time he pulled her to him at Carib cinema and all the times after that in his souped-up Ford Escort. Had there ever been a twinge like that with Bradley, or just his reassuring steadiness that bordered on boredom?

Before it hit her, they were in Patrick's hotel room, where she spent the next two evenings awakening sensations she had switched off after their first dalliance came to an abrupt end with her unplanned marriage. Nothing prevented them from expressing it all—nothing except the worlds they occupied, the lives they had separately built. In a display of passion that startled even her, Esther seemed to abandon all thoughts of her husband and daughter at home. Patrick was all she had imagined but never experienced while they had been together years before. His body was decisive and urgent; it brought a responsiveness they had only guessed at before. On the third evening, they mouthed quick promises, impulsive pledges to stay in touch. From an interlude she would not soon forget, a woman unknown to Esther walked away to confront the real life she feared would always fall short.

The next day, an unexpected Hurricane Gilbert loomed near the island and picked up speed as if a deadline popped into its head. The TV weatherman predicted a definite hit, but as usual, arguments raged among know-it-all Jamaicans about whether it would strike. Supermarkets and hardware shops teemed with people in search of essentials. In Sunday's twilight, traffic had ground to a standstill at all the major intersections. Cars spilled out of gas stations where their drivers paced around, or leaned on their open doors tapping their fingers, all the time in fear that the operator would say supplies had run out.

Her valuables stuffed into her grip and everything secure on her side of the Ulster Road house, an anxious Naomi waited for Bradley to pick her up.

"Is what yuh have in here, Miss Naomi? Mi can't even budge it," Bradley said, with a grunt as he lifted the suitcase to put it in the back of his little

Lada car. They were off to Duhaney Park, where Naomi would wait out whatever Gilbert brought.

***

On Sunday night, Air Traffic Control grounded all flights, and Patrick paced the floor in his hotel room at the Pegasus, scouring the fine print on his ticket to Fort Lauderdale.

Half-hearted showers started early on Monday, soon strengthening to a steady rumble and then a furious deluge, overflowing drains and gullies, washing away everything it could move. Giant fireworks lit up the sky. The soughing wind whipped itself into a frenzy of fierce gales that lashed hour after hour, bringing down small and large structures. They shattered windows and doors, cracked electricity poles, uprooted giant trees, and tossed them wherever they wished. Between frantic safety duties, house-bound residents peeked through masking-tape strips across shaky windows as Gilbert's rage tossed hapless roofs across the city, landing them in treetops, wedging them between sturdier structures.

Against the thunderous rage, thirteen-year-old Zarah turned into a fretful skittery bird. She hid, ran, and shrieked with every flash of lightning. Bradley consoled her, occupying her with board games and made-up stories. Naomi prepared dinner, and all three watched Esther tiptoe around the house like a shackled prisoner.

The rattle against the walls, the restlessness of Zarah, and the nearness of Bradley and her mother bore down on Esther, who longed to escape into the deluge. Her skin itched for Patrick, but her insides threatened to explode with shame and guilt. Her husband became someone to stay as far away from as possible, and except for Zarah's hundreds of unanswerable questions, Esther bore her turmoil in isolation–until she faced Naomi's insistence that something was "just not right." She did her best to sidestep her mother's probes, blaming Gilbert for her anxiety. Out of the corner of her eye, Naomi tracked her every move.

***

Across the island, people stepped out to face the remnants of Gilbert's rage: houses in shambles, giant potholes, satellite dishes and roofs lodged between uprooted trees and crumbling walls. Scores of people were unaccounted for and several were dead. Young people regretted their desire to witness a hurricane, and old people said, "Hurricane Charlie was a boy to this!"

As the weeks dragged on and everyone settled into new routines, Zarah nagged her mother for the attention she needed. A perplexed Bradley glanced at his wife, certain Gilbert's dislocation did not account for her preoccupation and bad temper.

"How many times are you going to ask what's wrong with me, Bradley? You don't see how life is hard since Gilbert?" Esther asked, her irritation palpable. "People on the radio talk all day about the hardship everywhere."

"Of course, I see," Bradley said, "and I hear everything, but most people trying, and even though things are bad, we managing better than plenty other people."

The knob on their bathroom door no longer turned at his touch, confirmation that his wife was no longer comfortable with him in her space. Reflected in the full-length mirror, her body sagged on their bed, shielding itself behind the unyielding, invisible wall between them.

CHAPTER 5
RED STAINS ON A WHITE TILE

Kingston, 1988

Three months went by before a few areas in Kingston got back electricity and water. But the landscape still bore wounds, and anyone could forgive a visitor for thinking building blocks with stones holding down tarpaulins were the roofs of choice. In the absence of television, the children of Duhaney Park discovered outdoor games that kept them outside until well past their old dinner times. Jaded couples looked with fresh eyes at each other, under skies lit up by the moon and the stars, no longer dimmed by the bright city lights. In the semi-darkness of kerosene and battery lamps, Bradley and Esther felt none of the romantic sparks some couples giggled and murmured about.

Although between the Pegasus sheets Patrick had convinced her they could and should have more than a few days together, Esther never expected or wanted to be in contact with him. Now she longed to hear his favorite words, "We can work it out; just give it some time." They plagued her, convincing her they could have more. But there was no way to talk to him. Relieved to be back at work, she was soon overwhelmed with arrangements to deal with the impact of the hurricane on schools. Damage was everywhere, complete destruction commonplace across the island's schools. But no distraction could dislodge the image of Patrick's face from her mind. Nothing could soothe her ache for the thrill of his skin against hers, his breath on her face, his hands everywhere.

"Daddy, Daddy, Grams, come quick," Zarah said between screams, "something bad happen!" They found Esther half-crouched over the bathtub. "Look, Daddy, blood." Her mother's skirt soaked up some of the thick red, and the rest formed an ominous pool. Bradley rushed to her side, in panic at his wife's distress.

"What happen to yuh?" Naomi asked, on her knees splashing Esther's face with cold water. Knees tucked into her stomach, she writhed and groaned. Her mother roused her with smelling salts, more aware of serious trouble as the minutes passed. Bradley took her to the bedroom, dark red stains trailing his footsteps across the bone-white tiles.

"Dis don't look good at all, Bradley. Yuh better take her to the hospital."

"No, no; it's okay ... the usual business; I didn't eat ... felt weak, that's all."

From the passageway, Zarah watched, her mind racing with thoughts that made no sense. Although in her head she understood some of her mother's words, somewhere else inside her, a dark feeling lurked–*I bet nothing will be the same after this.*

"What going to happen now, Grams?" she asked, her place under Naomi's arm feeling less safe than before. "Suppose Mummy gets worse?"

"Hush chile," Naomi said, fingers running through Zarah's hair. "Don't put all dat on yuh head at all. It will soon be awright." Naomi's voice reeked with uncertainty.

For weeks, she had eyed Esther picking at her food and rushing to the bathroom. Her body had changed in subtle ways only an experienced woman could understand. Despite the years since Zarah's birth, her grandmother hoped a baby might be on the way, but why the secrecy? How could the hurricane be the true cause of Esther's unusual behavior? When Naomi had asked what was troubling her after Gilbert, Esther made up the same improbable story about depression and worry, so Naomi left her alone. Now, her instinct said something awful was happening. Bradley woke to see his listless wife on a sheet soaked in blood, and there was no denial. They bundled Esther up and headed for the Accident and Emergency Department. With his wife settled down and past immediate danger, Bradley took Naomi and Zarah home.

A young doctor stood at Esther's bedside when Bradley re-entered the room a few hours later, just in time to hear his words. "I'm sorry, Mrs. Thomas. We couldn't do any more for your baby, but you will soon be okay. I'll just update the chart and the nurse will bring some medication to help you sleep; you will feel a little better after a good rest. I'll see you later today, and we'll decide if you have to stay for a day or two. Good night; sorry, good day, Mr. Thomas." Bradley's answer took its time.

"Morning, Doctor. Thanks for your help."

Across the room, Esther's face confirmed the fear that had overtaken Bradley after his rough mental arithmetic. His wife had lost a baby; he had not. With a distraught glance at the unfamiliar woman who fixed her eyes on the far gray wall, he left the room without a word.

CHAPTER 6
THE YEAR WITHOUT CHRISTMAS

Kingston, 1988

With few prompts, Esther admitted to the affair she called "meaningless," with the man she refused to name. "It doesn't matter who," she said, "it was my stupid mistake, and it must be hard to believe me, but I didn't plan it. I would never set out to do something like that. You will never know how sorry I am."

"Right; I hear yuh, but only one thing really matter," Bradley said, "yuh wanted something I didn't give yuh; is a pity yuh couldn't respect and trust mi enough to know yuh should tell mi...and I would do something about it."

Esther wanted to protest, to deny, to undo the hurt she had caused him, but the words eluded her. An unfamiliar force drew them into a grim rhythmless silence, broken only by heavy sighs and grunts. Against the margins of their bed, they abandoned their end-of-day planning and catch-me-up talks, groping for refuge in the empty television screen and pages where words ran into one another. After hours of broken sleep, Esther hugged her pain in the quiet of dawn, fingering her unspeakable grief. It made no difference that she was unaware of the baby conceived in her reckless encounter with Patrick, or how unlikely it was she could have kept her child. She still ached for the lost parts of herself. She bit down on her lips until fresh blood leaked between her teeth, but the tears still escaped, a mirror of the soundless well in Bradley's eyes.

It was almost as difficult for her to meet the stares of her mother, who saw to her physical needs and tried to provide the comfort and reassurances a miscarriage warranted. But it puzzled Naomi that Bradley and Esther did not seem to share the loss. What seemed like a sudden distance between them soon became overt hostility, and it was no surprise to find Esther in one of her many episodes of distress. "It must be awful to lose a baby; but yuh have to tek time and heal; and draw close to yuh husband. Yuh don't think this hurt him too?"

"It's hard to be close to him right now; I can't explain."

"Yuh might believe a man can't fully understand how yuh feel, but yuh know dat Bradley is different—"

"Mama, please stop. It's not him; it's my fault. I can't explain, and this will upset you, but yuh have to know. Bradley soon won't be around; we need to be apart for now, hopefully, just for a short time."

"Apart? At a time like this?"

"We have to do it; I can't say anymore now. Please just help us keep Zarah settled after we tell her; I know she will take it badly."

Memories of her daughter's anxiety and tension over the weeks between the hurricane and the incident on the bathroom floor helped Naomi stitch a patchwork of hints together, but she no longer wanted to find the missing pieces. All attention turned to Zarah, who sensed something awful was about to happen; and she waited–for what, she didn't even know; she knew only that she feared it more every day.

***

Schools reopened, and her new routines kept her occupied, but nothing could prevent what was ahead. Her father tried his best to explain as he drove her home, planting his words against the noise and the maze of lunchtime traffic.

"It won't make any difference to us Zarah; yuh will see mi every day."

"No, Daddy, stop it; Don't tell me that! I need you at our house like always."

"I'm sorry, baby girl; yuh mother and mi agree; it's just not good for mi to stay there right now."

"But why? And how long 'right now' will last? Me and Mummy need you ... and you know Grams will soon go home? Don't leave us, Daddy, please. Why the two of you have to agree on everything bad?" Her hands beat against the dashboard, and tears stained her cheeks as her wiry little body squirmed in the seat.

"Sit back, Zarah, right now!"

"How we can stay safe in the house without you?" Zarah's mention of safety struck a chord with Bradley. He had agonized about the same problem, but the situation was impossible, and he didn't know how to fix it.

"Yuh are a big girl now, and yuh can try to understand. Sometimes, parents can't explain what's going on; big people need time to work things out."

"Things like what? And what about what I need?" Zarah was no longer keen on bravery, and if being grown up meant accepting other people's awful decisions, she wanted no part of it. "Daddy, please. I don't want to be like the children at school who live all over the place."

"It won't be like that, I promise. Yuh will live same place in yuh own room at home; and every day, we will spend time together."

***

They agreed a Saturday morning would be least difficult for Zarah. Esther found work to keep her at the office, where she could be safe from all eyes. The last thing Bradley hurled into his friend's pickup with his stereo and music collection was an old suitcase stuffed with his clothes; the one he took to the rented rooms he moved into with Esther on the night of their quick wedding. With nothing left to say, Zarah never left her room. *What's the use of questions and promises to behave? What children say don't make any difference. Parents not supposed to tell lies, but nobody can make me believe they're not doing that.* After several knocks on the door, Bradley gave up. "Talk to you later," he said, loud enough to bring his daughter to the door, but instead of opening it, she turned the lock. He handed Naomi a telephone number for his cousin's house in Havendale. "Call me anytime, Miss Naomi, and we can talk. I'll stay there until I work out something." They squeezed each other's hands, and he was gone.

"But why Daddy have to go?" Zarah said, while Naomi tried to console her even as her own anxiety peaked.

"Yuh will soon understand, chile; right now, yuh mother still not well, but she have to work, so I'll be here to give a hand. I promise I will look after yuh and help keep everything together. Don't fret yuhself; everything soon get better." For the first time, the child looked into her grandmother's eyes and hated the lies that lurked there.

***

The Christmas breeze wafted through the trees and blew the sun-dried leaves across the sidewalks. Poinsettias shed their fading greens for the rich red coats they sported over the festive season. Most of the city and big towns had electricity and water, though telephone service was still creeping back to normal. When Patrick eventually called Esther at the office, she asked the telephone operator to say she was not available. His efforts did not last long; despite his protestations, he was still the old cavalier Patrick Naomi had warned her about many times years before. None of it mattered to Esther; like so much else, that was that.

For most of Jamaica, Christmas was a poor imitation of the usual festivities. Esther avoided all but casual conversations with Naomi. Her mother ached for a sign that could allay her suspicions about the lost baby and the absent husband, but she left it alone. With a sinister distance between them, the holidays were a disaster for Esther and Zarah.

CHAPTER 7
"TWO GLASSES AND ONE MUG"

In the new year, Zarah immersed herself in school and dancing, and the months swept by. Her fourteen-year-old logic led her to conclude that after girls reached her age, adults made no sense. She couldn't figure out what to make of all that had happened in the long months behind her. Did parents celebrate their daughter's first birthday as a teenager, come through a hurricane together, and then glare at each other with what looked like hate, until one packed up and left? And why couldn't her mother look her in the eyes? With no sign of answers, she took solace in her room, her retreat to the world of Nancy Drew and Sweet Valley High.

Despite Zarah's aloofness, and even hostility at times, Esther set about building a bridge back to her child. She did all she could to make Bradley's interaction with Zarah easy. As long as he stayed with his cousin, they continued to hope he might still return home. But when he picked up Zarah at school and took her to a different house, she knew it was a bad sign. She waited to see who lived there, but the front of the house seemed empty. With a shiny key, Bradley opened a door at the back. With gaps between his words, he showed her around, picking at the flesh in the corner of his thumb nail, peeling little edges of skin until there were signs of blood. His daughter had seen those telltale signs enough to know things were hard for him. They confirmed the sadness this awful new place already suggested. Pieces of his music system stood disconnected in the corner, and the records lay strewn all over the bedroom, unlike their neat categories at home.

"They call the place Meadowland," Zarah said, when she reached home.

"You're sure he moved all his stuff from Uncle Martin's house to that new place?"

"It looks like all of it is there, but is not much."

Their eyes went to the space where Bradley's music and its paraphernalia had always been arranged in neat categories on his home-made shelves–a space Esther never filled, no matter how many times she reorganized the small area. All hope of his return sputtered and died. Struggling to breathe, Esther reached out to pull Zarah into a hug, but her daughter broke away, ran out the door and sat on the back step. She wrapped her arms around her knees and rested her head on them.

Zarah ignored her mother's every overture. In her head, bits and pieces tumbled around, snippets of what her parents and Naomi had told her after the bathroom incident. She understood her mother lost a baby, but she never entertained the stories about "old disagreements" causing Bradley to move out. All she knew was she hated his absence, and her introduction to the dump where he lived. *How Daddy can feel at home at the side of somebody's house in one little room, and half a kitchen with his things all over the place. No space at all; I won't even be able to stay there with him sometimes.* When Esther tried again to embrace her, she pulled away and flew off the steps. As if disconnected from her brain, her arms sprang from her sides, and her fists pummeled Esther's chest. "Is you cause all this! Why you didn't leave instead of Daddy? I wouldn't even miss you!"

"Zarah stop it!"

"No, I don't want to stop it! Daddy living in a shabby little room; the bathroom is nasty, not even a mat on the floor. Two glasses in the little kitchen area ... imagine ... two glasses and one mug I give him for Father's Day."

"I know it hurts. Come, let us—"

"I don't want to do anything with you; leave me alone. You caused the whole thing."

Esther shoved her daughter's hands to her sides and drew her unyielding body close, as if to squeeze the anger out of her. "I'm sorry he left, but please understand; I didn't tell him to go."

"Seriously? Then what you did? Why nobody won't tell me why everything gone wrong?"

"Because we just can't; you wouldn't understand; when you're older I can explain but not now."

In that moment, the truth hit her–the time for her father to be back home would never come. And the last remnants of the little girl inside her disappeared; only the acrid taste of disappointment and anger remained. *So, this is what parents do; they promise you the world, and leave you stranded. I will never believe her again–and I will never do what she did to Daddy; imagine just chasing away somebody that love you!*

The bell rang to end the second period on Monday and, while her clique waited for the teacher to arrive with her endless drone about the history of the Morant Bay Rebellion, Zarah floated a few harmless questions about the latest developments with her friends and their parents. A slew of advice followed, about how parents behave and what she should do to insulate herself. "Don't upset yuhself, girl," said Toni-Ann, "from we get in a good high school, parents don't worry about us again ... only if we get in big trouble, or we get sick." Everyone was quiet as she filed her nails, until a sniffle intervened, "What yuh crying for now?" Toni-Ann asked, turning to Rachel. The girl hesitated, but she had to speak.

"You and Zarah lucky: at least yuh have fathers yuh see; from I was seven, my so-called father ignore me and Mummy."

"That's how all of them operate–more or less," said Toni-Ann, a new gravity in her tone. *No; Zarah thought; Daddy never ignored me, and before all this crazy business, Mummy wasn't like that either.*

With Bradley gone and Naomi back home, Duhaney Park longed for lightness and laughter. Although Zarah seemed less and less inclined to be near her, Esther still tried to talk to her about everything–except how she felt or whatever went on with her and Bradley. "Chief Organizer" was still her job title, ensuring Zarah had all the necessities. Her surprise treats still turned up in the school lunchbox, along with frequent inspirational notes. She persisted with her long talks about growing up and how to deal with issues, but although her daughter had to pretend to listen, her thoughts were somewhere else.

It was all part of Esther's promise to herself that she would raise no daughter of hers the way Naomi had brought her up. As a little girl, Zarah heard "the facts of life" in bite-size pieces, making her the expert among her friends on what they needed to know but never heard because their own mothers zipped their lips in fear, ignorance, or indifference. Zarah's responses had included words like "gross" and "yuck," but when the girls giggled after biology class or questioned what they picked up elsewhere, she always set them straight about the facts earning comments like, "How you know all that, Miss Zarah?" followed by "Girl, you don't know Zarah mother tell her everything?"

Since her disastrous mistake with Patrick, Esther was even more determined to be as open as she could be with Zarah, but the new situation made her timid. It was not just because of guilt and concern about what its repercussions would do to her child. Stories about teenagers rebelling, climbing through windows, and staying out until close to morning, increased her anxiety all the time. Zarah had never given trouble, but Esther was afraid her own actions, and the long period of tension, along with Bradley's absence, would tip her over to the wrong side.

Night after night, she woke in terror, heart racing and throat dry, overcome with fear her punishment would be one disaster or another. An unforeseen rage stood up in Zarah more and more often, setting Esther on edge. It was a fury of which Esther never knew her child would be capable, especially directed at her. Constant worry, and fear of Zarah's simmering resentment, blinded her to the darkening cloud that wedged itself between them. Nowhere was it more visible than in the teenager's eyes, where a light had gone out.

CHAPTER 8
A NEW COMPANION FOR ZARAH

Kingston, 1990s

Saturdays and Sundays brought Zarah's most dreaded moments. The days stretched out, and she felt as if she were in detention with her mother as supervisor. The eerie quietness in the house was unbearable. Gone were Bradley's music, laughter, and cheerfulness–his constant assurances something better was just around the corner. All of him was gone, and nothing could ever be enough to make up for his absence.

House cleaning and folding laundry were no longer times for games with Esther, who soon became a slave to bleach, Ajax, steel wool, and the straight lines Zarah hated: *Every piece of furniture, every glass, and cup–even the little figurines have to be spotless; stretch out like soldiers on parade at camp.* Ever a stickler for order in the house, Esther recited her rules and complaints, making her daughter sick. "Come back here, young lady; you turned the top sheet the wrong way; do it again. Anything worth doing is worth doing well." *Seriously? Who care if the hem on the sheet turn up or down? I'm not taking a bed spreading exam.*

With Bradley's spirit and lightness gone, and her mother replaced by this obsessed stranger with the eyes of a trapped animal, the house became a chilly box in which the fifteen-year-old was a misfit. Once the place for stories, board games, books, music and new dance moves, her room turned into a silent cave from which she excluded her mother every chance she got. Every excuse took her from picking bones from saltfish for Sunday morning fritters, and making poetry out of recipes while Esther collected ingredients and utensils for Sunday bake-offs.

Esther ran out of the patience and energy to induce and complain. Enrolled in a part-time program to get her degree in public administration, she came home later and later. There were study group sessions, weekend workshops, one seminar or another. Someone else was in charge of the cold Duhaney Park house: Six-feet-one, 230-lb. Miss Lucretia Bodden, a "mature, experienced woman" had ended Esther's search for help with the housework and Zarah's supervision. In a voice that matched her massive frame, Miss Lucretia announced her own rules, and Esther put absolute trust in her no-nonsense approach. Lack of respect for household helpers made it quite common for even young children to call them by their first names, but even if Esther had not instructed Zarah how to address the new helper, no one who needed to face the woman's forbidding eyes would have the temerity to utter her name without "Miss" before it.

When Zarah and her friends came from school to work on homework projects, they would run past Miss Lucretia, heading straight to Zarah's room, but the housekeeper would summon them right back for her stern admonition. "But what is this? Nowadays pickney don't learn manners at home again? Look how mi stand up right here, and all of yuh pass mi like a full taxi, without so much as 'good evening'? What use school learning and nice talking have, without a scrap of manners?"

"Sorry, Miss Lucretia, we never see you, Mam," the girls would say in a sing-song tone, snickering as they headed off to Zarah's room. Before long, loud knocks would bring an annoyed Zarah face to face with the grim Miss Lucretia.

"Tell mi something, Miss Zarah, is not homework all of yuh come in here to do? How schoolwork can go on in there with all dat chatting and laughing and chaka-chaka music? Mek dem stop the skylarking, for hard-ears pickney always eat rock stone."

"What she mean?" the girls asked in one voice.

"Who knows?" Zarah said with a heavy sigh. "Miss Lucretia is the queen of Jamaican proverbs that nobody can understand." Zarah's words brought the helper right back.

"It mean pickney who won't listen always suffer, so pay attention when big people tell yuh what is right."

By the time Zarah settled into eleventh grade, the routines were dry in their cement. Long lists of chores and reminders decorated the fridge door. Most days found mother in a rush to work and studies, daughter hustling to school with her father, and housekeeper managing everything else. Bradley transported Zarah everywhere, and Naomi's visits decreased. Almost every one ended with her handbag and a huff as she headed to the bus stop, after inevitable arguments with Esther about how busy she was with "the damn office work and the endless book work."

"You don't see it's all to make a better future for us, Mama?" Her mother flounced and hissed, anger camouflaging her deepest fears of the consequences of this coldness and distance between Esther and Zarah.

"A better future? What about now? What sense it mek to prepare for a better future, and right now this chile spend more time with the helper than with yuh?"

Zarah accumulated school reports with excellent grades and received accolades at every awards ceremony, easing the anxiety of her parents, who dispensed rewards and steady doses of praise. Unimpressed by their shows of approval, their daughter smiled, still harboring suspicions about everything good that happened to her. She stood still for their hugs and accepted their mementoes, but her eyes remained empty.

Aware their sixteen-year-old had accomplished more than most of her peers, and assuming the worst had passed, Esther and Bradley loosened their grip and paid less attention to her world; and Zarah was a clever girl. Her strategy was to build up so much credit with them through her apparent compliance and her accomplishments, they would stop breathing down her neck. But emotionally, she kept her distance. *No way those two will get the chance to turn my life upside down again.* Her room was her best friend, and she learned to keep conversations with everyone on the surface. Her solitude swaddled her in a secure space, where she staved off the danger of caring too much and battled to keep the strands of herself together.

Naomi sensed danger in Zarah's closed door and the wide spaces in the house. The situation troubled her because her own life had started after her mother Pearlie found herself disconnected and afraid just like Zarah. Of course, Pearlie had lived in a half-finished room with her parents Agatha and Mas' Winston, amid the destitution of a dry banana field in long-ago Oracabessa. Yet, even now, as Naomi considered the misfortunes she and her mother had lived through, an old sore festered between her ribs and stayed there until the nausea surfaced. The growing distance between Esther and Zarah brought back all her old fears. How could she let them know her story was theirs too—that they must learn the lessons from it? Lifting the thin veil between present and past, she let her mind travel to the world she could still see, through the eyes of her mother—a fifteen-year-old country girl with none of Zarah's privileges.

CHAPTER 9
THE WRONG CHILD

Oracabessa, Early 1900s

Oracabessa River was unrelenting; it flowed alone and unnoticed unless the rain stayed away, and the water dipped so low, the mud seeped into the children's water pans. Through centuries of snaking through ageless trees, bamboo roots, and cocoa leaves, it had borne witness to the beginnings of the island, the unspoilt beauty of its landscapes, the simplicity of its Taino Indians, and their near decimation through one foreign occupation after another. It had heard, too, the lament of Africans captured and enslaved by the British, intent on extending the glory days of King Sugar.

The river had cast its watchful eyes as the death of sugar loomed, ushering in the scramble to "free" slaves and rid their owners of responsibility for the thousands no longer needed to fuel production after King Sugar lost its dominance. Released into near destitution with little preparation and few resources, ex-slaves struggled for limited places on dying plantations in the sugar belt, but many refused to work in conditions still too similar to slavery. Others turned to plowing scrawny banana fields spread out against the splendor of a country left to languish. Undaunted, the river meandered still, through valleys and hills, emptying its tales into the cobalt blue of the Caribbean Sea, as it frilled and swirled around the skirt of Oracabessa.

Agatha had lived all her life in the sleepy town, never a day without the murmur of the river and the crashing waves of the sea. She believed in God and her father, whose two threadbare khaki suits bruised her fingers as she washed and ironed them. He wore one on his daily trips to the banana ground, one on brisk Friday night walks to the village bar. For his arguments with Parson Blakely every Sunday after service, she ironed his one white shirt. Of other men, Agatha knew nothing but what the older women warned young girls about: "Most man wicked and bad, or at least dem just come in and out of woman life like a shadow. Yuh have to just tek dem as yuh see dem."

Young Agatha never believed Mas' Winston would be a shadowy man in her life; her father said this was a solid farmer on whom Pastor relied for ground provisions for harvest service, the thanksgiving held every year at the Redemption Baptist Church. Apart from Christmas and Easter, this was the only time when the little church was lively and colorful. But Mas' Winston never stayed for the festivities. Before service, he deposited his green bananas and retired in the back bench where he sat every Sunday.

Afterwards, he slipped out and made his way home, where he picked up an old clay jar, washed it, filled it with water, and set off for the banana field. In the blue cambric shirt already worn out by his deceased older brother, he culled a few stems of red ginger from the back of his one-room house, replaced the jar from the previous Sunday, and sat until noon at the graves of his mother and father, alongside the one with their first-born son.

When Agatha was of age, Mas' Winston had a word with her father and received his blessing to take her home. The young farmer gave her the two children Eudora and Pearlie and left them all to "woman business." He labored long hours among his few fragile banana trees, stripping their barks and bearing their stains all over his hands and clothes. There was little to his life apart from his days at the two-by-four banana ground the last son of a long line of English merchants named Harker left Mas' Winston's family. Even as a boy, he had continued what his grandfather and father started, tending the stony ground, long after the Harkers returned to England and his parents died.

Agatha had her two girls a year apart in the one suffocating room, but Mas' Winston toiled little by little to add another. After Eudora and Pearlie came along, Agatha knew life would get harder, so she doubled her work to help her man. It was the future for which her father had prepared her all those years since her mother gave up the battle against a fever no medicine would cure. With Eudora perched on dried leaves, and Pearlie just able to sit up in an old wooden box Mas' Winston rescued from the factory nearby, a dutiful Agatha cleaned and wrapped every bunch of bananas to send to the station. There, the tallymen counted and checked them, as Agatha waited, her anxiety building as they rejected the bananas that failed to make the grade, and totted up the few pennies to pay for those good enough to make it past the inspectors at the banana stand by the seaside.

The young mother took meticulous care of her two baby girls, working hard to stretch the limited resources. But as the girls grew up, her brows became more knitted, and her fingers trembled. "What mek yuh hand shake so, Agatha?" the children's father asked, his eyes fixed on her as she laid out his every meal.

"Is nutt'n at all, Mas' Winston." Her hands and knees still wore cracks and scars from years cleaning the wooden floors with crude brushes withered old men hacked from dried-up old coconuts. He had never seen the shaking hands, so he worried until she convinced him nothing was wrong, and it would go away.

Every Saturday afternoon as she dusted the altar, Agatha drew as close as she could to the partitions between her and the older church sisters and stretched her ears to pick up their muffled conversation. Since overhearing them once when they were unaware of her presence, Agatha no longer doubted the favorite topic of the whisperers. They had trained their eagle eyes on Eudora and Pearlie from a distance, feigning pity for Agatha as they predicted the calamity that was certain to come.

"Yuh see how Miss Agatha two pickney look different?" Miss Esmeralda said, determined to stir the conversation. Her words were not out of her mouth when Miss Gloria's rejoinder came.

"Lord, Mam! mi never want to say it, but look how Eudora pale till she look like a little half-dunduss girl." It was the cue for each member of the Altar Guild to chime in with her own judgment.

"And the little one Pearlie black like charcoal; is how a thing like dat happen when Agatha and Mas' Winston have the color a little better than a nice dark-brown floor polish."

"Mark my words: Dat little girl will mek poor Miss Agatha fret until she dead."

"Is a good thing the big one Eudora complexion soon mellow; look like she will grow into a nice brown-skin girl with good tall hair."

"Dat is why old-time people say bad luck worse than obeah. Dat terrible problem happen to plenty Oracabessa family arready; sister and sister, or sister and brother, come out with different color skin and different hair, and it always cause trouble."

Agatha's "good luck" with Eudora seemed like a wicked irony that clinched the fate of her second baby girl. Church women who were observant enough (and there was no shortage of them) scrutinized the blackness of Pearlie's elbows, knees, and heels, and they nodded in agreement. In the eyes of many Jamaicans, these were sure signs of the dark complexion any "poor unfortunate child" would eventually have. The words gnawed at Agatha's heart like a dull knife and the women's predictions worsened as Pearlie's "bad hair" failed to grow and resisted every kind of hair oil known to Oracabessa. Mother and child shed tears whenever it was time to comb what Agatha called her "natty head, dry like a coconut brush." A stubborn sadness welled inside her when a tearful Pearlie murmured her fruitless consolation, "mi sorry mi shame yuh wid mi black skin and dry head. Just mek mi stay inside the house, and nobody won't see mi."

The young mother's heart opened and wrapped itself around Eudora, with no room left for Pearlie. The discussions spread from the church women to the shop and the market; all around them, the women spoke behind their hands, debating whether they should be sorry for Mas' Winston as well. "Miss Yvonne, yuh think Agatha give Mas' Winston a jacket?"

"Yuh think so? But she look so quiet, like she can't mash ants; my God, what a thing!"

"Den if Mas' Winston is not Pearlie father, wonder is who?"

They racked their brains to find out what else could account for one child with an albino's color, and the other one with skin the women called "black fi true." The wisest among the church women, who all possessed a direct link to God's truth, provided the final verdict. "Everybody know the

Lord is long-suffering and merciful," proclaimed Miss Meikle. "But even God have a limit, and the Good Book say is dat why Him visit the sin of the father on the pickney dem." Jaws hanging open, the women imbibed every word of the trusted Oracabessa chronicler, adding their own garnish to the speculations.

"Is true, Miss Meikle; and Parson say dat mean the badness of a mother can follow her pickney dem too." Emboldened by the scriptures, and serious about her duty to inform her church sisters of all she knew, Miss Meikle revived dead rumors about the transgressions of Agatha's mother, repeating hand-me-down stories without fear of contradiction. She finished with a flourish. "So is not poor Agatha fault what she do to Mas' Winston. She doom to badness from she born because her mother lie down with anything name man–even her father himself. And everybody know fruit don't fall far from tree."

"Yes, Mam, yuh right; Pearlie skin and hair is the punishment for Agatha sin."

"Mark my word," Miss Esmeralda said, "Nutt'n good can come from this."

It did not take long for Mas' Winston to discover the cause of Agatha's shakes, and instead of taking her to him in their narrow bed, he turned his back, leaving Agatha with no reason to wonder why. Desperate to prove herself as his devoted partner, she took in more bundles of dirty clothes from the white and brown families scattered on the hillside and in the better parts of the district. With her toddlers around her feet, she spent long mornings scrubbing clothes with corn cobs and beating the dirt out on the rough stones along the river's edge.

Blue was the first color the children learned–blue for the sky and the little square inch of blue powder Agatha crumbled in the water to make the men's shirts sparkle extra white after she bleached them on the river stones. *Look how mi try hard to scrub the banana stain out the clothes and not a thing tek it out. Mi hand nasty too. Is the curse dat mek Pearlie color and her hair stay so bad; an' it will never leave us.*

Criss-cross scars littered her firm hands–remnants of the many burns she sustained from the wood fire where she toiled every day to feed her little family. There, on the crackling red-hot wood too, she heated heavy black metal irons to press out the stubborn coarseness of the khaki pants and white shirts.

Proud banana merchants strutted through the town showing off the sparkling clothes invisible women like Agatha labored over, parading their superiority over the likes of Mas' Winston, a lowly laborer. They passed washer women by without a glance, but by night they tumbled into secret makeshift beds with other dark-skinned girls who served their dinner and scrubbed sheets for British wives too fragile for their husbands' coarse desires. Young girls had babies with much lighter skin than their own, but nobody in Jamaica worried about that. The trouble surfaced when, like Pearlie, a child appeared with skin that was too dark.

The women's whispers rose to a clamor, and Agatha distanced herself and her children, rushing away from church before anyone could come close to them. In time, she stayed away altogether. Pearlie was glad when they stopped going to church. At least at home, she could suffer without the hostile stares, bearing the agony of her mother's furious disappointment expressed with harsh blows for any minor transgression.

No effort of Agatha could dislodge the stone bulging between Mas' Winston and herself over the rumors, questions, and denials. Like his ancestors who spent their days leaking beads of silent sweat on bedraggled banana leaves, Mas' Winston was a man whose bare chest, mud-crusted feet and sharpened blade did all his talking. Averting his eyes from realities at home, he wielded his razor-sharp machete, across the sun-drenched shrubs, his heartache growing every day. He spent more and more time in the field and at the bar, and soon, from the look in his eyes, Agatha saw how much he needed the consolation neither she nor they could give him.

A new whisper spread as the chorus of church women wondered about the man who sat past decent hours, half-hidden on the back veranda of the "Godless woman from Spanish Town," who had moved to Oracabessa just a year before. There, the reluctant Mas' Winston sought refuge from the hurt and the doubt that plagued him, bolstering the wall between himself and Agatha–between himself and the child he doubted more every day. He stayed away from Pearlie as if to avoid the contagion and the accusation in her dark eyes. Little did he know his distance only aggravated the child's dismay at the inexplicable torment that had befallen them. When he approached Agatha's father for help, the old man turned on him.

"Yuh stay there and listen to the wicked old church woman dem. Yuh know how much people life mash up over dis foolishness about who sinful and who can get salvation? Mi know Agatha; and yuh supposed to know what yuh woman will do and what she won't do."

"But people say yuh never even know what Agatha mother was carrying on in yuh own house."

"Don't say one more word 'bout what happen in my house, Mas' Winston. Look to yuh own. Yuh think it right to doubt my daughter and hate yuh own pickney, an' mash up her life because of what fool-fool Jamaica people say 'bout which color skin make a person better?" Guilt overcame Mas' Winston, but his fear of Agatha's betrayal was much worse.

"No, but what yuh would do if people say yuh woman bring home somebody else pickney—"

"Yuh can listen to dem fool-fool people who believe every word dem hear? Dem see yuh and Agatha carrying on good and dem want to mash it up over foolishness 'bout skin color. All now, we don't get over how the Englishman sugar plantation mek us hate ourself and one another. Slavery finish but we fight and cuss one another same way over who have better hair and color." Mas' Winston wanted to believe, but how could the words of Agatha's own father stand up against the words of everybody else? Would a man not defend his own daughter? They were blood; he was the outsider.

Everything was slipping from Agatha's grasp, but what could a decent, God-fearing woman do, except pray from the safety of the riverside and leave it in the hands of the Almighty?

CHAPTER 10
"PLEASE, GOD,"

By the time the girls headed for the floorless little wooden room they called Oracabessa School, the family's dilemma was part of the town's folklore. Agatha tried her best to listen to the words of the brown-skinned schoolteacher from Kingston who'd pulled her aside a few times at the market. "Agatha, listen to me," the woman said, her tone urgent. "You are young, but you must know a mother cannot deny her own child who lie down in her womb for nine months." Incapable of trust in anyone to have her interest at heart, Agatha usually hurried away, but this was a day when she was desperate to grab the slimmest chance of support. *Miss Robinson come from Kingston and she is the teacher, so she know more dan mi.* She turned back.

"What yuh say, Mam?"

"The same thing I said to you before: Stand up for what you know is right! Love the daughter you brought into the world, even when people condemn you for it. Don't you know how everybody condemned me? Sticks and stones may break our bones, but not the words of hypocrites!"

Agatha longed to make those brave words her own; but this was the condemned woman whom everyone in Oracabessa knew for her "unforgivable sin." Rumor had it Mrs. Robinson's bookkeeper husband had slipped away in the night after he used church money for his private business, but his mother insisted he had to run from his wife. "Is dat miserable red woman him married and bring here to turn school teacher;

she think she better dan everybody because her skin light and she come from Kingston." Focused on her work, Mrs. Robinson ignored the rumors, certain her husband would come to his senses and return home. To everybody's consternation, it was a woman who moved into her house. The gossip mill churned out the news, peppered with charges.

"See? Mr. Robinson mother was right; him schoolteacher wife and her woman friend living in the worst sin the Bible ever talk about." They never stopped until they hounded Mrs. Robinson out of her job at the school, and even the dangerous illness of her friend could not quench their thirst for their punishment.

Every time Mrs. Robinson stepped through her front door or approached anyone in the street, the same hostile words met her, "Serve the two of yuh right; too wicked and sinful!" No denial could appease their rage; no explanation of the woman's illness could suffice–not until when Mrs. Robinson walked straight up to the church in the early morning sunlight and greeted them with a tirade a much younger Agatha had witnessed herself.

"Yes, all of you leaving church sanctified and pure, ready to condemn people like me. Of course the woman was my friend, and a friend to plenty people in her own church in Kingston–a much better one to me than any of you. But when she fell sick with her nerves from worries and distress over repeated lies people from her own church spread about her, nobody stepped forward to help. Your God didn't rescue her either, even though she served Him better than most of you."

The churchgoers huddled in fear and awe, some calling on God. "Strike her now, Lord." "Mek her drop right here and face yuh in the middle of her blasphemy."

"Well, she's dead now, so you can all go about your business and your Lord's business. I don't want any part of a God who makes people suffer for nothing, and who makes a wicked man like my husband go free while all of you hold him up as a saint, and me as the sinner." The onlookers held their breath, certain Mrs. Robinson would fall dead before them, punished at once for her sinfulness and blasphemy; but to their utter disgust, she walked away.

The old story was supposed to be a lesson for Agatha whose inner voice insisted: *How mi must listen to a woman dat cuss God?* "Miss Robinson, the people say yuh friend dead because of sin, and dem say yuh mad from dat day, and yuh must dead bad too. Yuh know dem can tell yuh every chapter and verse in the Bible, Mam?"

"Believe what you want, Agatha, but you will regret letting these ignorant people turn you against your own child. Black people shouldn't look down on one another because of skin color and other people's business. This foolishness ruins families all over this country." The woman's words rang in Agatha's ears. She longed to be fearless like her, but the more she watched the straight line of Mas' Winston's back in her bed, and the more she saw the scorn that lined his eyes, the more she donned despair like her old church hat.

On Sundays, Pearlie's eyes brimmed with tears, as Mas' Winston taught Eudora how to prepare the red ginger for their visit to the family graves, as he instructed her sister about the birds and the plants. His rejection wounded Pearlie like a hundred pinpricks under her skin. At school, she lived through the endless taunts of children emboldened by the certainty that even her mother was against her, and by the confidence in their half-a-shade-lighter skin.

"Go home, picky-picky-head Pearlie; nobody not playing wid yuh!"

"Because yuh too black and ugly, and yuh hair bumpy like jackfruit skin."

"Yuh sister say yuh so black, not even yuh Mumma an' yuh Puppa don't want yuh!" At recess, when everybody played "There's a brown girl in the ring, tra-la-la-la-la," Pearlie hovered on the outskirts–so far from brown, no one allowed her into the circle. She slinked away from her classmates when they joined their hands to play "Blue bird, blue bird in and out the window; oh Mary, I'm tired." She was too familiar with her own tiredness–the tiredness of waiting, praying for a change she doubted would ever come.

Up where the river was only a cool gush that took its time forming pools of water where the light of the sun danced, Pearlie found refuge. She wiggled her toes and caressed the whiteness of her hands, considering how much better it was than the black sides. She lay flat on her back as butterflies danced around the oleander blossoms. Her gaze focused on the image of her black face in the clear water, she prayed: *Please God; Miss Rose at Sunday School say yuh full of mercy, and yuh mek sick people get better; she say yuh bring back Lazarus after him dead. Mi don't want nutt'n so big, Lord, but tonight when mi gone to bed, please just mek mi skin turn brown like Eudora. Mi promise to behave good if yuh help me. Or mek mi wake up somewhere far from Oracabessa, so everybody feel better, especially Mama.*

CHAPTER 11
ONE EMPTY CHAIR

It was on the far bank of the river where Pearlie first saw her mother huddled with Lenworth, the man who worked with Mas' Winston in the field. She wondered what brought them there, but how could she have imagined she had caused this too? Pearlie tried to figure out what it all meant, but although she overheard them a few times, she could make no sense of what they discussed. Lenworth comforted Agatha when they spoke near the end of the field, assuring her of Mas' Winston's movements. "No, Mam, the church woman dem tell lie. Is only now and again Mas' Winston stay long at the woman yard."

Already distraught, poor Agatha believed because she needed to. How else could she hold on to the brittle hope that God would eventually end Mas' Winston's nightly absence; that He would give her relief from the gnawing pain between her ribs? Lenworth fed upon her need for any little consolation he could give; he was sorry for her, and it cost him nothing to lie. He had his own worries too and figured it would be just a matter of time before life would force him to get back the kindness he showed her.

Agatha learned to pretend one of her children was not there, and Pearlie learned to live with her invisibility. But she made mistakes too, wondering if, like Eudora's, her offences would make her father pay attention to her. Sometimes he did, but not with the prompt forgiveness he extended to Eudora. When Pearlie bounced the water jar from the kitchen step and its pieces rolled down the hill, Mas' Winston's leather belt lashed her back, and its metal buckle cracked against her knuckles. When he got angry because she stayed by the river too late, his tamarind switch peppered her shins and ankles with a rage much worse than the transgression. It was the same rage they saw when he stripped small bits of peel she accidentally left on the boiled bananas on his plate.

"Agatha, why the hell yuh won't mek sure Pearlie peel the banana good so mi don't have to eat the skin too? Yuh better just make Eudora peel them."

"No Mas' Winston, mi don't want Eudora hand stain up like mine; Pearlie own can stay." Stung by her mother's words, Pearlie stuffed her mouth with the last of the banana from her own plate and sat still until she could escape to spit it out behind the back door. Though forced to eat them, she never once swallowed boiled bananas again.

In the middle of the night, she woke in a bloody sheet, her belly aching as if someone had reached up and ripped something from high between her legs, leaving ugly stains on the sheet. "Mama, Mama, mi begging yuh to come help me; mi sick bad!" Agatha dismissed her with old newspapers and brown bags ripped in long strips.

"Go ask yuh sister what to do wid dem; keep yuhself clean and stay to yuhself. And don't mek no careless boy come near yuh now, for mi don't want no trouble wid yuh." The thin bed cover wrapped tight around her, Pearlie wondered what worse trouble could be ahead. *Is because mi so black and mi hair stay so bad why dis only happen to me? Prob'ly mi soon dead too.* In the next few days, Mas' Winston's impatience grew as he watched her pick at her food more than ever.

"Eat yuh food, Pearlie. Mi not slaving in banana ground every day to put food on the table so yuh can waste it."

"Yes, Papa," Pearlie said, forcing the dry breadfruit slice down her throat, struggling to make it past the lump of hurt living there, only to settle on the soreness of hunger and sickness in her belly. The girl knew no name for her oppression; she just longed for one day when she would stop being the cockroach everybody wanted to smash against the wall to avoid contagion. When she walked on the street, lewd men shouted veiled threats about what they would do with her, now they considered her almost a woman.

Her dark eyes sank under her thick brows as the unbearable burden bore down, and silence tiptoed beside her through the almost forgotten corners of the dwindling house. When it shrank so much it threatened to stifle her, the insistent loneliness dragged her along, bringing her home only when the darkness frightened her too much for her to remain by the river. On a stifling Thursday evening in August, her worst fright was to come.

Agatha and Eudora stayed late at Bible studies at a faraway church where they were comfortable because no one knew their story yet, and they never took Pearlie with them. Mas' Winston was out. Pearlie waited alone too long–again. It was that hour after dusk when the safety of light withdrew– the hour when evil travels under cover of the darkness that mirrors it. Pearlie knew she had no protection, so she willed her eyes to remain open until she knew somebody would soon be home.

She woke under a smothering heaviness; *Get up Pearlie; get up; this weight will kill yuh!* A scabby hand covered her mouth; skin as coarse as sandpaper rubbed against hers. Every inch of her body battled, but there was no escape from under the man with his gravelly voice. "Keep yuhself quiet an' shut up yuh mout'." He muffled his words, but Pearlie knew. *Why Missa Lenworth come to kill mi in mi bed, and mi never do him nutt'n?* Pinned down in terror in a room as silent as an empty church, Pearlie tried to resist, willing every moment to be her last. But the man fumbling above her was too massive for her to budge.

After an eternity, the sandpaper skin slinked away and its owner muttered, "Is Miss Agatha send mi to yuh. She owe mi plenty favor an' she know nobody else will want yuh. But people say a girl like yuh, dat never know a man yet, can fix this bad sickness dat mi have." Pearlie understood none of what he said–not until the threat came, "Tell yuh father, an' yuh will soon feel how mi cutlass sharp." Her arm would not move, and her feet stopped working. She turned her face toward the wall–away from the eyes red with the mingle of rum and ganja in the glow of the helpless moon that bore witness through the window.

Outside, Pearlie scrubbed every inch of her skin, awash with the cool river water, until Agatha's last piece of carbolic soap disappeared into useless suds. *Tomorrow, Mama going look in mi face and see dat mi do something nasty; prob'ly she will just send mi away.*

Pearlie stayed away from the riverside. It was too close to the banana field and the smell of sandpaper skin. Instead, she took herself across the shaky rope bridge, darting through the trees and bushes, snaking down the stony path, brushing the branches from her face until she came to the clearing on the way to the seaside. As the sun peeped through the thick sea-grape leaves casting shadows on her legs, the precious moments of peace calmed her. There, in her refuge, her palms moved up and down along her skin. To her touch, it had always felt perfect, even lovely. But it was not what her mother wanted; it was what made her different from everyone else in the house; and it was everything. Above all, it was where Lenworth's scabby skin rubbed against her, so it brought disgust. *What praying can do now? Miss Rose say sometimes God too busy with big people problem, so children have to wait until Him finish. Well, mi not waiting anymore. If what happen last week happen again, mi going lay down in the river or the sea until it tek mi away.*

On a clear summer evening one day before her fifteenth birthday, Pearlie did not go home.

***

Back from his long day in the field, Mas' Winston was impatient to eat, so he could get away from the house he now despised.

"Agatha, where Pearlie gone again?"

"Eudora, weh yuh sister gone?"

"Mi don't see her from wi leave school, Mama."

The chipped enamel plate at the fourth spot on the makeshift eating table remained untouched; the fourth chair stayed empty. Nobody spoke, as the three ate their daily green bananas, this time with turn cornmeal with a few flecks of salt fish. With the remnants of the meal, Agatha walked away and threw the words behind her.

"Mas' Winston, beg yuh to give dat girl a good beating wid yuh big belt when she come, for a tell her every day she not to walk down by the river when night soon come, and she won't hear what mi say."

Like a cigarette thrown carelessly into a dry cane piece, the news set the district on fire. However much the versions differed, the conclusion was always the same. The autoclaps the church women had long predicted for Agatha had come. "Yes, mi dear, dat likkle black pickney just vanish!" No one counted the days as they turned into weeks and months. No one noticed the moment it happened, but the December breeze gathered up itself for Christmas, and the heaviness inside Agatha surrendered. Her one black dress swung around her meager frame, and she could not wear it a day longer. Along with Pearlie's scant belongings, she folded the dress, briefly held it to her face, and with a handful of camphor balls, she stuffed it all into her mother's shabby brown grip. She set it on the fourth chair in the far corner of the unfinished third room, where neither she nor Pearlie's father ever set foot again.

Agatha did not know longing or regret, but a lump in her chest grew into an unbearable weight. Hour after hour, she stared into Oracabessa River, her hair uncombed, her frantic fingers picking at her skirt tail. The bugs and insects whizzed by, a harsh accompaniment to her indecipherable muttering. *But mi never know it would happen. Mas' Lenworth only beg mi one small favor to help him sickness, an' now Pearlie don't come home. Mas' Winston dash way her food, an' the nasty banana stain all over everything. Jesus tek the case.*

CHAPTER 12
PEARLIE'S LONG WALK

Unaware of time or distance, Pearlie trudged ahead without pause, her seaside haunt disappearing behind the rocky edge of the cliff. She was not conscious of a decision to walk farther than the usual trail. There were none of her usual tears. Since the night of sandpaper against her skin, and river water tainted by her blood, the ability to cry had abandoned her. With the sudden passing of evening into night, the darkness engulfed her. *Which way mi must go now? Out here feel good, and nutt'n worse can happen.* Amid the unexpected security of open spaces, the regularity of the crash of the waves onto the shore, and the salty spray on her skin, her resignation morphed into a strong sense of safety. Hungry, wet, and overcome with weariness, she came upon a clutch of shrubs and ripped off a few branches of thatch to cover herself in a spot where she could rest.

The orange glow of sunrise warmed her into wakefulness. The sea breeze gentled her skin, left bare by the blown-away thatch she had used for a blanket. *If mi go home now, it will be big, big trouble and more shame for Mama; Papa big belt going to batter mi. Prob'ly is God bring mi here. Him know Mama will glad if she don't have to worry over how mi shame her with mi black skin and mi natty hair. If mi don't go back, who going care?*

As she plodded ahead, confusion about her surroundings grew, so she followed a bend in the stony track, and her footsteps slowed as her gaze fell on it all. This place was different from anything Pearlie knew. The blue of the sky was without end; the sun at her back burned through the flimsy second-hand dress Eudora already had the best of, and the breeze swept the salt into her eyes. She searched for a smooth enough area and rested under a blue canopy that stretched as far as she could see—the ocean indistinguishable from the heavens. With their unbreakable rhythm, pools of aqua, green, and white ebbed and flowed, washing over the stones, punctuating the silence where her new cocoon cradled her. Here in this new world of color, where the ugliness and the hurt she had known all her life could never reach her again, an unfamiliar force took hold. She rose to her feet, and, with a new grasp of their meaning, she belted out the words Miss Rose taught them at church, "All things bright and beautiful; all creatures great and small ..."

Her scrawny body strained against the breeze shimmying along the roil of the sea. In an endless motion, the waves drizzled all over her hot black skin, drying into blotches of salt. Her bare feet stung, blistered by the long trek across burning sand and stone, but she had never loved them more. They had brought her to this place, where every color surrounded her, and a yellow bird wooed her with the idea that this taste of freedom could be hers, forever.

Here—where she had made a turn in her path of rocks and wild bush—a gathering-up of emotions churned through Pearlie, like the waves of the ocean. She had no words to describe them. Salty tears drenched her face as her mother's disappointed voice echoed in her head to the accompaniment of the whispers behind the church window, the giggles she had turned away from too many times. The ugly sneers of the children haunted her, and she re-lived the hurt of her sister walking away, the loneliness, the gifts only Eudora received, the church picnics with everyone but her, and the choking fear that was always in her throat. Above all, the weight of the nasty Thursday night two weeks before dragged her down, and the smell of useless carbolic soap filled the air.

She swallowed hard to catch her breath. *Not one soul ever tell mi 'bout a place like this, where mi don't feel shame. The breeze feel like it belong to mi, not like mi have to beg the owner for it. Why mi must go back an' mek green banana stain mark mi up again? God have mercy, and mi know Him will carry mi somewhere better.* Lips parted, she sipped from the cup of unborrowed air, and she waited. Certain for the first time that nothing ahead could be worse than what was behind her, Pearlie opted for the safety of the unknown and trudged across the stony ground to find it. Hungrier and weaker by the minute, she lay in the warmest place she could find–and she prayed. Amid the soothing beads of a fresh drizzle, sleep came and went, until the sun ushered in a new day, and saltwater caressed her skin, washing away despair.

***

Idlewild was a strip along the coast; the few families who called it home occupied houses that ranged from wattle and daub to concrete blocks with occasional steel rods. Bertie Scott was about to take his sunrise swim as he always did when there was no school. At the top of a small cliff, he had positioned himself to jump into McCarthy pool, when he glimpsed an unusual shape in the distance. Racing to the spot, he stumbled upon the cold shivery bundle, half-covered with salt and sand. Without a thought for who she was, or why she was there, the boy lifted her over his shoulder like a sack of flour and took her home.

CHAPTER 13
A STRONG COUNTRY FAMILY

Idlewild, 1932

Bertie's mother lay the limp Pearlie on her bed, caring for her as if she were her own child, until the fever passed, and a turn for the better seemed imminent. The family was poor like everybody else, but their spirit and determination helped them provide for their two boys and three girls, and become part of the district's backbone. Looking after Pearlie was not an unusual act; their little old house was stronger than many and had been the refuge of several destitute people. Mrs. Scott questioned her son about the girl, but he added no more to his first account. His mother intended to dig the girl's story out of her and get her home as soon as her condition allowed. She had taken in runaways before, and her priority was always to return them to their families.

As the days passed, this girl seemed mesmerized, and she uttered no words. The woman prayed over Pearlie, sang choruses in her ear, and rubbed her shriveling skin with camphorated oil, over-proof rum, and the bitter gel of the Sinkle Bible plant. She force-fed her with cornmeal porridge and settled her stomach with ginger and cerasee tea. Her sons and other youngsters from church walked miles, making discreet enquiries about whether any family had lost a young girl, but no one knew of one, and since they did not know her name, the searches were as fruitless as the efforts of the one police constable sent from Port Maria police station to look into the matter. As Pearlie had predicted, her family did not make a big fuss about her absence, and the constable in Oracabessa had few resources and no encouragement to search for her. Mrs. Scott knew the girl might run away again, so she made her comfortable and held back her questions. As if on guard duty, members of the family watched Pearlie like hawks, never allowing her to step outside their view.

The weeks turned into months, and Mrs. Scott soon noticed a few signs of trouble. Though her body was lean and revealed none of the usual teenage bulges, Pearlie was thick around the middle, and her bottom was heavy. She ate nothing but potatoes, arrowroot and cornmeal porridge, and yet, her food would not stay down.

"Come here, chile; we have to talk; we can't put it off no more." Pearlie did as Mrs. Scott said, still without a word. There were other changes too; her face had softened, and she seemed much more at peace with herself, which made Mrs. Scott hopeful even as she was about to disclose her suspicions. "Mi know why yuh run away; yuh get yuhself in trouble, and now yuh in the family way." Pearlie's response was the usual empty stare and a face without expression.

Making light of it so Pearlie would talk, Mrs. Scott said, "Look how yuh carry yuhself heavy, and three times now, mi see yuh jump up and flash lizard off yuh clothes. Everybody know dat mean somebody around here expecting a baby, and is not any of my girls." Another blank stare was all she got from Pearlie. "Yuh know what?" Mrs. Scott said, in a firm steady voice, "Come. Get the big straw hat mi give yuh and walk outside with me." Then she called after Bertie, who was on his way to the seaside, "Wait for us; yuh must show mi just where yuh find this girl."

The moment the sea-grape bush came into view, Pearlie broke away and sprinted across the stones, laughter, howls, and screams along the way. It was the first time they had allowed her so far from the house, and Mrs. Scott wondered if she had done the right thing, or if the strange girl was losing her mind. Pearlie headed straight for the spot where Bertie had found her almost three months before. The two watched her transform into a little girl, frolicking across the rocks and heading toward where the sea narrowed into McCarthy Pool.

"Run, Bertie, run! Catch her before she reach the water." But the boy had already rushed toward Pearlie. He was about to grab her, but he had a hunch, so he let her go as far out into the sea as would be safe. "No, no; bring her back," his mother pleaded. Bertie remained still, his eyes on Pearlie. The water was at her waist, then her shoulders, and an immense wave was closing in. He braced himself in readiness and stood close by as the water rose into a crest before crashing over Pearlie, dragging her from the shore. The girl screamed, gasped, and thrashed about, guzzling water and coughing it up.

"Jesus Father, she dead now!" his mother said, the echo of her cry everywhere. Although he could not explain his thoughts, Bertie knew what he was about; he believed if nothing else could make Pearlie talk, the idea she might drown would do it. The sea almost swallowed him once, and it changed how he thought about many things. He let Pearlie go down a second time, and just as the wave was about to submerge her the third time, he grabbed her from behind, hoisted her above himself, took her screaming to the shore, and lay her at his mother's feet.

"Thank yuh, boy; thank yuh. I should know yuh wouldn't make anything happen to her. But the sea is a serious master, and mi 'fraid she would drown. Yuh make mi proud. The Lord sure to bless a kind soul like yuh." A bedraggled Pearlie was on her shaky feet. Mother and son walked her to the house, where she changed into dry clothes, sipped hot mint tea, and gazed into space. After dinner, her first words found their way out.

"Mi thank yuh very much, Bertie; mi thank the Lord because two time now Him put yuh where mi nearly dead and yuh save mi. Miss Scott, please, mi begging yuh, Mam; don't send mi back. Is Oracabessa mi come from. Is Pearlie mi name, but mi begging yuh please not to call mi dat and make people carry news to mi family. All of dem hate mi and dem don't care if mi dead; mi know dem never even look for mi good. So, please, Mam, don't send mi back. Mi promise yuh to work hard and help yuh, and mi will tell yuh what happen to mi and how mi find mi way here."

"Yuh own family hate yuh?" Mrs. Scott asked, relieved to hear Pearlie speak, but fearful of what she would reveal. A fresh round of sobs gave them both a slight breathing space until the woman's gentle prodding brought out the story. It was one Mrs. Scott knew well, for it was common across the country. Though people did not always mention the actual cause, Pearlie was not the first girl who ended up on someone's doorstep because she was too black for her family to love her. So inconsolable was the young girl, Mrs. Scott could not bring herself to ask about the pregnancy she suspected.

"Yuh can stay, Pearlie, but yuh must promise to talk the truth all the while. I am a God-fearing woman, and this is a Christian family. Yuh can't stay in this house and keep secret."

"Me promise, Mam."

Two weeks later when Mrs. Scott confronted the looming signs of the other problem, the girl's answers were no surprise.

"Yes, Mam; sometimes mi belly pain mi, and bad feeling come over mi."

"And what about dat business every month?" Mrs. Scott's discomfort with the topic left her voice barely audible, setting the tone for Pearlie's answer.

"Business, Mam, is what yuh mean?"

"Every few weeks, don't something happen ... down there?" A furtive glance made its way down the girl's skirt. "Don't yuh mother tell yuh about yuh ... yuh health? Or prob'ly she call it yuh nature?"

"Yes, Mam, is true; but she never say nothing else; only dat mi must stay to miself. Is a long time mi don't see it. And to tell the truth, so much things happen to mi of late, mi never even remember it."

"Is not so it work; it look like yuh getting a baby. Dat is why yuh don't see it again."

"Baby? Me, Miss Scott? How dat can be, Mam?" Full of mystery and hesitation, the explanation followed, accompanied by question after question about the man or boy who did a terrible thing to her. The only answer was a faraway look and a loud silence, punctuated with several wistful sighs. *So is Mas' Lenworth mek mi get baby then, for is only him alone come near me.* It was plain to see the months ahead would be hard for them both. How could anyone prepare a fifteen-year-old girl for the hardest job she would face, and the one about which she knew nothing?

Chapter 14
Her Name Is Naomi

Idlewild, 1933

"Mama! Mama! Pearlie ready!" The eldest Scott girl was at her mother's bedside, and the process was underway.

"Send the boys for the Nana; she know Pearlie time is near, so she keep herself ready. Freddie, get up and help mi change the sheet; and please boil up the water in the kerosene pan." It was time to move Pearlie, who lay in a huddle of twists and turns in the bed she shared with the two sisters. When the Nana arrived, she took one look at Pearlie and announced, "... not tonight at all; this poor little mother have a long journey before her." She lay out her accoutrements in the narrow passageway and advised everyone to get some sleep because no one could predict how long the night would be, or what it might bring.

Every hour, the Nana fed Pearlie with fresh thyme tea and rubbed her with herbs steeped in an array of oils. She swathed her belly with yards of white calico, softened by rigorous washing and rolling. Brisk massages followed, urging the baby to settle in the right position. Over twenty-six hours passed, and the whole family prayed as the last moments of Pearlie's labor seemed certain to rob them of both mother and baby. But the two women took turns praying and kneading, feeding her sips of cool water from the clay jar. Just past sunset on Friday, the little head made its appearance. Tiny as she was, and long as her arrival had taken, the infant's confident scream ripped through the quiet of dusk, and Mr. Scott and his children broke into loud laughter and applause under the naseberry tree. The Nana cut the navel string, tied it, and cleaned it, smothering it with grated nutmeg and ashes, before disappearing with the baby. Mrs. Scott cleaned up the exhausted new mother and left her in bed, aware she was still not out of the woods. As they waited, they prayed.

It was another twelve hours before Pearlie woke, as if from death. "Thank yuh, Jesus," was the only response from the woman who'd spent all those hours at her bedside. Too weak to lift her head from the pillow, Pearlie could manage only a whisper.

"What yuh say, chile?" Mrs. Scott asked. "Talk up, mek mi hear yuh. Lawd, mi glad yuh come back to us."

"Miss Scott? Is yuh dat, Mam?"

"Yes, little one, is me. Yuh think mi would leave yuh and go anywhere before yuh wake? How yuh feel?" Pearlie's hand felt for the mound that had been her belly. Overcome with panic, she tried to get off the bed.

"Jesus, Father! Miss Scott, what happen? What happen to—"

"Don't worry yuhself; everything awright; mi soon come back," Mrs. Scott said, stepping into the dim light of the Home Sweet Home kerosene lamp. Pearlie continued to feel her belly, raising up to scan the rest of her body; her eyes went to the door and the sound of Mrs. Scott coming back.

"Don't get up; mi bringing yuh little girl baby to yuh."

Just visible amid the folds of the delicate bundle was a sight that stopped Pearlie's breath. As if they belonged to the towel, the two smallest eyes she had ever seen peeped from a face no bigger than the biggest spoon in the pantry. The girl, who a few moments before had been as helpless as a leaf in a whirlwind, struggled to get up from under the sheet.

"Mind yuhself, Pearlie; yuh not in good condition, and yuh have to rest now." But Pearlie would have none of it. Not yet able to sit upright, she stretched her eager hands for the first thing in her life she knew nobody could take away from her. One tear trickled along Pearlie's face, and Mrs. Scott, certain hers would be next, reached for her kerchief.

"Mi don't believe it. She is my own for true? Thank yuh, Lawd. Miss Scott, this is the first good thing that happen to me. No, wait; is not true; yuh and yuh family is the first. Yuh know how much mi thank yuh, Mam?"

"Yes, mi know, but yuh are just a little more than a baby yuhself; yuh don't see much life yet. Still, yuh right; this is truly a God-bless day–and the Lord bless yuh to bring a little baby in the world. What name yuh going call her?"

"Naomi ... is Naomi she name, and she musn't have no pet name. Everybody have to call her the right name–Naomi."

"Lie down, Little Mama; and keep her right beside yuh; make yuh little Naomi head rest in yuh elbow. How the pain?" The pain was different from any Pearlie had known, and it lasted so long it seemed as if life had dodged her, leaving her afloat in some kind of trance. But now, it was like something from another place and time.

"Pearlie, what about her last name? Yuh never even tell us yours, but the baby need one."

"But she is my own alone, Miss Scott; she not to have nobody else name."

"She need a last name–her father name."

"What? No, Miss Scott, never! She don't have no father." It was the most expressive version of Pearlie the woman ever saw, and, as if the accomplishment of giving her child life had emboldened her, she said, "And mi not calling her mi last name, for somebody might carry news to the Oracabessa people 'bout me. Miss Scott, please, mi can give her yuh name, Mam?"

"Don't worry over it right now. Is nine days before yuh have to give her a full name; is dat time she will be somebody with her own soul." It was enough for Pearlie, who gazed into the eyes of her beautiful new dolly baby as if she might disappear. Pearlie banished the unwelcome thought that the nasty sandpaper-skin Lenworth had planted this gift inside her.

Mr. Scott buried Naomi's navel string along with the burned placenta near to the breadfruit tree and planted a small hibiscus tree right over the spot. "Is Naomi navel-string tree this; it mean no matter what happen, Naomi will always have her own place right in this yard," he said. The joy of Naomi's breath on her chest was all Pearlie had yearned for but never known. The men of the house created a makeshift cover over part of the side veranda, where the young mother had her privacy, at rest on a rickety homemade cot. On a table beside her mother, Naomi slept in an old bureau drawer padded with old sheets and towels. The family Bible found its place above the infant's head to keep away evil spirits. Beaming with gratitude, Pearlie cared for her space as if it were a mansion.

When it was time to baptize the baby, there was no money for a trip to Port Maria Church. The Franciscan nuns from Kingston ran a small mission in nearby Boscobel, and a priest visited every month for Sunday Masses and baptisms. Fearful someone would recognize her, Pearlie stayed away from every church, and now it was in the old school room where she waited with her infant, until Bertie gave the signal the small congregation had dispersed.

"What is the name of this child?" Father's voice startled Pearlie; as she shuddered, the baby screamed.

"Naomi, Father; she name Naomi." The day was sultry, the vestments were weighty, and it offended Father that all these Catholic godmothers like Mrs. Scott kept bringing careless young girls to christen babies with no fathers. The stiff white collar squeezed his fat red Irish neck, and big splotches covered his face.

"Naomi what? Tell me her full name." In fear of his displeasure, Pearlie thought of the miles she had walked to escape the darkness of Oracabessa. With a new certitude, she spoke,

"Walker, Father; is Naomi Walker she name."

Mr. Scott brought home second-hand planks, zinc, and other scraps from the old estate where he worked; and when he gathered enough, he and his sons started a room on the side of his land, to give Pearlie and Naomi their own little space. From the seaside, the Scott boys brought twelve of the biggest smoothest stones they could carry and forced three of them under each corner of the room to raise it from the ground and keep it dry. When they plastered white-wash all over the wood and everyone chipped in to move mother and baby from the back veranda into their new home, Naomi was two years and three weeks old.

"Me and Naomi thank yuh, Sir; yuh and Miss Scott, and all yuh children help us very much. Missa Scott, yuh soon see how we keep our little room clean an' pretty."

It seemed like no time at all, before a rambunctious tomboy replaced Baby Naomi at the center of the family, who all loved her as if she had been born to them. Her screams and giggles filled the yard as they tossed her in the air, chased her around the trees, and caught her as she jumped from the low branches of the fruit trees. With a glow all over her face, Pearlie looked on, absorbing the love and care everyone showered on her child, who faced none of the agony she had grown up with on the banana ground in Oracabessa. As the images of her mother and father flashed before her, she re-lived her long years of pain. *Hmm; wonder what dem would say if dem see mi and Naomi now.*

Pearlie had never seen Lenworth's face in daylight except from a distance in the banana walk, so she could not tell whether Naomi grew with any of his features. But none of that mattered to her. She loved her daughter's smooth chocolate skin, her eyes set wide apart under her brow, the curl of her mouth, especially when her little girl wanted to have her own way. Nobody in the house ever saw anyone work as hard as Pearlie. Mrs. Scott taught the young mother to sew, and making clothes for Naomi from the Scott girls' hand-me-down dresses became one of her favorite pastimes. She could make a tasty meal from anything. From the wood fire outside her room, anyone nearby could smell all kinds of treats–from stew peas peppered with Scotch Bonnet, to mackerel run-down, to guava preserves and marmalade from the bitter oranges that weighed down the trees near to their room. At her side, Naomi learned it all, as long as she was not gallivanting around the yard, lapping up Bertie's attention. She thought he must be the kindest person in all of Jamaica.

Not one day did Pearlie ever cook green bananas; When Mr. Scott cut bunches from the tree by the side of the house and offered Pearlie, she refused them all. "Thank yuh, Missa Scott, but is one thing mi and Naomi don' eat."

"What? How yuh don't eat green banana and yuh come from Oracabessa where every yard have at least one banana tree?" he asked in dismay.

"No, sir. Mi don't want it near mi or Naomi. Is plenty years mi mother couldn't get banana stain from the clothes and her hand. She say banana stain never come out. Is a bad thing, Missa Scott an' she never mek mi light-skin sister get it on her hand, only mi one. Dat is why since mi leave Oracabessa mi don't peel banana, and mi don't eat it. Banana stain is a curse, and prob'ly it don't finish with mi yet."

CHAPTER 15
THE BOY AT DEVON HOUSE

Kingston, 1990s

Zarah had donned the image of the preoccupied teenager for good, claiming to be busy with dance rehearsals, off to meet her friends, or at the homework table. It was part of her resolution to stay away from emotional attachment to her parents and avoid the hurt of another betrayal. On Saturdays Bradley dropped her and her friends at their Devon House hangout for their usual ice cream and compensation snacks after hours at the dance studio or extra classes at school.

When her friend Ebony's birthday came, Bradley left them there as usual, nodding agreement with Zarah's reminder, "At least two hours, Daddy, please." The girls bought their chicken patties and scampered in and out of the famous I-Scream shop, balancing top-heavy cones leaking their favorite flavors between their fingers. They captured a nearby kiosk and began their review of weighty matters at school and at home. Toni-Ann said, "Shh ... don't look; a guy coming this way."

Nicole straightened her blouse and pushed out her breasts. Ebony sneaked a look in the mirror on the back of her hairbrush, and Shari grabbed her eye liner. Zarah licked her cone. The boy sauntered over as they all tried hard to smother the giggles and feign nonchalance while studying their shoes, eager to see which one of them would be the newcomer's target.

Zarah did not waste time looking up. No boy ever glanced in her direction, for she had perfected being invisible. Although when she was fourteen Esther finally allowed her to straighten her hair, she still hauled it back into a thick ponytail spread out in spikes from her scroongie. Unlike her friends, she could not bear to pluck her thick eyebrows, which she quite liked for their arch and the way they came together in the middle. They stood out in what was an otherwise plain roundish face with no other distinct features except the hint of a smile, mostly absent ever since the trouble at home.

Her jeans were floppy, and her T-shirts hung on her like an extra-large garbage bag. At first, her mother said she could not waste money on new clothes as often as Zarah outgrew them or stopped liking them, so a size too big was always the choice. Zarah resisted, but oversized clothes soon served the purpose of hiding how unfeminine she looked. She cultivated a plain appearance because she wanted nobody buzzing around her; she could not imagine what she would do with any boy interested in her. *Anyway, it would only be a matter of time before it would go wrong, and someone would walk away leaving the other one to suffer.* While her friends craved the experience of getting involved and even falling in love, her parents had proven it was certain to end in pain, and there was already enough of that in her story.

Everybody acknowledged Zarah was the group nerd, and they laughed at her for being too "serious with yuh head always in a book." As Ebony often said, "No boy not coming near you, Miss Speakie-Spokie English lady; how any boy going understand your big words?" Esther insisted Zarah would do better at school if she spoke "good" Jamaican English, and with all the words they learned from Scrabble, she excelled at it. But it was more than Esther's efforts; learning excited Zarah; words intrigued her, and she collected them. Her head between the pages of a book was one of her favorite positions, and by the time she was fourteen, she had read three or four times as many books as any other girl she knew.

Every week, she wrote her five favorite words and synonyms on a poster and stuck it on her wall. They helped her understand some of what was happening inside her, and although she was not as careful about speaking standard English as Esther had drilled into her, her wide vocabulary helped her with school assignments. When her activities waned, or her thoughts worried her, she scoured the thesaurus for unusual words to describe the emotions in her secret notebooks. Some she collected because she loved the sensation they created as they rolled off her tongue: *mellifluous, scintilla, peremptory*; others because of their gentle tones–*murmur, meander, swish*, or because of their connection to chemistry–*solvent, synthesis*, and *covalent*. Then, there were Jamaican words–words that captured ideas like no English word could; these she learned from Louise Bennett; like *boonoonoonos, fenkeh fenkeh* and *bangarang*. The girls teased her about her words too, but they copied many of them and kept them handy until it was time to write essays or prepare for exams.

The boy strutted past the feigned indifference of the girls ahead of him, for he knew which girl had caught his eyes. His back arched against the metal post nearest to Zarah, he spoke in a flat drawl as if they were the only two people around. "Yow, nice girl, bet yuh is my favorite flavor ice cream yuh licking." Startled at how close his face was to hers, Zarah pulled away.

"Excuse me?" she said.

He inched away but continued to speak as if he had known her forever. "Girl, tell mi is only the ice cream why yuh voice sound so cold." Zarah licked her favorite coconut flavor and tapped her feet on the grass. Her silence did not prevent him from continuing. "So, tell mi something, it did hurt yuh?"

"What? Did what hurt?"

"When yuh drop from heaven." The girls' laughter rang out, but Zarah responded with a smirk.

"Seriously? No, tell me you didn't use that lame line." The girls snickered even more, but he had no eyes for them; he straightened up and leaned against the post, one foot stuck high behind him, his face pulled up from Zarah's, so she could look up into his wide eyes and the two teeth sticking out beyond his thick upturned lip. The smell of cologne lingered even when he pulled away and leaned against the tree again. She could not tell if it was a good one; it was not like her father's, but she guessed the boy was trying to be a man. Unconscious of any interest in him, Zarah paid no attention to the boy's looks, but it dismayed her that his presence, and his raspy voice made her feel like somebody held a flame against her skin, almost close enough to burn it.

Huddled at a safe distance, the girls could no longer hear their murmurs, but they took turns inching up to their friend to monitor the progress of the accidental date. One of their rules was that the prospect of a new guy with a little potential should always take first place over their gossip, so Zarah knew the girls would give her time and space. He was right beside Zarah, nattering a mile a minute about his bike, his basketball team, his sneakers, and the music on his Walkman. In between, his flood of questions rolled off his tongue so quickly, she found it difficult to answer and soon decided she had had enough. Determined to avoid giving the slightest suggestion of interest, she gathered her stuff. "We have to leave soon; I'm going over to my girls." He leaned in and handed her a slip of paper with his scribble: Damien: 9279656. Zarah breathed in the last whiff of cologne.

CHAPTER 16
"WHO IS HE, ZARAH?"

Kingston, 1990s

After her Devon House incident, Zarah's extracurricular activities multiplied. Key Club, choir practice, students' council events, and group sessions at the library for research assignments crowded the huge new timetable she hung on her wall, drawing the constant attention of a mother impressed with her daughter's multiple interests. It was just what Zarah intended. Nicole, one of the Devon House crew, gave everybody advice about how to manage parents, and she schooled Zarah in techniques to hide secret activities.

For weeks, the girls got updates about Zarah's progress with Damien whom she chatted with on the phone. After one secret liaison at the library, Zarah dropped a bombshell. "Damien is funny and everything, but him not my type. At first, I thought we had potential, but no, I can't bother." She made up the story because she was intent on seeing more of the boy, and her instinct warned he would not be one to comply with house rules. There were so many at Duhaney Park, it would be best not to mention him to Esther, who would trot out one of her grim reminders, "Anybody who should be your friend should be able to come home with you." Her girls were always at Duhaney Park, and they could not keep secrets, so she wanted them out of her business, and she faked the breakup.

Zarah felt like her own person keeping everything about Damien to herself. That was the thing about him that had struck her from the start. He was daring; he did what he wanted, and if it meant breaking rules, he didn't care. If she could learn how to be like that, the rules would not be so oppressive. Their time together became her escape. It took her away from girlfriends whom she found more and more annoying as they giggled and squirmed in the cafeteria, trying to pry into every detail about her movements. Damien made her smile; no, he made her laugh from deep down until her stomach walls hurt. *Like Daddy used to make us laugh at home.* What he said was not always that funny, and from anyone else, his jokes might have bored her. It was his silly lopsided grin, his cracking voice, how the corners of his eyes wrinkled when he came out with the outrageous words and stories he was always making up. He brought lightness to Zarah, sparking the belief life could be fun again. Most of all, her desperation for connection to somebody–anybody–drew her to the boy.

The old talks with her mother echoed in her head, but she dismissed every memory of their agreement about avoiding secrets. *That was before everything went crazy; before they let me down and kept their secrets. I have rights too; I will keep Damien to myself.* The surrounding heaviness diminished, and Zarah drifted farther from her mother, whose mind was now set on becoming all she could be–and ensuring Zarah would become even more. By the time Esther spotted the first clues of trouble, an uneasy calm had settled over Duhaney Park.

"Goodnight, Mummy; I'll be up late to study. Geography test tomorrow."

"Give me a minute," Esther said, shoving a pile of bills and paper from her bed. Zarah hovered in the doorway, eager to escape without another long talk.

"Anything you want to tell me?" Esther asked, patting the space for Zarah to sit. Zarah ignored the signal.

"No, Mummy, like what?"

"About a new friend?"

Zarah felt uneasy, but she bluffed. "I have all the friends I need; plus, you know I don't have time with all the things I'm doing."

"Okay," Esther said, in a steady voice, "so, who is he?"

"Who is who? Where these weird questions come from all of a sudden?"

"Leave out the dodging; just tell me who you spent all this time with, on these calls I have to pay for." Zarah glued her eyes to the imitation-wood tiles that recently replaced the old terrazzo tiles in the bedrooms. *No wonder Mummy picked them, dull straight lines all over.*

Esther stood next to her, the telephone bill in hand. "See? Calls to and from 9279656, morning, noon, and night: 20 minutes, 40 minutes, one hour and 15 minutes."

"It's somebody I see at the bus stop and the library sometimes; we talk about the music we like, or basketball and schoolwork." Her lips twitched; she straightened up to get as close as possible to eye level with Esther, and her tone changed. "So, talking on the phone or at the library is a crime now? I can't have somebody around me who is interested in what I like?"

"We discussed this a thousand times: You don't keep friends on the street; you bring them home–boys and girls alike. You must have a reason for breaking the rule this time."

"Rules and more rules; that's all we have here. Ever since Dadd—" Her grumble stopped abruptly and she turned to go through the door. *What's the point, anyway?*

"Where you think you going? I'm waiting to hear who this is, where you know him from, and why he is a secret. You can tell me; or I can tell you." Zarah saw this was no joke, and instinct said there was more ammunition than the bills to make her mother take that stand.

"Mummy, it's a boy. I met him at the bus stop one day when Daddy couldn't pick me up. It happened a few times, and sometimes I see him at the library."

"At the library? And what about Hope Gardens, Devon House, Half-Way-Tree and Tropical Plaza?" Her mother waved the notebook-turned-diary Zarah kept under her mattress. "Look how far those places are from where you live! How long have you been lying and hiding? And you are up and down with a boy on a bike? You crazy, or what?"

Zarah grabbed her notebook. "So now you spying on me? Reading my private notes? Good one, Mummy–after all the old promises about my space and privacy, and encouraging me to write what I feel. Now I know that was just to give you something to use against me."

The outburst astonished Esther, but she stood her ground. "You know that's not true; those promises were part of an agreement, but I see you forgot your side."

"Like the agreement some married people make when they decide to change everything?" Esther flinched at the veiled accusation from the girl who never missed an opportunity to blame her for her father's absence. Esther hoped that with all her efforts at exposing Zarah to movies, discussions about relationships, and even the stories everywhere about break-ups, she might have let go of some of her bitterness about her own parents' divorce. But her resentment had lingered. As always, it hurt Esther, but she was not about to allow Zarah to break rules by calling on a ready-made excuse.

CHAPTER 17
LET'S TALK ABOUT IT

Kingston, 1990s

Remnants from the confrontation about Zarah and Damien floated in the Duhaney Park house for weeks, but Zarah soon accepted her parents would have to meet Damien if she intended to continue their friendship. Bradley came over for *the talk*.

"Yes, Miss Thomas ... no, Sir. I would never carry Zarah anywhere on the bike, Sir." Damien's head bobbed up and down as he tried to peep across the room for encouragement from Zarah, but she looked everywhere else. Esther called in Miss Lucretia and outlined the once-a-week visits she would supervise while Esther was out. The helper puffed up her chest as if she would burst until the moment Zarah left to show the boy out.

"Mi understand what yuh want to do, Miss Esther. But mi don't feel good about it. A boy like dat one is bad news. Mi hear what him say a while ago, but anybody can see him don't mean one word. Him don't come off a good table at all. Mr. Bradley, mi sure yuh can see the cut of him jib arready. Him soon turn Miss Zarah into a woman before time!" Miss Lucretia's words captured what Esther sensed when she first set eyes on Damien, but after a long talk with Bradley, they agreed to give the arrangements a try.

Esther backed up the plan with renewed efforts to reach Zarah. Their daughter going too far, getting pregnant, hurting her reputation, interrupting her education, and enduring endless suffering were not the only concerns Esther and Bradley had. On the talk shows and at PTA meetings, in office lunchrooms, and in Sunday sermons, stories abounded of families in crisis over defiant teenagers, STDs, drugs, and inappropriate relationships no parental efforts could end. Parents argued about whether harsh punishment, more rules, or limited freedom worked with wayward teenagers.

Esther and Bradley questioned themselves and each other about whether parents could tell teenagers about their own mistakes and still get their respect or obedience. But their situation made it too challenging. They had told Zarah everything she should know, in theory. But how were they supposed to help her manage herself and the bold flesh-and-blood boy on their doorstep? The courage to share her own experiences eluded Esther. If her lips could have done so, they would have uttered the words to explain her own longing for more than Naomi ever allowed, for more than Bradley could give. They would have warned Zarah against the force that misplaced her mother between the perilous white sheets next to Patrick; the agony, the relief, and the guilt over an unplanned baby, the hurt and the irreparable damage her recklessness had rained upon them. How could she share all of that with her child to warn her of what could result from the wrong decisions about this boy?

It occurred to Esther that similar fears and confusion must have been at least partly responsible for some of the darkness in Naomi's eyes over the years; for her refusal to explain issues that set them at odds as Esther had grown up. In the stillness of her sleepless nights, she replayed the desperation and panic she had always detected in Naomi's cryptic warnings about what would happen if Esther brought "any big-woman business home." Similar feelings and words threatened to force themselves upon her every time Zarah broke another rule or put up an argument against her parents' decisions. Why did nobody tell her the words to substitute for Naomi's crude warnings? Could Naomi help her unravel those mysteries for Zarah?

***

Wary of the tension at Duhaney Park, Naomi had withdrawn to her refuge at Ulster Road. Esther's divorce, the problems with Zarah, and the drawn-out conflict over what Naomi saw as her daughter's preoccupation with her job and career had left her exhausted. With all the shifting circumstances around her, she had distanced herself, with the hope she could find a sense of predictability. Every morning, she pulled on her combat gear and stood up to face the enemies of loneliness and the unfinished strands of her life that threatened to dislodge her peace of mind. The care of her plants in the old paint cans along her strip of yard brought unspeakable contentment; the feel of fabric gathering under the special presser foot attachment on her new Singer sewing machine calmed her. And at church, the feel of the keyboard under her fingers enlivened her, so she practiced for hours to perfect the new-fangled hymns that always seemed to have more words than the melody could manage.

In one of the few rituals that remained intact, Naomi sat on her wooden kitchen stool and shelled home-grown gungu peas for her Saturday soup, until minutes to nine, when Esther walked in from the taxi with her market supplies. On the side of the sink, the pig's tail and salt beef lay soaking in the blue-rimmed enamel bowl that survived their journeys from Boscobel to Oracabessa and then Kingston. As they sorted fruits and vegetables, Esther pointed to the old-fashioned beef mill with its pieces laid out to dry on the windowsill. "Mama, you don't throw away this old thing yet?"

"Why I should throw away things that have use? What yuh call 'this old thing' save mi from that big money yuh pay for mince."

"Awright; I hear you. I picked up some nice butter beans to cook with the oxtail next week." Before Naomi could slip in her thanks, Esther went on. "So, Zarah told you about a new friend?" She was pretty sure her daughter would have shared her version of what happened, but she knew no other way to broach the subject. Astride the fence between breaking Zarah's trust and being honest with Esther, Naomi kept her response brief.

"Yes, she mention a boy; Damien, I believe."

"She told you all about their meetings and hour-long phone calls? The lying and hiding is the worst part; she never used to do those things." Naomi's silence troubled her. "It really shocked me and Bradley to find out what they were up to." Turning to her mother, she planted her feet in the same spot where they had shared so many important moments–tense, hilarious, uplifting, devastating moments, some that put them on the brink of irreparable conflict. She expected any minute now, an accusing finger would rise before her, blaming her for everything. But Naomi remained quiet, and Esther picked up a handful of peas. Only the shuffle of their fingers against the dry pods interrupted the hush.

It was Esther who braved the moment.

"I suppose you believe is my fault because I'm at classes on Saturdays sometimes, and Miss Lucretia is not there, but we should be able to trust our child."

"I didn't think that at all. Zarah is wrong, and she shouldn't tell lies. But we all know the devil find work for idle hands; nowadays, young people will use every chance to find out what they can get away with."

Another long pause. "You know, Mama, sometimes I have to wonder ..."

Naomi waited, filled with hope that some of the issues they had always found hard to discuss were close to tumbling out. And she feared what they might be. Esther moved closer to the window, her fingers on the delicate lace curtains, her breath halting as she wiped the tear that would betray her.

"These still look good, eh?" she said, "after all these years." Money for the curtains had come from Esther's first week's pay—her "gift" to their first rented kitchen in Kingston. They had faded with the years, but now they sparked mixed emotions in each woman. Naomi watched and waited, but Esther still played with the curtain and stillness reigned. The women longed for another time—before they ever had kitchen curtains and before life was so complicated.

"I can see yuh struggling," Naomi said at last. "Everything look hard sometimes, but whatever troubling yuh, just follow what is inside. From Zarah was little, yuh talk to her about everything. Mi not sure if that is the best way, and mi never do dat with yuh. Prob'ly it was wrong, but mi do what mi tink was best. Just like how yuh do what yuh believe is right."

"I feel like nothing works."

"Yuh ever tell Zarah about our life, and all what yuh and mi go through ... when we ... yuh know?" The crunch had come: Naomi could not bring herself to acknowledge the old challenges. Some things had not changed.

"Yes, I know what you mean, but I didn't tell her. I tried over and over; I just can't get it out."

Words eluded mother and daughter, but a single thought dogged them both: nothing had prepared them for the hard moments of being mothers.

Naomi walked over to the sink. "Do yuh best; dat is all anybody can do; and pray. Wait ... yuh know what? Ask Bradley to bring Zarah over here tomorrow. Mi will tell her what mi can, about where we coming from and some of the hard times we go through to come to where we reach. Prob'ly it will mek her tink twice before she mek dat boy mix up her head."

Esther agreed, but she wondered how her mother would manage that kind of talk. After all, this was the same Naomi who had bungled such moments with Esther during their own hard years. Memories of their conflicts always ushered in bitterness and depression, so she had struggled to bury them and find different ways of raising Zarah. Had her efforts been just as futile?

Naomi sensed what might be in Esther's mind, so she said, "We can only try, but don't worry yuhself because I won't tell her yuh private business. That is up to yuh and Bradley."

***

On Sunday, Naomi skipped the last verse of the recessional hymn and hurried home to prepare a special lunch for her fussy granddaughter. In the kitchen, she stood in the same spots where Esther had fingered the curtain and swallowed her words. A cloud of doubt and anxiety enveloped her as she considered what Zarah needed to hear. As a mother, she had done what she picked up along the way in the days when nobody knew much. She knew she had never been enough, and now the sourness of her failures with Esther swirled in her mouth, merging with the bitter taste of her own inadequacy as a mother, and the contribution of those legacies to Esther's shortcomings.

Through the side window, she watched Bradley plant a kiss on Zarah's forehead and walk to the car. Naomi knew he was on duty, so he could not stay to talk, and she returned his vigorous wave. *Lord help dat poor man get over all that happen to him.* As her granddaughter walked up the short path to the door, Naomi sensed the weight on the child's shoulders. Memories of long talks with Pearlie during her last days flew into her head. Like an omen, her mother's warnings against the fearsome curse of Oracabessa's banana stains assailed her. Over the years, her strong faith had calmed the fear of stains and curses, but today, nothing could dislodge her sense of lurking danger and insufficient time. Her fingers found the St. Jude medal in her pocket and her words for her granddaughter carried a lightness she did not feel.

"Morning, little one."

"Hi, Grams." Zarah threw her backpack on the table and hugged Naomi without conviction.

"Is only dat sulky look and half-dead hug yuh can greet Grams with?" Her effort at lightness did not budge the load Zarah brought in. "Come … tell mi why yuh don't sound like mi one granddaughter today."

"I don't even know, Grams; is just a lot; I wanted to stay home; and Mummy say I have to stay here because she won't be there, and the new rule is I can't stay in the house all day by myself."

"What yuh think cause dat?"

"Really, Grams? Both of us know I'm here because Mummy tell you everything, and she want you to talk to me. She will never trust me again." Zarah sipped water and lay on the bed, hugging the Limacol fragrance of her grandmother's pillow.

"She use to trust yuh though; everybody use … all of us trust yuh, so what change?"

Alert as ever, Zarah noted her grandmother's quick attempt to correct herself, but she let it pass. *Of course, she has to be on the side with the big people now.* Half of her wanted to end the discussion, but if not Grams, who would listen to her?

"Remember I told you about my friend? Well, Mummy found out I was talking to him after school sometimes at the library; other places too, and on the phone. Now we can't talk at all unless I follow her new rules."

"Yuh didn't tell mi yuh was hiding and telling lies … and now yuh mek it sound like what yuh did wasn't serious."

"So, you agree … I'm the worst kind of daughter, just like Mummy thinks."

"Nobody believe you're the worse anything, but yuh must admit when yuh wrong, and face the consequences. When yuh break trust, it tek time to build it back."

"So how come this only apply to young people, Grams? What about when big people break our trust?" Zarah had never used such a sharp tone with Naomi, and her grandmother pounced.

"No, chile; calm down and remember who yuh talking to. Trust is trust; and yuh might believe yuh parents break yours, so yuh can do the same; but two wrongs don't make a right. And another thing: Yuh think yuh can keep vexation in yuh heart forever? Yuh going use it to excuse everything yuh do wrong?"

Eager to put more space between them, so she could be free to say what she wanted, Zarah moved away and fumbled with the window.

"No, Grams, and sorry for talking like that, but what I don't get is how after she and Daddy change everything, they expect me to stay the same. My whole life is different, but they want me to stay forever like the same little girl."

"Listen; we can't change who we are every time we don't like what happen to us, an' it don't mek sense to blame somebody else when we let down ourself."

"You mean like how Daddy left? Like how Mummy not the same anymore? She should be the one having this talk with me. But nowadays ... well, we don't talk about anything important, and I know is because—"

"Because what?"

"Because all the time, I tell her she drove him away, and the whole situation get worse from that. She don't like when I say it, but is true."

Naomi gave her the look that meant, "Here we go again"; she hoped the message would sink in, but Zarah continued.

"How come after all this time, nobody expects me to figure out what happen between them? Parents always say, 'when you get older, we will explain.' So how old I have to be, before they level with me–about forty-seven? Why I don't have a right to know, but they must know every detail about what I do?" Naomi swallowed and kept her thoughts to herself; *better just mek this chile get all of it off her chest.*

"Now, they are like good old friends, but that don't help me; I still don't have Daddy in the house, and anyway it's too late; plus, who knows what else might come? Who knows when she might do something different?"

"Like what?"

"Who knows, Grams? She can do whatever she wants; I mean … is not even like she's really there; she controls the house through her warden Miss Lucretia … and now, just because I have somebody I can talk to, she wants to control that too."

"Yuh must know if any boy is buzzing around a girl chile, parents have to set some rules. Anyway, look from when yuh father leave the house; how yuh can stay vex forever over it? If yuh go on like this, it will tear yuh up inside and spoil things with everybody dat love yuh. Bradley never leave yuh; him and yuh mother part, for whatever reason. Yuh and mi neva like when it happen, but wi don't have to know what cause it. Still, the two of dem work hard together to bring yuh up the right way. He's around yuh all the time. Why yuh can't mek yuhself happy with the blessings yuh have?"

"Trust me, Grams … is a long time I been trying to get up one day and don't feel vex; I don't even know what I vex about, or if is something else." The certainty in her voice wavered, and a tear sneaked from one eye. Naomi consoled her, recalling the many times she should have done the same with Esther. Why had she been so ignorant about how to manage the young life entrusted to her care? She had no answer, but she had a chance now. *No matter how hard it might be, I will tek dis burden from Esther and mek Zarah know our story.*

As the afternoon wore on, Zarah swallowed slow mouthfuls of her curry chicken dinner, eyes wide and her jaw dropping as Naomi garnished her talk with stories of Pearlie's misery, Naomi's struggles in Idlewild and Oracabessa, and her flight with Esther to Kingston. She pressed her grandmother for details about her poverty and her pain, the tribulations and fortitude of the women whose blood she shared, one consolation in her mind: *Those legacies belong to Grams and Mummy, but this is the 1990s; they won't be mine.*

CHAPTER 18
A SERIOUS TALK WITH BERTIE

Idlewild, 1946

As Naomi got older, Pearlie earned a little money from sewing for people and selling guava jelly, marmalade, and baked sweets. She seemed to lose herself in the smoke from the coal stove, and Mr. Scott warned everybody to be careful whenever Pearlie lit her fire. "Stay far," he said, "if yuh stand up careless, she will stew yuh!" The first time Pearlie earned a few shillings, she tied all of it in a kerchief and handed it to Mrs. Scott with pride in her eyes. The woman's heart brimmed with joy as she stuffed half the money in her bosom, covering the rest in a dry calabash where she always kept a little money for the rainy days that were sure to come.

Afraid somebody would recognize her, and carry news to her family, Pearlie stayed away from the big Saturday market in Oracabessa. She set up a table on the roadside near the church closer to Port Maria. Naomi skipped along and sang the little song she made up. "Come buy Mama jelly and mar'lade please, Miss Nice Lady." Stories traveled through Idlewild about the blessings Pearlie and her "nice little Naomi" brought to the community. "Miss Scott everybody know is a reward from the Lord because yuh was so kind to Pearlie," the women said.

"Yes, is a blessed day carry her to us. She have a good heart, and her little girl bring light in the house." But Mrs. Scott worried about Bertie, who showed no interest in his future. He helped his parents with their small backyard field and sold produce at the market, but that was all.

On a steamy washday, his mother sat under the shady breadfruit tree, her legs wrapped around the wash-pan, her skirt tucked underneath her. *Sqrrish ... Sqrrish ... Sqrrish* went her fingers against the soap-slippery clothes, the sound every girl had to make to prove her washing would measure up. From the corner of her eyes, she watched Bertie as he sat under the star apple tree, his stare fixed on Pearlie across the yard, her oily fingers parting Naomi's hair into one-inch squares, and plaiting each one to a fine point. "Come here a minute, Bertie."

"Yes, Mama," he said, ambling over as he sharpened the Y-shaped twig to make a new slingshot.

"Siddown here beside me; an' listen good to every word."

"Is what happen, Mam?"

"Nutt'n don't happen, but dat is the problem. Yuh should be meking something happen for yuhself because yuh are a man now. Yuh must look to yuh future and do something to mek yuh way." She hated the thought her words might hurt her son, but she could not stop, and her warnings streamed out, until Bertie protested.

"But mi love her, and mi save her life two time arready; one day she will belong to me."

"Don't mek mi hear yuh say dat again, boy! How Pearlie can belong to yuh? Yuh great-grandfather and him father before him was a slave, but all dat done and over wid long time! People not like sheep and goat no more. No man don't own anybody again."

Bertie had not explained himself well; he knew he had no rights to Pearlie's love; but his untried heart craved it more than anything. Day and night, he longed for her—beside him, under the naseberry tree, in the deep blue of the warm Idlewild sea water, on the narrow bed he slept in next to his brother's breath. He yearned to take her to the little church one day and later give him a baby just like Naomi. "So yuh don't tink she want dat too?" Bertie asked, his voice breaking. His mother stared from her son to the young woman, who bore little resemblance to the shivery waif he had rested at her feet so many years before.

"Pearlie can't help how she feel, Bertie; her life was too hard when she was a girl. To tell the truth, mi don't believe she can feel what yuh talking about at all. Too much bad things happen to her, and her heart dry up. Dat happen when people don't get plenty love when dem small."

"No, is not true. Look how Pearlie love Naomi; and mi will give her enough love."

"Boy, yuh too young; yuh don't understand life at all. Love for her little girl is not like loving a man. Mi don't think Pearlie can love any man." Mother and son remained silent as Bertie tried to take in the most profound words they had shared. But in the days ahead, he agreed to find work at the new construction site in Oracabessa, where preparations were in progress for a new house for a rich man who was in love with the island and planned to escape to its sunshine from the bleak winters in England.

Mrs. Scott's suggestions held no appeal for Bertie; the part that did the trick was when she pointed out what his absence might cause. "When yuh go to Oracabessa every day, and come home after Pearlie gone inside, she might miss yuh. People say when yuh leave somebody sometimes, dem heart might beat harder for yuh." Her meaning escaped him, but he liked the sound of Pearlie's heart doing something for him. If going to Oracabessa could bring Pearlie closer, it would be worth it.

A week later, he set off for Oracabessa before daybreak to join the line of men who waited every day to enter the property. He soon got a break to join the crew, and later moved from handyman to sweeper, and then joined the crew to demolish the old house. As construction progressed, the simple structure bothered the men, who mumbled among themselves. "But how a rich white man from England can come here an' build this plain little house?" And when Commander Ian Fleming named the property Goldeneye, some did not understand the "eye" part, but they endorsed the rest because for about one hour a day, everywhere in the area turned orange and gold as the sun dozed behind the clouds, and twilight covered the land.

Bertie marveled at the man who sat for hours at his desk, an old machine rattling under his fingers. When Commander went down the cliff to swim and snorkel with his famous friends who visited from all over the world, curiosity drew Bertie close to the house, where he peered through the jalousie windows that let the sunlight in, along with the breeze and the birds. He wondered how words could float into the man's head and how his fingers could form letters from the clatter of the typewriter keys to drop word after word on each page. Little did Bertie know he was witnessing the birth of stories about the Goldeneye exploits of James Bond–Agent 007.

Pearlie continued to work like a woman possessed. She was a fierce protector of Naomi, whose rapid growth was too much for her. Naomi was at school in the days, and the Scott girls remained in St. Ann to work after their studies at teachers' college, so the two women grew closer. Pearlie did miss Bertie; in fact, it surprised her how much. But his mother was right about her damaged heart. Despite her strong connection to Bertie, and though she had never tasted the love of a man, Pearlie longed for something more between them. Still, she never allowed herself to show what she felt. What Lenworth did had tainted her for life, and she could allow no man, especially one as good to her as Bertie, to get near enough to discover the stains the man with the sandpaper skin left inside her.

Ever since Naomi's birth, the pain in her abdomen had been constant and dreadful remnants of Lenworth's nasty legacy oozed from her body. As close as she was to Mrs. Scott, they had not spoken, since the early days, about how she got pregnant, or who Naomi's father was. Pearlie carried a heavy burden inside, and Mrs. Scott felt it was enough of a price to pay for whatever the poor girl might have done. Now, she had no words to tell the older woman of her new plight.

Very often, Pearlie struggled to get up from the bed, and when she did, her hands and feet would not work in the right way. Small objects slipped from her hands for no reason, and sometimes she fell without warning. The interminable pain tormented her body and her mind, but the most alarming part was the occasional loss of her eyesight.

Mrs. Scott knew the situation was grave, and when the matron at Port Maria Hospital said "bad blood" with her hand over her lips, it was no surprise. Lenworth's syphilis had remained latent in Pearlie's body, and the arduous labor with Naomi had aggravated her condition. The matron spoke solemnly, "Take her home and give her whatever you have to ease her pain; she might not have long with you."

"The poor girl don't even reach thirty, Matron," Mrs. Scott said, "and only one small part of her life mek her happy."

Pearlie's condition alarmed Bertie, and he spent all his spare time close to her. Determined to protect him from her body, she let him into her heart bit by bit, and they stubbornly held on to the little they could share. But he was not the only one she wanted to tell important things. Home early from school because of an expected storm, Naomi found her mother next to her own special tree.

"Evening, Mama, what yuh doing out here yuh alone? Come inside; teacher say plenty rain soon come."

"Nutt'n don't happen; tek off yuh uniform; put down yuh bag and come back; mi want to tell yuh something important." Naomi almost dropped her bag; as young as she was, she knew those words often brought bad news.

"Mi don't do nutt'n bad at school, Mama."

"Mi know dat. Just come back out when yuh tek off yuh school clothes; carry the lemonade on the table."

Eager to hear what her mother wanted to say, Naomi was back in a few minutes.

"See mi here, Mama; what yuh have to tell mi?"

"Don't yuh know mi always tell yuh what mi know dat can help yuh get through in this world?"

Naomi sat up straight; her mother started none of their frequent talks in such a serious tone.

"Yes, Mama."

"Is plenty important tings mi don't understand. Mi talk too bad and mi glad yuh soon can talk better. Mi wish mi did know more, but mi hope yuh always remember mi try mi best."

"Of course mi know, Mama, but what yuh mean by more things?"

"All what a mother like Miss Scott know; things a mother suppose to tell her little girl. Mi sorry mi never get more schooling."

"Mi don't understand yuh at all today."

Pearlie could not explain the strange feelings that had nagged her for weeks. All she knew was the same old-fashioned vagueness and the peculiar language of older women everywhere. This time, the matters would be even harder to share, for Pearlie herself understood little about life, and she had buried so much, so deep and so long, it was hard to unearth it. Anxiety made her start and pause, searching for words that eluded her.

"Why yuh don't tell mi plain and straight what yuh want to say?" the child kept asking as her anxiety grew. Pearlie tried again, and Naomi fell silent as her mother spooned out her stories about the Oracabessa house and the long dark night that was her life in the district where her skin made her an outsider.

"Yuh understand what mi telling you, Naomi?"

"Yes, Mam, but why God mek yuh suffer so?"

"Mi can't tell yuh dat, mi chile, but listen to mi good. Yuh getting big now, and yuh have to watch yuhself, especially when certain people come around yuh. Behave yuhself and go to school as long as yuh able, so yuh will know more dan mi."

"Mama, mi love school, and mi behave good all the time, but which people yuh talking about?"

"Bad people all over the place, but remember mi tell yuh dis: Mi go through plenty bad things, but God help me, an' him mek yuh bring a bright light in my life when everywhere was dark. Mi family bad treatment and other wickedness dat happen can never rub out, but mi ask the Almighty Father every day not to mek no stain leave on yuh."

"Yuh mixing mi up, Mama."

"Don't worry yuhself; yuh will understand when yuh grow big; and try yuh best, but if one day yuh find yuhself in Oracabessa, don't put yuh foot near any banana ground near dat riverside, don't make no banana stain get on yuh, or yuh clothes, for dat stain will never come out, and is a curse, so it will mek trouble follow yuh." As they drew close, and their fingers intertwined, Naomi sensed a deep fear in her mother. The smell of rain filled the air, and they walked together inside.

"Mama, is true dat Miss Scott know plenty more things than yuh, but mi still only want yuh as mi mother, so please mek yuh sickness get better."

Every day, they looked across small spaces at each other, both fearing the time when Pearlie would vanish.

CHAPTER 19
THE HOMESPUN CALICO DRESS

Idlewild, 1946

"Morning, Naomi; yuh mother wake yet?" A beaming Pearlie stepped out, wearing one of the few good church dresses she owned.

"Lord have mercy, girl what a way yuh look better today; is like yuh getting over everything. Thank our Almighty Father. But where yuh going, dress pass tidy so?"

"Bertie carrying mi somewhere," she said, stifling her giggle. "Please don't vex, Miss Scott; is only dis one time." Bertie waited, his face alight with excitement. An old donkey moved from one foot to the other, his back padded up with Pearlie's sheet and pillow.

"Bertie, what yuh doing with this poor girl? She look good today, but don't forget she is very sick."

"Is awright; mi keep her safe, and the fresh air good for her."

"Dat might be true, but yuh putting her on dat old donkey?" his mother asked, with a smile on her face. She looked down and laughed.

"Wait... is what yuh have on yuh foot, boy?"

Her son was wearing his father's old brown-and-white wing-tipped Spectator wedding shoes, the brown tips polished to a sheen and the uppers gleaming with his mother's whitening.

"Awright; go where yuh going; but just make sure yuh don't carry Pearlie in any danger."

"Don't worry, Mam," Pearlie said, "Mi feel good today and Bertie right; the fresh air good for me. We coming back before Naomi reach home from school, and it will be awright."

Bertie took all the care he could, loading Pearlie side-saddle on the donkey and wrapping an old blanket around her. Excitement and pride filled his mother's heart as her son showed a gentleness uncommon among men in her day. She smiled as she watched them trudging off into the distance. *Give dem a little time, please, Lord; mek mi poor son have something good to remember wid this poor girl.*

Bertie dragged the donkey with its precious rider, all the way to Goldeneye. He had begged the housekeeper to allow him to take his sick friend to look at the property. As they approached the gate, Pearlie giggled like a little girl.

"Why yuh excited so? Is just a pretty little place mi want to show yuh."

"Mi just feel like something good soon happen."

After they looked around Goldeneye, Bertie took her to the top of the steps above the cove, allowing her to glimpse what was down by the seaside.

"Mi have to go down there, please."

"Yuh sure? Mama will kill mi if mi mek anything happen to yuh."

"Bertie, look here; yuh know mi not going live long, right?"

"But why yuh have to say dat now?"

"And yuh know how mi thank yuh with mi whole heart for all what yuh do for mi and Naomi, right?"

"Yes, Pearlie; but why yuh sound serious so?" Feelings he had suppressed for too long flew from his mouth. "Pearlie, mi don't care no more; mi just going to say wat mi feel. Mi love yuh from before Naomi born ... from mi see yuh cover up under the sand. Is only one thing why mi go to Oracabessa and work; is because Mama say mi mus' leave yuh alone. An' mi don't know what mi mus' do; or why so much bad things happen to yuh."

"Me believe all what yuh telling me, but it too late. Miss Scott know what she saying; is a good thing yuh did leave mi alone. Everybody know what sickness mi have, an' it mek mi feel shame. Mi don't want to bring no shame on yuh."

"Don't worry yuhself over it; mi love yuh, and mi know is not yuh do this bad ting to yuhself. Mama explain to mi. Come; mek mi carry yuh down the step."

To the seaside they went, the old donkey trotting along.

"Bertie, look! Look!"

"What? What yuh showing me?"

"Is right here mi did walk sometimes when mi climb down the cliff and run from where the bad pickney dem tease me! Is only right here mi could find a little peace before mi leave the banana ground and come to where yuh find mi in Idlewild."

"What? Yuh sure, Pearlie? No wonder the first time mi come down here, the place feel like mi did see it before. Is because yuh tell mi how it look down here." The two sat in silence, interrupted only by the distant sound of waves breaking and the swishing of the foamy water roiling its way through the sand. Pelicans soared and swooped, streaking across the stunning blue sky and breaking into the water's surface. Bertie spread the blanket over his lap and laid Pearlie's shrinking body across it. She wiped the sweat from his forehead as he pulled her closer to his chest. Each absorbed the steadying thrum of two heartbeats poised between knowing and fearing.

***

That night, Pearlie's old dream returned, bringing back the memories of waking in terror and praying for morning, in her narrow bed next to Eudora's in the shrinking Oracabessa house. It had gone away after Naomi's birth, replaced by a dream of green fields where she and her little girl cooled each other from streams of clear water emptying into the ocean. Now it was back: There was no Naomi; alone and afraid, the young Pearlie thrashed around as the vast river of thick black banana stains edged up the length of her body. She jumped from her sleep as it swirled near her head, ready to drown her.

The dream's meaning was clear to Pearlie, and she knew it was time.

"Miss Scott, mi have to get everything ready."

"Ready for what?" Mrs. Scott asked, unwilling to hear the answer she already knew.

"So mi begging yuh one more favor, Mam–only one."

"We don't have plenty, but we will do what we can for Naomi."

"Yes, mi know, Mam; but Naomi not going to go far in life if she believe she don't have anybody to call family. Mi always beg yuh not to send mi back to where mi come from, but the Lord tell mi Naomi have to know her people." For the first time since turning up destitute on the stony expanse behind the Idlewild house, Pearlie shared more of the deep secrets of her life in Oracabessa, this time revealing the names of Agatha, Mas' Winston, and her own sister Eudora.

"Please, after mi—when the time come, carry Naomi to Oracabessa and mek her know dem."

"Yes, mi promise."

For two days, Mr. Scott pointed to the sky. "See dem there again." His wife had tried to ignore the seven ominous John Crows circling over Pearlie's room, but the flapping wings confirmed her ugly fears, and it was time for her to accept. Reaching up to the top of the cabinet, she took down the calabash with all the money Pearlie had given her. Down from the kitchen stool, she bounced into Naomi. "What happen? Why yuh face look so?"

"Miss Scott, mi can stay home from school? Mama sickness on her bad, and mi don't want to leave her."

Daughter and mother huddled together all day. The yard buzzed with people from the district gathering with food, drinks–whatever they knew would be necessary. As dusk settled over the small room, and the peenie-wallies scampered in and out the window, Mrs. Scott raised the tune and tracked the words in her uncertain voice. Villagers huddled and joined the singing, stretching every word to its full measure:

When I soar to worlds unknown, see thee on thy judgment throne,
Rock of Ages, cleft for me, let me hide myself in thee.

"Bertie, carry Naomi over the house and make her lay down in my bed; stay with her and come back when she sleeping."

"Why, Miss Scott? Why mi have to leave mi mother? Yuh don't see she feel sick?"

"Is for the best, chile," Mrs. Scott said, but a distraught Naomi fought and screamed, intent on staying by her mother's side, so they finally left her where she had always slept with Pearlie.

Familiar with the smell of death, those who could, waited. And as they waited, they sang. In the still hour past midnight when animals and insects shut down their calls, the last watchers repeated their solemn chants. Mrs. Scott glanced at Pearlie and then at the women close by, signaling what they already knew. Naomi lay protected in sleep, unaware of who she would be at daybreak. Bertie put her in Mrs. Scott's bed and dragged himself back across the yard to sit with the woman he had loved for so long.

Naomi stirred at dawn, and she was alone. On tiptoes, she made her way from Mrs. Scott's room, and ventured down the passage to the back door. Her hand was on the doorknob when she heard it: *Drip, Drip, Drip* went the sound breaking through the confusion of a girl who had no time to figure out what lay on the other side, for only her mother was on her mind. *Drip, Drip, Drip* as the slabs of ice leaked to the ground. Naomi jumped back from the door. Gathering herself, she slowed down and cracked it open. Then she saw it.

At one end, the narrow sheet of zinc rested upon an enormous stone; at the other, a smaller stone bore its weight, so the entire sheet tilted toward the steps. On it lay a log-like shape swaddled in stiff white.

"Naomi! Come back," Bertie shouted, reaching for her hand just in time. "Don't go out there."

"Is what out there? The whole place wet."

"Don't worry over it," Bertie said, his hands and voice shaking as he rushed her the other way out through the front, into the arms of his mother, who broke the news. Naomi fled to her navel-string tree until dusk took her to Pearlie's bare bed. For two days, she uttered no words.

Pearlie had washed and ironed the dress she made from two yards of cheap calico, trimmed with blue bias binding at the neck and on the sleeves. All over the blouse, she had embroidered the sky and the seaside, stitching one pelican with its wing touching the neckline. It was the scene etched in her memory from the day of her long walk from the darkness of Oracabessa to the rocky expanse near the spot where Bertie found her.

Bertie dug her grave out of the rocks and sand, under the sea-grape bush where he had found his shivering bundle so many years before. Naomi, Bertie, and his parents marked the spot with a circle of pink conch shells and a guava jelly bottle filled with red hibiscus and white ram goat roses.

A trail of red ants made their way around the spot where Pearlie lay, free at last from her long acquaintance with grief.

CHAPTER 20
EUDORA'S GIRL FROM THE COUNTRY

Oracabessa, 1947

Life without Pearlie was beyond the worst fears of Naomi, a fourteen-year-old with half herself missing. What would become of her if the situation with the Scotts changed? The thought crossed her mind every day despite their constant reassurances: "We going to do what we can to help yuh; work hard at school and keep up with the Sunday school teaching with Sister Ignatius. She was always a good friend to Pearlie, so she will look out for yuh. One day, yuh will see the reward."

Almost a year to the day of her death, the time came for Mrs. Scott to reveal Pearlie's dying wish.

"No, no, Mam, please don't carry mi to dat place. Please mek mi stay with yuh; mi not 'fraid to stay in Mama room."

"We can't do better. Mi have to do what mi promise. We put it off until now, but Mr. Scott boss send home most of the workers, and nobody else not giving him work because him not young again. We can't do better ... we moving to Highgate to him family." All day under her navel-string tree, Naomi polished her shoes with the red hibiscus flowers.

***

Along the paths close to Oracabessa River, the story of Pearlie and Agatha had faded from many memories, but rumors spread like wildfire that strangers were asking about the family of a young girl who had run away years before. Mrs. Scott's church connections learned that Pearlie's light-skinned sister Eudora was the postmistress closeted in a little corner of the grocery shop in the square. People said just like Pearlie, Agatha had drawn into herself after Mas' Winston disappeared for good, leaving her to gaze at the withering banana field, until Eudora tucked her away in the back room of her own cramped house.

It was a busy Friday afternoon when Mrs. Scott dragged a protesting Naomi to the postal agency. Gripping the child's hand in hers, she sidled past the people in line, straight up to the window. Eudora pulled and pushed letters, stamps, staplers, scales, and her other work accoutrements, looking up from time to time to assess the length of the line forming in and outside the shop for service after lunch break.

"Pleasant hafternoon, good people of Oracabessa," Eudora said, her voice ringing through the little space. "Please form a horderly line and get out whatever yuh need to carry out yuh business today. We want to get through early because is Friday." The English lady from Kingston who had come years before, to train the three candidates for the job had planted the idea in Eudora's head that becoming the postmistress would "require her to be a cut above other people." Eudora knew her light skin and curly hair, along with her Sunday school teaching, made her the favorite, but "speaking properly" would also be essential. The parson's wife had supervised Eudora's diligent daily practice to rid her speech of the "flat tone and countrified bad talking."

All these years later, her efforts at "speaking proper English" never wavered, though a high squeak and regular collisions of tongue and teeth prevented the words from coming out just how she wanted. Nor could she keep track of which words had aitches and which ones did not, so her own aitches went any and everywhere.

Observing her aunt through the chicken wire, Naomi tried her best not to giggle, but when Eudora appeared in full view, she could not stop herself.

"Yuh sure is Mama sister, Miss Scott? Mi know she suppose to have high color, but she red for true, and she talk like she better than everybody else."

"Stop yuh noise," Mrs. Scott said, stepping up to Miss Eudora's workstation and puffing up her chest as if it could push the right words out.

"Yes, my goodly lady? What do you want today? Stamps? Postal horder? hairmail henvelope? I know you don't come from Oracabessa, so prob'ly you don't know you must join the line. If you come about post office business, be pleased to find your place be'ind all these goodly Oracabessa people who reach before yuh."

"No, Mam, we don't come for post office business," Mrs. Scott said in a quiet voice, hoping her whisper might give Eudora the hint to lower hers. Intent on impressing Eudora with her best English, she measured her words, drawing a snicker from Naomi.

"Well, Mam, we … this poor unfortunate girl and mi have to talk to yuh when yuh have a chance; but is a private matter."

"Talk to me private about what kind of matter please, lady? You and that girl is unknown to me."

"We can wait outside till yuh take a little break, Miss Eudora? I will explain."

"Well, if you want you can wait; but stand one side, for you can well see the line is lengthy."

Mrs. Scott dragged Naomi outside to wait in the shade of a breadfruit tree.

"Miss Scott, yuh don't see how this woman miserable, Mam? She mek mi more vex every minute, and mi hope she not mi auntie at all. Please mek we just go back to Idlewild."

"Keep quiet; the woman doing her work, and she don't even know what we come to see her about."

"Remember, Mama was sick bad; suppose she never know what she was saying when she tell yuh to bring mi here?"

"Stop it; yuh mother know full well what she was doing."

It was almost an hour before Eudora presented herself with a flourish outside the shop. As she listened to Mrs. Scott's story and looked from one visitor to another, her face went from pale to paler. When she finally spoke, her words were fraught with doubt and fear.

"You mean somebody call herself Pearlie and use my mother name and mine?"

"Yes; when her time draw near, she ask mi to bring Naomi to Oracabessa and she tell mi who her family is. Mi and mi husband was not sure about the matter, so we tek it to the Lord in prayer, and we give Naomi as much time as we could manage. But now mi husband find himself without work, we have to come to yuh because we moving to Highgate, and we cannot carry Naomi, or leave her alone in Idlewild. We want to do what Pearlie ask us."

Eudora rubbed her hands in her apron again and took out a kerchief from her pocket, wiping the sweat from her forehead and her cheeks. The little blue flowers on the kerchief turned a bright brownish red with the caked-up powder. Naomi giggled at her aunt's blotchy patchwork face.

"I don't rightly know what you want me to say, Lady. That is a very large problem for true, but—"

"Miss Eudora," Mrs. Scott said with even more conviction, "we hear yuh mother Miss Agatha is not too well, and Naomi can help her out when yuh have to work. Pearlie teach Naomi the right way. She look after her little room and tek care of herself, and she can be a help to yuh—"

"But Miss Scott, remember about school—"

"Keep quiet when big people talking, girl." Eudora's shriek made Naomi back away, but she advanced, wagging her finger in the child's face. "It look like you don't get one scrap of home training." Naomi slinked away, leaving an embarrassed Mrs. Scott to face their questioner.

"Naomi not herself today, Miss Eudora; coming here like this is very hard for her. Her mother do her very best to bring her up the proper Christian way."

"Lady, before you say one more word, tell me something: Who is the father of the girl?"

The dreaded question came without warning, and Naomi approached the two women, knowing her time was coming. *Watch how Miss Scott going stammer now because the woman ask her about Mama business.*

"Well, to tell the truth ... but Miss Eudora—"

"No, lady, no 'well' and no 'but'; just answer the question."

"I am very sorry, but is one thing Pearlie never tell me, no matter how much time mi ask her."

Recalling her mother's firmest words, Naomi stretched herself beyond her height, and spoke in her boldest voice.

"Mi mother say mi don't have any father. Mi never have one, and mi will never have one."

"Foolish girl, everybody have a father. Anyway, Miss Scott, I cannot help you or this girl, and is time to go back inside. Postmistress work is very important."

"But, what about Miss Agatha? Yuh not even going to make her see her own granddaughter?"

"You think I can just take this unbeknown girl to my mother and tell her this tall story? And with no father name? You look like a fine upstanding woman. What kind of plan is this you want me to agree to?"

"Miss Eudora, is Idlewild we come from; how we can just turn around and go back, with not even a good word from yuh about this girl seeing her own grandmother? And not to cause any offense, but people say yuh are a very important woman in Oracabessa Church."

For the first time, a brief smile flashed on Eudora's face. "You hear so?"

"Yes, so mi wondering if yuh considering about yuh Christian duty to help people who not fortunate like yuhself, especially yuh own family."

"Well, my Christian duty is ... I mean it is very important; but you will have to come back another time, after me and my mother have words over this peculiar business."

"But yuh don't tell us when to come back!"

Eudora was already halfway to her post when she threw the words at them.

"Week after next Monday when is not end of month or market day."

Naomi's eyes burned with humiliation, as she ran into the street. "Mi not coming back nowhere, Miss Scott; look how she shame mi and yuh. And mi don't care if mi have to stay by miself in Idlewild."

In the end, the chance of Naomi's presence being good for Agatha's condition, and the prospect of help in the house seemed to make a difference to Eudora. But the reference to her Christian duty did the trick. Visions of praise from her pastor and admiration from the entire community tilted the scales against her outrage at the thought of having Pearlie's fatherless child in her house. In another month, Naomi was "Eudora's girl from the country."

***

The move to Oracabessa brought fresh grief to the misplaced teenager. Idlewild without Pearlie was like a desert without a hope of water, but at least the Scotts did all they could to help her manage her loss. Once she moved to Oracabessa, her eyes lost the tiny glow that had struggled to return to them, and her feet dragged her along as if there was nowhere she wanted to go. Everywhere she turned in Eudora's house there was a rule, and even the air she breathed felt like her aunt doled it out in teaspoons to ensure she did not take too much. When all the chores her aunt left for her every day were behind her, she walked around the yard without purpose or hope, just an endless longing for her mother, her friends from Idlewild, and her exciting days at school.

Agatha showed no interest in her, or where she came from, or what became of Pearlie. The old woman just stared ahead, singing snippets of church songs and brushing from her ankles what she alone could see. When her grandmother did speak to her now and again, Naomi could not understand her muttering about banana stains and curses. Disappointed and resentful, the teenager did not care to have a relationship with her aunt, especially after Eudora announced Naomi would not be going to school even after the Christmas break. There was no school around for children past fifteen years old, so Naomi's chance to fulfill her promise to Pearlie was disappearing.

"What yuh say, Miss Eudora? How yuh mean mi not going to school? Mama say no matter what happen, mi have to finish out mi schooling so mi can have a better life."

"Is not everybody must go to school long. Mama send Pearlie there, and it never stop her from putting herself in trouble till she have to run away."

Naomi seethed at the lie, but her mother had made her promise never to mention their terrible treatment of her in Oracabessa.

"But Miss Eudora, yuh promise mi yuh would mek mi go when January come and now yuh saying this foolishness."

Eudora did not budge, and this was the last straw for Naomi, who was already angry about her aunt's refusal to send her to Boscobel when the priest and the nuns offered Mass on Fourth Sunday. The broken promises stole the two things Pearlie had begged Naomi to stick with, no matter what.

CHAPTER 21
THE BEST ICE CREAM

Boscobel, 1948

Tension stretched out between Eudora and Naomi, but she never took her eyes off the girl, especially after her husband Rufus said Naomi was old enough to go out sometimes. Weeks after his suggestion, Eudora tried a novel approach.

"Come in here a minute, Naomi!"

"Me have to finish pressing the clothes, before the fire burn out and leave the iron cold," Naomi said.

"Come when you finish." Whenever Eudora called her in that tone of voice, Naomi expected a complaint, so she braced herself and joined her aunt in the kitchen.

"Yes, Mam? Yuh want something?"

"You finish with everybody church clothes for tomorrow morning?"

"Yes."

"Well, I decide something; you can go to service at Boscobel; you might learn something, and you will tell the Lord and me thanks for the good fortune that bring you to this house." Naomi could hardly believe what she had heard, but her attitude shifted, displaced by a sliver of hope.

"Yes, Mam; thanks; when mi can go?"

"Very well; next week, take Mr. Hibbert's early-morning van so you can have time to talk to the Sister Lady; then go straight to the service, and after it finish wait for him to bring you back. I don't want you keeping company with anybody outside the school yard, for you might chat my business with people. You understand me good?"

"Yes, mi understand everything."

Every Fourth Sunday, Mr. Hibbert's van to Boscobel pulled up outside the grocery shop and chugged through the fresh morning mist, taking Naomi to her new oasis.

***

Naomi had been attending Mass for about three months, and apart from getting her out from under Eudora's glare, the best thing about it was knowing she was doing one thing Pearlie wanted. On the Sunday after Ash Wednesday, she struggled to keep her mind on the gospel readings. She felt the eyes glued to her face, and she yearned to glance at their owner. At last, the recessional hymn began, and as everyone filed through the narrow aisle, she peeked in the boy's direction. They made their way from the school room, each glancing at the other in a wordless ritual that overflowed with meaning.

After the next Mass, as Naomi waited to speak with Sister Ignatius, a subtle warm breeze lingered close to her back. She stepped gingerly out of the side door, her hand almost brushing against him as her words sailed across the room, "See you next month, Sister Ignatius."

"Morning, nice girl," the strange boy said in just the voice Naomi imagined since she had noticed him leaning against the wall, three rows from the makeshift altar. His skin was the color of the rich dark sugar Pearlie used to sweeten her marmalade and guava jam. A little silver cross gleamed on his chest where he had left his shirt button undone.

"Morning, is who yuh calling nice girl? Yuh know me? Kindly move and make mi pass; mi have to catch a bus," Naomi said, putting on a less than friendly tone. Back in Oracabessa, the days dragged along, but the silver cross danced in her head, making its way through the clutter of washing, cleaning, and hopelessness.

Meanwhile, at the Boscobel school, the drummer boy from the mento band nagged Sister Ignatius with questions about the girl who talked to her at Mass on Sundays.

"Miles, what is the matter with you, boy? Keep your mind on your schoolwork and your music. Remember your parents are planning to send for you soon. Joining them in America will change your life forever."

Miles had been Sister's student at the little Catholic school where his grandmother sent him when he was too young for elementary school. But even when he moved on to the all-age school, Sister kept a close watch over him, determined to prevent him from getting into any situation that could endanger his parents' plan.

Driven by the urgency of what they had no words to name, Naomi and Miles continued to hover, and not even Sister's rosaries and warnings could impede the plans they whispered in the breeze, or the crude notes they pressed into each other's hands as Naomi rushed to catch the bus after Mass every month. Easter now behind them, she tore up the last note from Miles, setting out the steps they had planned. Friday found her completing her chores in half the usual time, and feverishly working on all the jobs Eudora expected her to finish on Saturday morning. As usual after dinner, her aunt stood in the kitchen to make sure Naomi was cleaning up.

"I notice you wash and iron and tidy up everywhere; what happen?"

"Well, mi was thinking ... like how yuh always say Friday is a hard day at yuh work, mi could finish what mi have to do and then—"

"And then what? What you want to say?"

"Then Saturday morning, mi could go to market for yuh because mi know yuh don't like the crowd down there. Is dat why mi try finish all mi work today." As hard as the words were to utter, waiting for Eudora's response was much worse.

"Well, well. Wonders never cease. To tell the truth, I pray all the time for a day when you would show a spoonful of gratitude. Thank God, this day is here; I cast my bread on the water, and now it might come back." Naomi had no clue what her aunt meant, but it did not matter.

Every Saturday, Miles took the bus from Boscobel to meet his new friend outside the Oracabessa market, bringing a new light into Naomi's drab life. Shoes in hand, they walked along their favorite spots by the shoreline. They feasted on the fish and bammy breakfast his grandmother packed in enamel carriers, feeding one another with the food and the hope spread out on their table of sand. The seed of belief struggling to stay alive in Naomi's heart soon grew into a shrub, convincing her that the future held more for her than Miss Agatha, or Eudora, or the endless work in her bleak house.

When they tired of the seashore, hills and valleys on the other side became their playground as they explored paths to the shallows of Oracabessa River. Naomi shared the secrets of her mother's agony in the house at the side of that other little field and the inevitable curse of the banana stain. "Don't worry 'bout dat," he assured her, "what happen to yuh mother not going happen to yuh."

Still, every time he suggested a longer walk toward other places he knew, she dragged him away, shunning every area that resembled the field Pearlie had described. How could she explain her mother's misfortunes, or why her warnings against stains and curses still rang in her ears?

"Miles, yuh believe one day we can leave this place and go somewhere better?" she asked over and over, always with a tremor in her voice.

"Of course, we leaving here one day. My mother and father in America, and dem working hard to send for Grannie and me."

"So dat mean yuh soon leave mi and gone."

"Don't say dat; it mean after mi learn a good trade and can play better music, mi can send for yuh."

"Yuh lucky; mi wish mi did have people like yuh family, somebody mi could talk to like yuh grannie."

"Don't fret; Yuh soon talk to her yuhself."

To Naomi's ears, his words were like a song her mother hummed in the little room at Idlewild, and they awakened her yearning for the reassurance of Pearlie's company. A few weeks passed before they perfected another plan to elude Miss Eudora.

***

"Grannie, see mi bring Naomi just like yuh tell mi!"

Miss Myrtle's skin was velvet black, every inch of her face wrinkled like the prunes the island women soaked in wine all year to put in their Christmas puddings. The old woman rose from her bench under the ackee tree and wrapped the girl in her ample bosom. Then, she shoved her away, looking her up and down twice, before a warmer embrace followed. "Miles, yuh find a proper friend at church; mi glad for yuh. So yuh is Naomi? Why yuh look so frighten? Come inside."

"Thanks, Miss Myrtle," Naomi said, taking the woman's hand and following her. His eyes gleaming with pride and relief, Miles walked a little way behind them, whistling.

"Come, siddown right here at the window. We can catch the cool breeze."

Everywhere smelled of Miss Myrtle's Limacol toilet lotion, and Naomi wished she could stay forever with them in the cozy little house down the alley. Reminders of her son in America were everywhere, and they never stopped talking about the plan for Miles and her to join him. "So yuh think yuh and Miles soon leave, Miss Myrtle?" a wistful Naomi kept asking.

"Is a good while now mi son suppose to send for mi and this boy, but it don't work out yet and the Lord alone know if or when it might come to pass." Her words filled Naomi with the hope that Miles could help her leave Oracabessa one day, but deep inside, an ugly fear lurked that his parents could snatch him away, and his promises would come to naught.

"We hope so chile, but to tell the truth, sometimes mi don't mind if we don't go too quick. Mi hear dat dem treat black people bad over America, and mi 'fraid for the cold."

Naomi's visits multiplied, and Miss Myrtle fed them with the tastiest food Naomi ate since she used to gobble down all the special treats Pearlie brewed in Idlewild. Pride in her eyes, Miss Myrtle showed off cheap mementoes her son sent home every Christmas since he and his wife took the long journey from Jamaica to make a better life. The old lady shared special treats he sent and glowed when she spoke of how he helped them with a little money as often as his meager earnings as a garbage man allowed. When the treats included Miss Myrtle's favorite grape nuts, she made Miles bring out the green wooden bucket, and he made the best ice cream Naomi ever tasted.

Every few weeks, Eudora heard an extra reason for her niece to be in Boscobel. And every time Miss Myrtle was about to leave for her prayer meeting, she warned her grandson, "Now, listen, Missa Miles, mi don't want yuh troubling this nice girl before the two of yuh know what yuh doing, for it will mash up her whole life. Yuh father soon send for yuh, and him will walk from America to deal wid yuh if yuh ever fall this girl and put us in trouble."

"Me know, Grannie; mi not going do Naomi anything, Mam." Miles said.

The brief hours with Miles, and their visits to Miss Myrtle were the best times Naomi had experienced since leaving Idlewild. Whenever she felt tired, or sick, or desperate to escape Eudora's misery, she reached for the bottle of Limacol Miss Myrtle gave her and doused it all over her face and head. Now and again, she allowed herself to hope a day was near when she could truly let go of Pearlie's dire warnings.

CHAPTER 22
A NEW LIFE FOR NAOMI

Boscobel, 1950s

Naomi's escape came, but not in the way of her hopes. The Oracabessa River churned with its extra muddy water after weeks of rain. The air was heavy, and dusk fell early on Friday. Clothes, shoes, and personal items littered the sidewalk outside Eudora's gate. Naomi was so busy dodging the wild stones her aunt kept hurling, and she was so frantic to grab some of her clothes, she could not find words to utter a protest. Miss Eudora's high-class talking disappeared as she laid into Naomi, sounding like any Oracabessa fishwife.

"And never yuh show yuh face around dis place again. Look 'ow much mi do for yuh since the lady beg mi to take yuh in after yuh mother dead, and leave yuh. Mi should know yuh would be like Pearlie–sneaking out from the house all the while until she get a baby. All this time, yuh say yuh want to help mi out, an' yuh gone to Sister and church; and look what yuh and dat worthless boy was carrying on." Between her shrieks, she rained blows all over Naomi's back with her husband's belt as the two children danced around her, gleefully mimicking her words.

"Stop now, Miss Eudora, mi begging yuh, Mam. Mi know yuh vex, but please don't send mi away. Yuh can give mi more work. Mi really and truly sorry. Where mi going to go? Yuh know Miss Scott gone, and all her family leave Idlewild long time."

"Why yuh never consider dat when yuh was sneaking away like a common slut to see dat oily half-coolie boy? Yuh think yuh could keep yuh secret from me forever? Well, mek him find a place for yuh now ... yuh and yuh bastard pickney … and don't put one foot near this yard with yuh disgraceful belly! Go 'bout yuh business and don't even walk on this road again."

***

The main street into Boscobel overflowed with villagers celebrating Emancipation Day, the annual August 1ˢᵗ holiday to celebrate the abolition of slavery. Young and old danced everywhere, dressed in bandana fabric and multi-colored head-ties. Miles was playing in the mento band, so Naomi picked her way through the crowd, carrying the bag Eudora had thrown out with almost everything she owned. The lead singer whispered to Miles that "his girl" was at the back of the stage.

"What yuh doing out here so late? Yuh auntie know yuh leave the house?"

"Miss Eudora throw mi out; she find out mi expecting; some of mi clothes burn up and she fling some out in the road. What mi going to do?"

"Awright, don't cry."

"Miles, yuh don't see? Is this Mama was trying to warn mi about, and is this why she tell mi not to go near banana field and get the curse."

"Naomi, no curse not here, and nutt'n not going trouble yuh. Mi never want this happen either, but is not yuh alone."

"But yuh grannie always warn yuh not to put us in trouble; now mi know dis is what she mean. Where mi can go now?"

"Stop worry yuhself; we will find a way. Yuh don't have to beg yuh auntie nutt'n. Mi will look after everything. Wait right here mek mi tell Missa Brown mi have to carry yuh home. Mi coming right back."

Outside Miss Myrtle's house, the two huddled together, not knowing how to face the old lady, not knowing how to admit they had brought trouble to her doorstep. Miss Myrtle soon heard their mumbling and came outside, so there was no delaying the news.

"We sorry, Mam; we very sorry we never listen to yuh, and now God punishing mi. Mi deserve punishment, but mi don't have nowhere to go,

and what going become of mi if mi run away like Mama? Mi only hope the
Lord don't punish the poor little baby."

"Yes, Grannie, wi sorry; but don't worry yuhself. Mi will try mi best like
yuh always tell mi."

"Miles, is yuh wrong. Yuh is the bigger one, and mi warn yuh from long
time about man-and-woman business. Now yuh must tek up yuh
responsibility. And Naomi, yuh must stop talk like yuh mad! How a baby
can be punishment? God don't like what yuh and Miles do; yuh should wait
until the right time. But even if Him vex, Him not meking the innocent
baby suffer. Yuh auntie feel disappointed, but she don't mean what she say.
Go back and tell her yuh sorry." When Naomi explained all Eudora said and
did, Miss Myrtle understood the situation was grave.

"Well, yuh going stay right here, and we have to mek the best of the
situation for yuh and the baby."

***

Determined to keep his promise, Miles toiled week after week at the Jacobs
banana plantation in Oracabessa to provide for his little family. Before
Naomi spent any money, she turned over the few pounds and shillings Miles
put in her hands, as if they were the last ones she would ever hold. A woman
a few miles away in Galina opened a small craft shop in her front room and
sent messages to all the district churches calling "decent churchgoing young
women" to come to her so she could teach them to make a living. Eager to
play her part, and well trained by Eudora, Naomi battled her morning
sickness and readied herself for the mail van to take her every day to the pink
and burgundy house adorned with fringes of intricate white fretwork on the
wraparound veranda. Her days stretched into drawn-out hours of chewing
ginger while navigating three-inch long needles through miles of plaited
straw. She turned circles until they became parts of quaint hats, bags, and
mats the tourists loved to show off after returning home from their
vacations.

Not a word passed between Boscobel and Oracabessa. Naomi sometimes felt ashamed that her departure mirrored Pearlie's own experience of fleeing from home, rejected and pregnant, though she had no way of knowing it until much later. But her daughter was happy to be rid of the house and the ugly memories. Pearlie had wanted her child to know her relatives, and now she knew them. Naomi slammed the door shut on her Oracabessa connections.

As the heat of the summer bore down on them, and sleep became difficult for Naomi, a peculiar dream about Pearlie troubled her, but Miss Myrtle dismissed her concern.

"Stop worry yuhself about yuh own mother coming in yuh dream; she know yuh soon have yuh own baby, and she want to tell yuh she watching over the two of yuh."

"But why her finger in mi face like she warning me?"

"Which mother yuh know don't warn her children?"

"Is true, Miss Myrtle; yuh right."

Envelopes with red, white, and blue borders showed up at the postal agency with much more frequency. Naomi eyed Miles as he spent his spare time poring over his mother's letters. He had stopped sharing her excitement about her son's "nice girl." Grim warnings crawled between the words on the paper, right along with the reminders about plans coming through soon to get him into "a nice big trade school in Brooklyn." The evening when Naomi squeezed past him and sneaked a look at the latest letter, she walked away swiftly, tears brimming at the stern warnings all over the page against "dat girl yuh tek up wid down there."

Naomi never paused until she found the stash of letters bundled in the old school bag he had kept hidden under the mattress. His long day in the field provided more than enough opportunity for her to digest the withering words. "We are black, but not like that; yuh will do better over here with a nice brown girl beside your cool complexion. And if yuh give her a baby, yuh will have to leave the two of them right there in Boscobel."

The offending sentences sweated in her bosom until Miles put the first foot through the front door.

"What she mean, 'if yuh give her a baby'? How yuh tell mi long time yuh mother know mi expecting? So now, dem sending for yuh, and yuh going leave mi right here wid mi big belly!"

"Why yuh read mi letter?"

"Because mi know is something mek yuh hide dem."

"But yuh know from long time mi waiting to go and—"

"What the two of yuh fussing about again?" Miss Myrtle asked, troubled by their frequent arguments.

"Is nutt'n, Grannie; Naomi, stop this foolishness and come outside."

"Leave mi alone; him not telling the truth Miss Myrtle. We fussing over the letter dem from him mother. She telling him to leave mi and this baby and go to America. Dat is why him don't show mi no more letter."

Miss Myrtle had nothing to say; embarrassment burned her eyes, and she squeezed them shut to block the image of the woebegone girl glaring at her woebegone grandson caught between two worlds. *Miles is mi own blood, and it hard to believe it miself, but mi know him going do dis girl and her baby what him own mother and father do to him. Generation after generation is the same. It look like this problem pass down from slavery days.*

"Lord help us," she said, walking away.

The letters stopped—at least, Naomi saw no more. Miles reassured her he would not go through with his parents' plans, but his mother was determined to rescue her son from "dat girl who would do anything to better herself–even tie yuh down with a baby that might not be yours." His mother's alluring word pictures stirred his confusion, promising "plenty place to walk about, bus and train that come on time and can take yuh anywhere, rich people with big lawns yuh can cut on the weekends and make good money, a big rich place where yuh can learn real music and live without the burden of a baby, and a girl like that who won't help yuh get anywhere in life."

The girl whom Miles loved, and still promised to take care of, soon disappeared. In his mother's letters, she was "a girl without family, not a girl to bring in our family." In the suffocating Boscobel alley, a hideous shrew took Naomi's place, stalking every step Miles took, hurling accusations and desperate pleading in turn. She was always vomiting or sleeping, and she chased him away when he tried to comfort her. Soon, words made no sense, so to avoid Miss Myrtle's wrath as well, the boy stayed away with his friends. By Christmas, the last letter came—in it, a shiny ticket for Miles to a better life in America. Pearlie's words haunted Naomi, who was now certain she would follow the same path as her mother. *Mama, why yuh never tell mi how mi could get a baby and how mi would suffer for it?*

CHAPTER 23
THE WHITE SLIPPER SATIN FROCK

Boscobel, 1950s

Struggling to see over her swollen belly, a bereft Naomi rummaged through the old clothes and fabric she had been saving. Her fingers closed around the two yards of white slipper satin Miss Myrtle gave her to make the dress for her marriage to Miles. How many times had the two of them sat under the naseberry tree, caught up in feverish planning of wedding details?

The fabric slid to the ground, and Naomi glanced at it, her eyes filled with wonder: Would an envelope trimmed in American colors ever come? Would his breath brush against her skin again? Was there a God who could hear her prayers and send him back to her? Glancing at the rise and fall of her belly, she stuffed the slipper satin in the box and folded herself around the pillow.

"Mi know it hard, Naomi, but yuh have to carry on; sew yuhself a nice frock and put it up until yuh time come to wear it with pride. God know why him tek Miles from us, but Him know dat boy is yuh husband as sure as if the two of yuh did stand up in church."

The old woman's consolation bounced from the wall, rolled down the steps through the back door, and Naomi rose from the bed in a frenzy.

"Mama was right, Miss Myrtle! Dat banana field was nutt'n but a stain and a curse. If God care about mi, why Him tek away the few good things in mi life? Look how Miles promise to stay with mi, and how him mek mi feel safe. Wi never mean to cause trouble, and now him leave mi alone to bear everything."

"Don't say a thing like dat. Miles do wrong, and the pain hard to bear, but never yuh question the ways of the Almighty."

"But why God have to mek us lose who we love?"

"Is not God mek we lose dem. People go when the time come; we don't own one thing or one soul in this world—not even ourself. Prob'ly yuh poor mother dead to mek yuh know how yuh should live."

"What yuh mean?"

"Ah, mi dear, yuh have yuh life before yuh; one day, yuh will see."

Getting little or no sleep, Naomi struggled through the days at the craft shop and by evening, she stumbled around the house, wrapped in a cloak of grief. Her anguish was for Miles, but sometimes it was impossible to distinguish it from her sorrow at the absence of her mother to shepherd her through this new darkness. A dull throbbing ache settled under her breast whenever her baby moved; and right along with it, Pearlie's words assailed her. "Naomi, look how Massa Death coming to tek mi away, and mi don't have anybody to leave yuh with. Promise mi before yuh have any baby, yuh will have the father to stand up beside yuh." *Mama must be turning over in her grave. Lord Savior, if this is the punishment Eudora promise for what mi and Miles do, why mi alone have to bear it?*

Miss Myrtle and Sister Ignatius consoled the distraught girl and prayed with her every chance they got, but in her seventh month, Naomi marched away from the makeshift church, screaming at both, and at God, "Mi finish with dis praying to dis God who never answer." Blanketed in despair and anxiety, she found herself at the shoreline where Miles had walked hand in hand with her, weaving the threads of their seaside dream. A deep sleep wrested her away until only the steady pounding of the rain splashing mud on her back woke her to the unmistakable vision of Pearlie. Yet again, her mother's words replayed details of the implacable banana-stain curse, and despair enveloped Naomi. *Life too hard, Lord. Is better mi just lay down right here, and yuh can tek mi and dis baby right now.*

***

The night was thick when the loud banging took a frantic Miss Myrtle to the front door. "Naomi, where yuh was all this time? How yuh stay so? Steady yuhself and come inside quick." The old woman went into action– Limacol and smelling salts on the kitchen table, a head soaked with Bay Rum, a twisted old pot on the little one-burner kerosene stove, and towels and dry clothes stuffed into Naomi's trembling hands.

Miss Myrtle's old hot-water bag warmed her on the outside, and the hot chocolate with the oil and nutmeg swirling on top, streamed through her insides, dispelling the chill and helping her find words. "Sorry, Miss Myrtle, mi never mean to stay out so long and mek yuh fret, but mi telling yuh what happen right now."

"Is awright; mi just glad yuh come. And when yuh settle down, yuh can tell me. When yuh having baby and yuh reach a stage like this, yuh must tek better care of yuhself. Things can go wrong, and we don't need no more problem."

"Yes, mi know; but mi have to get it off mi mind; mi feel awful over it."

"What yuh do?"

"Me don't do nutt'n, but when the big rain catch mi out by the seaside, mi feel like mi want to lie down in the mud and mek de two of us drown. Mi feel bad over it, Mam, but mi was begging God to jus tek the two of us and stop the suffering."

"Girl, how yuh can ask God to tek yuh life and this poor baby life? Suppose poor unfortunate Pearlie did tek her life, yuh know yuh wouldn't get a chance?"

"Yes, Mam."

"No matter how things hard, every mother have to fight to give dem pickney life."

"Mi know, Mam; after mi talk to God, mi hear Mama voice plain, and she talk about the banana stain and the curse."

"Yuh sure is yuh mother talk about stain and curse, Naomi? Mi believe is the devil mixing up yuh brain. Mi don't believe a mother would put curse in her daughter dream when she expecting. Pearlie know dat would bring bad luck."

"Yes, mi sure. But she never stop. She ask mi how mi little baby going live if mi don't give it a chance, and she say mi mustn't tink about the curse but do what is right for mi baby. Same time, mi tell God mi sorry, and mi pray the right way. But mi drop asleep right there until mi get up and run come home to yuh. Miss Myrtle, mi realize now mi have to protect mi baby. Miles gone and leave us, but mi not going nowhere; mi have to fight life for the two of us, and for yuh too, Mam, because yuh treat mi very good."

***

When the little girl screamed into the bright February morning, Naomi and Miss Myrtle laughed, recalling how certain they had been that the child would be Richard Miles McIntosh, as his parents had decided. With the father long gone, mother and grandmother busied themselves, ignoring the name, and whatever else did not relate to the baby's care. On the fourth night, a loud cry disturbed the old woman's prayers.

"Miss Myrtle, yuh can please come here, Mam?"

"Mi coming...but is what happen?" the old woman asked, shouting from her room.

"Mi get the baby name: Esther Rachel Walker."

"Dat is two strong name straight from the Bible. She will get plenty blessing and be a blessing to everybody."

For the first few months, Esther kept them on their feet. As if sensing the surrounding anxiety, the baby was impossible to settle.

"Why she bawling so?" Miss Myrtle shouted from under the ackee tree.

"She won't feed, and she won't keep quiet. What mi suppose to do?"

"Yuh must calm yuhself; the baby know yuh on edge, and is dat mek her miserable."

Exhausted and confused, Naomi wondered how she could manage. She was battling to bury her own agony under the light Esther was supposed to bring, but the light flickered constantly, and her footing was gone.

Across the small space separating their rooms, Miss Myrtle wanted to console Naomi and help her with the baby, but her own burdens weighed her down. Next to her bed, her Bible bulged with snow-filled Christmas cards, photographs, and letters, but since her son and his school friend married and left Baby Miles with her, neither of them ever came back home, and now Miles was gone. What would become of her? True, she was not in the first half of her life like this deserted young girl, but only a modicum of relief came with knowing this. Her church sisters and prayer meetings buoyed her spirits. and when none of these worked, she sang in her softest tones at the back door.

What a friend we have in Jesus,
All our sins and grief to bear.
What a privilege to carry
Everything to God in prayer.

"Yuh believe what yuh singing, Miss Myrtle?" Naomi asked.

"What kind of question is dat yuh asking me? What else we going do but believe and never lose hope in the Lord?"

"Never lose hope? Mi don't even know how to look after mi own baby. Look how much time mi turn to Him; look how mi beg Him not to mek Miles leave. And him still tek himself gone to America. Four months now, Miss Myrtle, and not one word. God might hear yuh, but it look like Him don't know mi, so who mi must tek mi worries to?" Naomi curled herself at the old woman's feet. How could she explain that the only thing on her mind was the endless litany of God's unkept promises?

With time, her worries about managing a young child subsided, but her betrayal by Miles never left her consciousness, and without Miss Myrtle's whispers, Esther would have known nothing about her father.

CHAPTER 24
"I'M A MAN OF GOD."

Boscobel, 1950s

Naomi's work at the craft shop in Galina brought her peace of mind, but trouble soon loomed when she kept spoiling the straw mats with their new complicated designs. Relief came when her employer opened the enormous box with a used machine from Montego Bay.

"We get a big order for the new hotel; see what you can do with this. It have a foot pedal and plenty fancy parts." The first time Naomi cut a dozen fancy bandana bands, stitched and attached them in ways that brought new life to the hats, her eyes and the eyes of the other women lit up.

"Well, at last we find out: stitching and decorating is your calling," the shop's owner said.

Esther was a fixture on the floor as Naomi worked. She played with all the empty cotton reels and sometimes she sat on her mother's feet getting a bumpy ride as Naomi pedaled. When she was old enough, she went for a few hours each morning to the infant school a few yards down the street from the craft shop. They settled on the routine in the Boscobel house. Miss Myrtle took care of whatever she could manage, and the woman next door helped her if she did not feel well.

A proud Naomi registered Esther at Boscobel Primary School when her daughter reached six. Miss Myrtle was still a tower of strength for them both, but Naomi soon detected signs she was worried.

"Come here Naomi; mi want to talk to yuh."

Lord, is what happen now? Mi don't remember one time when words like dat ever bring good news. She braced her shoulders and prepared for the worst, slowing down her kitchen chores to delay the inevitable bad news. But Miss Myrtle was just getting over a serious case of bronchitis, and the thick red peas soup would get cold, so she had to stop stalling.

"Thank yuh, mi dear. Yuh have a kind soul; yuh bring Esther to keep mi company in this old house, and yuh stay here with mi all these years even though Miles and him father treat yuh so bad. Is mi own son and grandson, but God know mi have to talk the truth."

"Don't worry yuhself; drink up yuh soup, and yuh will soon feel strong again. Mi getting on all right, and Esther doing good in school," Naomi said, with all the reassurance she could muster.

"But mi getting older and even yuh not so young no more. We have to think about the future and make a plan," Miss Myrtle said.

"Don't worry; mi have a plan; if is awright wid yuh, mi staying right here. Esther at school and mi have mi work. And yuh not going nowhere, so even though mi don't cook so good, yuh still have to drink mi soup."

Her efforts at keeping the conversation light broke the tension, but Miss Myrtle's eyes held a message Naomi was not ready to hear. The woman's demeanor reminded her too much about Pearlie's last days, and her own experiences gave her no appetite for planning. *What the use mi mek plan for tomorrow and it always go wrong?* Little did she know the old woman had planted her own seeds for the future–not only for herself, but for everybody in the house. Miss Myrtle was just biding her time because she knew the day for their sprouting was near.

***

A long busy week at the craft shop was over. On her way from the bus with Esther, Naomi looked forward to a relaxing Friday evening. Then, she made out the man on the porch, and approached with hesitation, fearing bad news.

"Good evening, Miss Naomi," the familiar voice said, "and a good evening to you, little one."

"Good evening, Pastor," Esther said, trying to hide her anxiety.

"Pastor Bloomfield, pleasant evening to yuh, Sir. Miss Myrtle awright?"

"Yes, this was a better day than last Friday when I came to see her. So, you are just leaving work ... and your little girl coming from school?"

"Yes, after school, she stay with mi until time to come home."

"Good; well, I hope you can spare me a few minutes, Miss Naomi."

"Of course, Pastor. Mi have to check on Miss Myrtle and give dem something to eat and come back. Yuh will have some ginger tea or lemonade, Sir?"

"Thanks; the lemonade sounds like just what I need on this hot evening. But just a minute before you go in; Miss Myrtle said I can talk to you about a very important matter." *Nearly the same words again!* Naomi almost walked into the wall.

"Of course, Pastor; we can talk inside. Mi hope Miss Myrtle is awright." The pastor nodded and when she came back with the drink, he raised the glass with shaky hands, sipped the lemonade, and waited until she returned with one of her own.

Naomi stifled one yawn after another as a convoluted story dripped from the pastor's lips about the connection between his family, Miss Myrtle, and the old house.

"So, Pastor, yuh telling mi yuh brother come back from Cuba and want back this house? Then where Miss Myrtle going live, Sir?" *And where mi an' Esther going to live? Wonder if him telling mi this long mix-up story to mek mi know we soon have to leave here?* The older woman hovered by the doorway, her anxiety rising.

"Naomi, Pastor know the whole situation; him make a very nice suggestion to mi a long time now, an' mi hope yuh will consider it good."

Naomi's eyes went from the old woman to the parson and back, and her feet shuffled as her brain grappled with the thought of hearing anything more confusing than what they had said so far.

"Yuh listening Naomi? Parson say we can come live with him because him brother coming back for this house, and since the pastor wife unfortunately pass away years aback, is him alone live in the big house up the hill near Oracabessa."

"Mi very glad for yuh, Miss Myrtle, but mi don't understand what yuh mean by 'we.'"

"Is not mi alone; is mi an' yuh and Esther."

"But what him mean by dat? Mi going up there to keep house? How mi can do dat and still go to mi work? And what him church people dem will say like how I am a young woman with this little girl?" The memory of her years as Eudora's girl from the country clouded her vision, and she had never forgotten how Pearlie described how the church women in Oracabessa had stirred up the community against her and her parents.

The pastor stepped in to help the old woman explain the proposition, and in one move he was too close to Naomi, who stepped away, folding and unfolding her arms.

"Keep my house? No, no such thing, Miss Naomi; Miss Myrtle means ... what she's saying is ... well, to put it plainly, Miss Myrtle gave me permission to ask if you will come as Mrs. Bloomfield." Naomi did not know how to pick up her fallen jaw.

Miss Myrtle jumped in, "Yes, Naomi, Pastor ask mi long—"

"Leave it to me, please, Miss Myrtle; it's only right for me to finish this. Sorry, Miss Naomi. Of course, this is not the way for the whole matter to come out, so give me a chance to explain myself, please." He paused until Naomi slowed her pacing.

"You know, Miss Naomi, Miss Myrtle is a straightforward woman, and she's been worrying a long time over you and the little girl. I see how you manage the house, and I know you are a decent young woman, so that is why I want you to come as my wife if you will have me." *No...How mi can married to this old man dat mi never even talk to about one thing except Miss Myrtle condition? What the two of dem think?*

On and on he went, his words tying him in circles–painting a grotesque picture in Naomi's mind. He had watched her suffer through the betrayal by Miles; her steadfast commitment to Miss Myrtle and her little girl had impressed him, and he had watched her blossom into a young woman with purpose and devotion to her work. Miss Myrtle punctuated his words with "very true, Pastor."

But mi don't understand Miss Myrtle at all; she just chipping in with her penny worth, agreeing wid every madness this man talking.

She sank into the old corner chair, twisting the tassel on the faded cushion this way and that. Like a father awaiting his son's late arrival home, the man paced from one end of the room to another, his head bowed and his hands behind his back. The older woman wandered into the kitchen, knowing the hope of a secure future was slipping away. In that moment, without warning or reason, Naomi lost her clarity about how outrageous the pastor's idea was. *But suppose this is God answer to Miss Myrtle prayers.*

"Miss Naomi, I am a man of God, and I have talked many times to the Lord about this. I will treat you very well. Many years passed since Mrs. Bloomfield died, and believe me, I have a very hard time alone in the house."

Lord, how mi must know your voice different from the devil own?

"I truly need a wife but not for the house. The church helps me very well with that, but it is not enough."

"But, Pastor, you know—"

"With respect, Miss Naomi, I know what I see, and Miss Myrtle tells me only good things. You will make a wonderful wife, and I promise to do everything in my power to give you and the little girl a steady life." *Mama always tell mi to get a husband to help mi through life. If this is a good man the Lord send to give mi and Esther a chance, how him don't say one word about love? Don't love should come into this argument somewhere?* A taunting voice in her head countered, *Oh, yuh mean him should talk about love like Miles? Where dat love gone to now?*

"Look, Miss Naomi: I know all this must be a shock to you, and it didn't come out quite right, so don't upset yourself. You don't have to tell me your answer right now. But believe me, I pray about it every day. Suppose you think it over and talk with Miss Myrtle before you say any more?"

Two visions of her future danced before Naomi. In one, she grew old hoping and waiting to feel, just once more, the tremor of excitement that came with Miles's love and the promises he had dangled before her. But she knew now that if it ever came again, the unremitting torment of losing it might follow. In the other, she saw herself and Esther–secure with the man God sent to guide them to safety and certainty, along with Miss Myrtle.

There would be no love, she realized, but there would be no excruciating loss either. There were more and more words from Miss Myrtle and the pastor, fewer and fewer from the confused Naomi.

As they turned in for the night, Miss Myrtle reminded her of the mysterious ways in which the Lord performed his wonders. "Naomi, yuh might believe it is wrong to married to a man older than yuh; but think about it; the parson is a big man in the church and him have a wife before. Him not going to give yuh trouble like a young man without experience; one who bound to drink rum and run after young girls. And who know if one of dem won't raise him hand to yuh?" Naomi pondered the words, and despite the long period since her last conversation with the Lord, she decided it was as good a time as any to resume her contact and ask Him to show her the right way to a lasting refuge from her mother's stains and curses.

CHAPTER 25
A SILENT SITTING ROOM

Oracabessa, 1950s

Every morning when Naomi opened her eyes in the pastor's rambling house on the hill, the world felt as unreal as the morning when she had worn her plain slipper satin dress to stand with Esther at her side and stumble through her promise to "love, honor, and obey" Pastor Bloomfield. They had all they needed, and it was a joy to see Esther running up and down in the grass in the back yard. Miss Myrtle no longer stayed in the little room in the alley, waiting to feel better. Relieved of the worries she had been keeping to herself after hearing about the trouble with the other house, she was busy in the pastor's ample kitchen, cooking her special treats, and Bible study and prayer meetings re-entered her routine. Once a month, Naomi went to Mass and while Esther spent the hour in Sunday school, her mother brought Sister Ignatius up to date on their new life.

"You made the right decision for everybody, Naomi. Now, you don't have to worry about the future because the Lord knew His plan for you all these years; He was just waiting for the right time."

No one could have guessed what it was like when night fell over the somber cave the house on the hill became. A single evening routine prevailed: Four sat down to dinner; the pastor droned on and on with the long prayer over "this blessed food and the blessed hands that prepared it with loving care for all who sit at this table." Everyone ate in silence and all four rose, but only after every plate was clean, "because God does not tolerate waste when so many all over the world are dying of starvation." Miss Myrtle and Naomi cleaned up; the old lady slipped away to her room; Esther did her homework and went to bed. Separated from Naomi's window seat by what felt like a distance fit for a mansion, the silent pastor sat in his big black chair poring through long Bible tracts he annotated and passed on to Naomi for reading and comprehension questions he plied her with. When she finished those and answered to his satisfaction, he reviewed the English and grammar exercises he gave her to work on during the day, so she could read and speak better. *So, this is God's plan for all the years before me?*

It was not as if Naomi lacked gratitude for the chance to learn and improve. She relished the security and the opportunity; she enjoyed the open spaces that becoming "Mrs. Bloomfield" brought her. Esther's newfound freedom in a yard with plenty of playing space, and access to a few friends, opened a new chapter for her, and Miss Myrtle seemed to thrive in the new environment. But why did her new status have to sentence Naomi to this heavy chill hanging over the room like years of unnoticed cobwebs? Her husband watched her; she watched him. She served glasses of water cooled in the earthenware jar; he sipped and read. She brought him a nightcap of dry crackers and hot cocoa with nutmeg and brandy; he gulped and read some more.

"Well, thanks for your help with the readings, Naomi; and you did well with subjects and predicates this evening. Time to turn in; it will be early-morning visits to the sick tomorrow and then a full day at church. May the Lord bless and keep you, and carry you through a safe night."

"Thank you, Pastor and blessings to you."

What Naomi could not have guessed was how closely the evening rituals mimicked those during the pastor's first marriage. He had been the student then, and the teacher was the fair-skinned woman from Mandeville whose relationship with him ripped her family away because in their eyes, he was "too black and unrefined." After their courtship at theological college, where she lived because she was the resident principal's daughter, the first Mrs. Bloomfield spent her years polishing her husband to fit in with the family's sheen, but no reconciliation ever came. When her parents refused to relent even as she prepared to have their first grandchild, the stress brought her a bout of eclampsia grave enough to snatch the infant and its mother before they could reach help. Burdened with loss, remorse, and the weight of the family's blame, the grieving pastor shut down all his emotions, turned entirely to the Lord and the church, and shunned any kind of pleasure.

The old-fashioned clock in the sitting room chimed every hour, as Naomi lay in a bed as lonely as an abandoned house. Her body ached and her heart yearned for someone to fill the space next to her. The distance between them did not exist only because Pastor was almost twice Naomi's age, or even because they had nothing in common; in her eyes, the man appeared incapable of joy; he seemed ignorant that such a thing existed. Pastor thrived in his world of alleluias, praying by rote, caring for the poor, and lambasting his congregation. Knowing he provided Naomi, Esther, and Miss Myrtle with what they needed gave him immense pride and confirmed his decision was right.

If anyone wanted proof, he could point to the old woman he had helped, the soul of the child he had "rescued from deprivation," and the "decent young woman saved from a future of certain sinfulness." Above all, he could see the wife he was molding to stand at his side, as he eyed higher positions in the church. He saw none of Naomi's displeasure, but inside her, an ugly feeling churned, stirring the fear that she had not eluded the curse against which Pearlie had warned so many times.

As one year dragged into two and then three, every word her husband uttered aggravated the sourness in Naomi's mouth, bringing up her long-buried images of Miles. Resentment of one man fed into resentment of the other until it was impossible to distinguish between them.

Miss Myrtle said from the beginning it would look bad if a minister's wife did not go with him to church, so every Saturday morning found her in the front bench, surrounded by churchwomen instructed to "make Pastor's wife welcome and comfortable." But his kind of worship gave her no fulfillment. Accustomed to the quiet reflective moments of her Catholic Mass, Naomi hated the loud "Alleluia, Amen; praise the Lord" that punctuated every prayer, every verse of scripture, and every other sentence in the sermon. Half the women moaned and groaned as if they would pass out, and nerves rattled inside Naomi as he preached, swaying back and forth, wiping sweat from his forehead, screaming and raining damnation on the unrepentant.

Some elders complained she was not involved in church outreach, she never helped with the choir or Sabbath school, and during worship, she looked uninterested and cold. The complaints reached the pastor, and he brought them to the sitting room.

"Things have to change, and I want you to stop worshipping at that dratted Catholic church of yours."

"But is the same church mi go to from mi born; why mi must stop now?"

"Because it doesn't look right for the wife of a man in my position to worship at another church. And remember, pay attention to your verbs and pronouns if you want to get rid of that bad talking."

"But mi … I worship at your church too."

He strode back and forth across the room like a soldier, the old wooden floor moaning under his heavy footsteps. "Naomi, everybody except you know the Catholic Church is where the high-color Jamaicans worship and some of the few better-off black people. Look at me. I'm your husband. Do you think I could take myself up to any pulpit in a Catholic church, and call myself a preacher? When you go there, you are telling my church people you are better than them; it is not good for them to believe that is the message coming from my wife." His complaints bristled with the long-held rage against his former in-laws, whose prejudice against him robbed him of his wife and child.

"But yuh know is not true; I tell yuh from before we married how mi grow in dat church and mi have to mek sure Esther grow up there too. I promise my own mother not to leave the church dat do plenty for us when we need help."

"Well, I am the one taking care of you now, even giving you lessons to help you talk better. You don't see they are working just like all the other ways I'm helping you?"

"Yes, mi learn a lot, and mi thank yuh for yuh help, but why mi musn't go to mi own church?"

"The same reason that you should learn not to say 'me' in the wrong place. An upstanding parson must have a wife who can speak to people and sound educated; and the same reason I'm telling you to stay away from that church because it shows disrespect to your husband."

"No, Parson, sorry yuh so vex over it, but if is so yuh feel, mi can go back and work, and yuh won't have to support me."

"Work in that little straw shop? And bring down shame on me? Ungrateful Naomi! You know ingratitude is the ugliest of all sins?"

"Well, if yuh shame of how mi talk and ... yuh going shame if mi work, and ... and if mi not grateful enough, prob'ly mi should find somewhere and go—"

WHACK! The blow landed on the bone just below Naomi's right eye, and she was sure she heard it break.

Awakened by the loud voices, Esther cowered behind the curtain, but she could bear it no more. "Leave mi mother alone. Leave her!" As he turned around to raise his hand again, Naomi gathered up the shaking girl and ran all the way to the back of the yard, scattering the cackling chickens along the way.

It was the first of many battles that sent them fleeing from the house and caused Miss Myrtle to lock her room door against the pastor's outrage. The vexatious spirits gnawed at Naomi, sending her to one novena after another.

"Then, Mama, when God going answer? Look how long we suffering and meking novena. Why we have to live here?"

"Esther, have patience. God not sleeping."

Three months had passed since Naomi defied the pastor and returned to her job. She left as soon as he stepped out early every morning and rushed home before dusk brought him from his community visits. The house was spotless; Esther took care of Miss Myrtle's needs and did all her other duties. A responsible thirteen-year-old, Esther supported her mother in every way, helping her with the household chores and taking care of the animals, so the pastor would have no cause to complain. She read to Miss Myrtle after school and finished her homework, so she could meet her mother at the gate when the bus brought her from work in Galina.

On an evening like any other, Naomi arrived at the gate, but Esther was nowhere in sight. A strange apprehension overtook Naomi as she closed the front door; an eeriness clung to the walls and curtains, trailing her weariness into the kitchen where she deposited her bag of groceries. Why was Pastor's special glass in the sink hours before he should be home? In the instant her mouth opened to call, Esther's voice filled the house.

"Stop Pastor! I say to stop it; Mama soon come, and mi will tell her!" The panic in the child's voice drew her mother like a rocket to Esther's room, her shoes flying off halfway there. Naomi sensed a kind of evil around her worse than anything she had suffered at the hands of her husband, and she knew what it meant. *No! Lord Jesus, help mi; don't mek mi kill this man tonight!*

A silent rage was her constant companion, and in that moment, it gave her a strength frightening even to herself. She hauled Pastor Bloomfield from halfway across the bed, freeing her child from his odious weight.

"Tek yuhself outside! And if yuh ever come near this chile again, sure as fate, yuh will be a dead man!" Like a trapped animal with no idea where to conceal himself, the pastor fumbled with his unbuckled belt, his eyes bulging and his body swaying as it did in the worst moments of his most horrible warnings and admonitions from the pulpit.

Esther jumped off the bed and curled herself in the corner, watching him grab his hat and slither away through the door.

"Tell mi the truth right now; Parson ever come near yuh before?"

"No, Mama, but mi was so frighten when mi see him come to the room door, mi never know what to do. Please mek us leave this house."

"Don't worry yuhself; we leaving."

***

Within hours, Naomi and Esther stood before Sister Ignatius in Boscobel. "Jesus, Mary, and Joseph, have mercy on us. What yuh doing here, Naomi? What brought you and this child out so late? Come inside."

"Good night, Sister Ignatius; thank God we mek it to the last bus. Sister, we have a terrible problem, and we have to leave Oracabessa. Mi hope yuh can help us, please."

Upon hearing the full story, Sister stepped away and fell into quiet prayer. Only the rustle of her rosary beads broke the heavy silence until she spoke.

"Stay here with us tonight. And tomorrow we can decide what to do."

For Naomi, the only decision was how to get away from the house for good, and where to go. She knew they could not risk staying in or around Oracabessa. The pastor's shame and bad temper would make him blame Naomi or her child, and keep them in torment behind his closed doors. After working out a plan with Sister, Naomi and Esther made their way to the house on the hill the next morning when they knew only Miss Myrtle would be there.

They were half-way through the door when the old woman confronted them. "My God Naomi, where yuh tek yuhself and this poor little girl and gone from last night? Mi don't sleep a wink because when mi come home from prayer meeting to find the house empty, mi know a bad thing happen. Then, before day light this morning, parson leave and don't say one word."

"Sorry, Miss Myrtle, we couldn't do better. Mi have to deal wid a problem, and mi know Sister Ignatius could help mi. She mek mi and Esther stay wid her because it get late and we couldn't get any bus to come back." Naomi decided against telling poor Miss Myrtle what Pastor did. She understood the woman was at the stage of her life when she held few real options. Abandoned first by her son and his wife, and later by the grandson she had raised with little help, she depended on the pastor completely. Although Naomi had come to believe he might only have used the old lady for his plan to get her as a wife, she had to avoid jeopardizing Miss Myrtle's situation because the old woman had nowhere else to go.

For Esther and Naomi, leaving was vital. She could suffer more quarrels and beatings, but she could not forgive the horror he had tried to commit against her child. Miss Myrtle listened to Naomi's story about a job with the sisters, and a better school in Kingston for Esther. She knew for a long time the marriage was deteriorating, and she had helped Naomi meet her husband's expectations. But she figured this was worse, and she would never hear what it was. It was easier to accept Naomi's lies than to face her own suspicions.

Naomi wept at the thought of leaving the old woman who had been like a mother to her for so many years. She worried about whether the pastor's rage would extend to Miss Myrtle, but the safety of her own daughter was uppermost in her mind.

With Sister Ignatius's prayers, packed lunch, and two rosaries pressed into their hands, Naomi and Esther climbed the steps into Randy's Red Rider Bus before morning broke and traveled around the perilous corners of the Junction Road for hours, until the last stretch of road rose into Stony Hill and then rumbled down Constant Spring into Kingston.

Half-Way-Tree clock struck ten on Wednesday when the red bus pulled up at its last stop. "Look, Mama, look how the road big and wide, and car coming from all different direction. How we going to cross over?" With the clock and the square behind them, they read Sister's directions one more time, looked from side to side, sprinted across a second intersection and continued walking.

As if standing there from the beginning of time, Holy Cross Church rose into the morning sunlight like a promise. Grasping each other's hands as if afraid one would disappear, Naomi and Esther sighed in unison, breathed in the city air, and walked through the widest, sturdiest gates they had ever seen.

CHAPTER 26
ESTHER COMES OF AGE

Kingston, 1960s

Amid the rustle of rosaries and vespers, life at the convent brought relief from the disillusionment and turmoil at the Oracabessa house. No one recovered from its culmination with Pastor Bloomfield's fall from his lofty perch as "the generous man of God" who had promised Naomi a life of security for herself and Esther. It had taken a while for the rumors about Naomi's departure to spread, but they did, and with them had come other allegations about Pastor's untoward activities with young women. The wagging tongues of his church women didn't rest until he had no option but to flee to the other end of the island.

Uprooted from their lives and the dregs of those promises, Naomi and Esther tackled the challenges and opportunities of Kingston, hoping to erase the ugliness of recent memories. The convent high school opened Esther's eyes to what life in Kingston might make of her, but it did not erase the realities of who she was. True, the education was more advanced than in the ill-equipped rural school, but her foundation was weak, and her mother lacked the knowledge to bridge the glaring gaps that came to light in the high school setting. Coupled with constant badgering from most of the girls about her "bad talking" and the fact that she lived at the convent, Esther sensed she was less than the other students who littered their sentences with ideas, experiences, and long words alien to hers. Although everyone dressed uniformly from head to toe, other students owned fancy accessories Esther lacked, and they never stopped flaunting them.

The worst days for Esther were those earmarked for visits by parents, which for most girls meant mothers and fathers dressed in professional clothes and speaking like upper-class Jamaicans. Many were fair-skinned or Chinese, or they had financial means way beyond Naomi's, and it showed in their bearing, their ability to influence the sisters, and the impact they made on the school. Who would buy all the raffle tickets the sisters expected Esther to sell and gain points for her class? What could Naomi talk to her classmates' parents about when they all visited their children's classes on Parents' Day? Apart from Oracabessa's riverside and seaside picnics, sewing her mother's scraps, and raising chickens, what hobbies could Esther share with the few girls who asked? Her differences set her apart, and from the distance between her and them, the girl watched and built a new vision of what she wanted to be.

Hustling to work and repay the generosity of the sisters, Naomi could find neither the time nor the wherewithal to take on what sounded to her like Esther's childish whining. Her reaction was often scathing.

"Girl, yuh realize the good fortune we have? Look where we come from and look where we reach. Yuh think yuh would talk so good if we never leave Oracabessa? What more yuh could want than a school better than any in St. Mary, kind sisters who help us out so much and give mi a chance to earn a little money from mi sewing?"

Hope of a better time flickered when the needlework job became vacant at the craft training center, and they moved out of the convent to the two rented rooms on Maxfield Avenue. There, at least they could go about their lives without the eagle eyes of thirty habit-clad nuns watching, and they could spend time to themselves. But not much changed, and Esther's later adolescent years brought a kind of unpredictability that unsettled her and irritated her mother.

Knowing only a few people in Kingston, and having little exposure to how rural parents managed children, Naomi found the new phase of her daughter's life baffling. Esther's apparent dissatisfaction with their lives, and even with Naomi, bordered on annoying.

"Look how much better yuh life is than when mi was your age and be thankful for the blessings we get. Don't hanker after what wi can't have, and disappointment won't come to yuh."

Esther was not sure how much better her life was than Naomi's had been; she knew little about the times before she had come along. The rare hints from Naomi about her early life always came with a simmering bitterness that made Esther feel her own presence in her mother's life was mostly a cause for regret.

"I know we come far Mama, and I am grateful, but what about other things?"

"Leave other things till dem time come. The Bible say, 'sufficient to the day is the evil thereof.'" Words from the Bible always closed down such discussions, and every time they landed, Esther turned away more bewildered.

Though each one fought to conceal it, the exchanges between them became the source of constant contention. To hide her confusion and inadequacy, Naomi took refuge in silence, sidestepping her daughter's concerns and brushing off any question about her feelings, her life in Oracabessa, and whatever she considered "big-woman business." She never told Esther much about growing up. When the teenager sought help to deal with her first period, which arrived with no preparation, Naomi went through the motions, sighing and grumbling between her warnings. "All what yuh learning won't change some things, and this is where all the trouble start, so just keep yuhself to yuhself."

"What yuh mean, Mama? I cause this? and what trouble I ever bring in here?"

Naomi's eyes traveled in every direction except toward her daughter's face, and the mysterious warnings continued. "And mark my word: Don't mek neither man nor boy come near yuh. Yuh might believe yuh big now, but don't even think about carrying any woman business inside this house until yuh ready for the hardship and trouble it sure to bring." No one taught Naomi the tone, or the face, or the words uttered; they seemed to come on their own from some unknown cell secured in a mother's brain for moments like this.

What was a girl supposed to make of it all, Esther wondered.

Esther knew the years at the pastor's house helped to change her mother into someone without hope, someone afraid to express what she felt inside. Her efforts to find out more about their early lives, or share her hopes for the future, always brought the same reaction. Her mother's mouth would shrink into a firm line, along with the usual pronouncement, "And we not talking no more about those things." There was never any point in asking another question after the mouth became the line, and Naomi summoned the invisible curtain. Esther drew into herself, Naomi's back stiffened, and the unspoken conflict reigned.

Naomi wanted to spare Esther all the pain in her own life, but she could not think of how to communicate any of it. Pearlie's warnings about the enduring curse of the banana stains lost some of their power, but remnants still walked with Naomi when she considered events in her life. The few times she tried to share the warning with Esther, the teenager countered with, "But how can you believe in all that when you say God is in charge?" Her mother had no answer, but in her silence, the old conclusion persisted. *Well, if is not banana stain or some other curse, is something evil dat follow us from the beginning, and who can tell it still not hanging over us?*

Naomi's love for her was something Esther never had the confidence or the words to assert or question; the girl assumed that mothers–and presumably fathers too–took care of children and provided for them, but it was hard to remember Naomi professing love for her, and she never consciously attached the name of love to her actions. It seemed somewhere along the way, her mother had turned off a switch inside.

Questions haunted her about Naomi's family, about why Pearlie ran away from home, what led to her death so young, why Eudora sent Naomi away, what made her mother marry the wretched Pastor Bloomfield. Bits and pieces about these events slipped in and out of conversations along the way, but the facts were elusive; Naomi seemed to have locked the book about life before Kingston and thrown away the key. Of her father Miles, Esther had little knowledge beyond Miss Myrtle's secret sketches, and after they ceased, the chapter about his role in their lives remained closed. Esther was sure there were explanations but how would she ever hear them? Once they had heard that a group of church sisters had rescued Miss Myrtle from Pastor Bloomfield's scandal, contact with the kind old lady had ended. By the time high school was behind her, Esther vowed to be a different type of mother, especially regarding whatever puzzled her and caused arguments with Naomi. But first she would be a woman like the mothers who visited school and looked as if they worked at serious jobs in offices all over Kingston. These were women who appeared to know many important secrets she had yet to discover.

To become like them, she must build on the crucial lessons she had learned by observing life at school, at the church, and in the convent. If she hoped to get where she intended, she would need more than a high school education, and she must speak good Jamaican English around certain people and places. Although some people claimed she was "nice looking for a dark-skinned girl," she knew winning beauty contests or getting easy passage to any job would never be on the cards for someone like her. The Girl Friday stint at the church office could be only a stepping-stone, and it would not do for long. She wasted no time before checking out other possibilities. The subjects she passed in her school-leaving exam qualified her for a junior clerical job in the civil service, and with her favorite teacher's help, she went after it. Success came, but it took over two years.

"Well, I hope yuh will feel more satisfied now, and yuh will just settle down and stop yuh constant planning and complaining." Naomi said.

"Of course I'm satisfied, Mama, but this is not enough. I don't plan to be a junior anything for long."

After they moved from the convent, Naomi remained the same outwardly; but a change seemed to come inside her. She seemed sure of herself and less haunted by invisible reminders of experiences she wanted to put behind her. Since earning her own living and mastering skills, she never knew she had, she walked with a purposeful stride as if she could take on anyone and anything. Embracing the church mightily, she stitched a fierce faith into the lining of her life, and this gave her a self-assurance Esther had not seen before. And then there was the new source of pride in Naomi, who had imbibed Sister Sue's music lessons, and was due to start playing in the chapel.

Able, at last, to combine their income, they rented two big rooms with a small kitchen and their own bathroom at the side of a house at Ulster Road. The faded old picture of Jesus with the bright red heart sticking out of his chest survived all their moves; it occupied a prominent position above the little 4-seater Formica-top dining table with the matching red plastic chairs. The situation got better as Esther settled into work, and she savored liberation. New interests occupied her, and she "forgot" to mention late evenings out, decisions made, purchases tucked away in her room. Her mother's grumbling took on new life.

"Mi can see all the money yuh spending on clothes of late, instead of saving for tomorrow. Prob'ly yuh have to dress to match yuh Kingston life and the way yuh talk nowadays; but yuh could help more with the light bill instead. I notice yuh drop Bible Study a good while now and Sunday mass gone too." The grumbling turned into quarrels. Her mother's frankness impressed Esther, but not when she was the target. Stoking Naomi's fire with her own caustic barbs, she took aim at the woman she claimed, "belonged in the ark or at the convent with God's army, or way back in the backward Oracabessa you left but never left you." The distance between them grew, and with a fierce determination, Esther saved–more than anyone could guess because plans were never far from her mind. She would move out as soon as she could afford her own rent; she would take evening classes, and she would not be stuck in this job for another six years.

On a Friday evening after choir practice, Naomi came home to something unexpected. In the little sitting area at Ulster Road, Esther presented Bradley Thomas–a young man who picked up somewhere that the way to a woman's heart was through her mother. A telephone company technician, he had met Esther while working on a problem with the phone extension on her desk. For weeks he badgered her, refusing to accept her apparent lack of interest. One date led to three and by then, there was no escaping Naomi, who stood at the mail box when he deposited Esther at the gate and promptly offered icy lemonade with potato pudding.

Soon, Friday nights found Bradley at the Formica kitchen table telling jokes and stories that made Naomi laugh more than her daughter had ever seen. Intent on endearing the indifferent Esther to him, he invested almost equal time in impressing both women, engaging Naomi in long discussions about her favorite topics. Even when Esther seemed distant and preoccupied, he hung around Naomi's kitchen, plying her with questions about her sewing, her cooking, her church music, and of course her daughter. With no prompting from Esther, Naomi imagined a pleasing end to her daughter's yearning for more. Rings and white lace occupied a regular space in her dreams.

CHAPTER 27
"DON'T FLY PAST YUH NEST."

Kingston, 1970s

The decade of the seventies well underway, it was obvious the promises of Jamaica's 1962 declaration of independence had miscarried, and newspaper headlines teemed with images of violence and crime, splattered between hardships and political division. The 7:30 news on the little black-and-white TV, for which Esther skimped to pay the rental fee, featured the Kingston gang wars, political laborite-comrade claptrap, and exploits of the West Indies cricket team, which Naomi followed religiously. Whether Bradley and Esther were there, or she was alone, her grim pronouncements after the news were predictable: *Same old foolishness every day in this poor country; look how long we claim we get self-government and then Independence, and until today we don't mek much progress. Mama never know things would be like this, but mi wonder if she was right about the curse of dat nasty banana stain. Is like some people don't move one step from the banana ground an' the cane piece. Must be a mark on people who come from slavery, for we always too backward.*

None of her dissatisfaction with the news could dull her hopes for Esther and Bradley. Quiet, full of laughter, and obviously besotted, the young man would have spent every moment with Esther if she allowed him. Although he was not earning much, he lavished tasteful little gifts on her, and while a finicky Esther treated him casually most of the time, Naomi prayed he would not leave her. He brought a lightness into their lives when lingering tensions seethed. Whenever trouble loomed in the couple's relationship, the watchful mother prayed harder, begging the Lord to open her daughter's eyes to what Bradley offered, and assuring the young man "it will all work out in the end." No matter how close Esther seemed to ending it all, he never wavered in his devotion to daughter or mother.

It was just an ordinary evening when lemonade stood chilling in the fridge for Bradley, and Naomi rushed to the front door to greet her favorite visitor. But there was no Bradley. Instead, a sputtering red car disappeared around the corner. Esther stood there straightening out her blue cotton shirt dress, trying to wipe the excitement from her face.

"How yuh so late? Overtime again? Where Bradley is?"

"Evening, Mama. Bradley didn't bring me; I went to a show at Carib with friends from work. One of them gave me a ride home." Her casualness only spurred Naomi to probe further.

"I hope is not that boasy-looking high-color boy drop yuh home; the one who bring yuh here the other day and keep buzzing around yuh like a hungry-belly fly." A feeling sounding like panic crept into her mother's words, and Esther could not bring herself to admit the truth.

"No," she said without pausing; sensing her mother's deadening glare in the back of her neck, she gave up. "Awright, yes; Patrick brought me; and yes, I went to pictures with him."

Naomi grabbed her shoulder, spun her around, set her own hands on her hips, and stretched her neck until her eyes were level with Esther's.

"Mama, just let me pass, please. I need to change."

"So, what yuh think yuh doing? What about Bradley? Yuh tell him yuh change yuh mind?" The look on her daughter's face said she had done nothing so definitive, and Naomi went on. "So, what? Yuh plan to turn into one of those wild Kingston girls who paint dem ass red and hang out all over town with a different man every week?"

"I look like one of those girls to you?"

"Yuh may not look like one yet. But everybody know that having two men one time is what girls like that do. Yuh plan to bring disgrace on yuhself and me? Yuh don't realize how we lucky to reach where we reach?"

"No ... yes ... I don't even know which question to answer."

"Is yuh own self yuh have to answer. And mark my words girl, yuh meking a big mistake; sure as fate yuh will regret it; and don't yuh ever forget this: Yuh see dem smooth high-brown Jamaican men like the same Patrick? Dem want one thing and one thing alone from people like mi and yuh. Don't believe dem flashy fair-skin boy with fancy car going married to anybody with skin darker than dem own. Jamaican man always looking to raise dem color." Esther could not move; the doomsday warnings were nothing new, but the bitterness and contempt were more than she could stand.

"You heard me say I want to marry anybody?"

"So, what yuh want then? Mi don't know this careless boy Patrick, but mi sure him can never hold a candle to Bradley."

"That might be true, but at least I want to find out. I'm in my twenties, and if I follow you, Bradley will be the only boyfriend I will ever have. How I can decide if he is the right one if I never—"

"If yuh never what? Try out more than one?" Naomi hurried to lock the door behind them. "Yuh think choosing a husband is like buying shoes? And by the way, who yuh raising yuh voice at? I'm still yuh mother and yuh still live under my roof, so don't yuh fly past yuh nest!" Her forefinger was an inch from Esther's chin as she reached high gear.

"Imagine, this careless boy drop yuh off at the gate and drive off with a noise like some old truck, making the inquisitive people around here know yuh business. Bradley ever leave yuh at the gate yet?"

"No, he always comes inside; so that mean I should be with him forever?"

"Is fancy car drive yuh want? Just imagine how the people chatting us arready. Yuh giving them enough to chat about."

Esther was already heading for her room when she swung around, and the unedited retort flew out of her mouth, "What am I giving them to talk about? The fact I don't intend to live like some nun from the country? That I am a normal young woman doing what normal people do?" She brushed past her mother and breathed in the smell of onion, garlic, and lime that all the Johnson's Baby lotion in Kingston had failed to get rid of. The smells set her on edge, reviving memories of rough kitchens with dozens of flies, and dirt for the flooring; of hot cocoa without enough sugar; of her mother's misery all the years on the hill, her mother's nasty pastor-husband edging up on top of her, the endless tension and the eventual escape to Kingston.

All of it gathered itself into the rage that flew out of her mouth before she could step on the brakes. "You think I want to be like you, with nothing in your life except work and church and kitchen smells? How I can follow the foolishness you always talking about banana stains and curses, when you made your own decisions that yuh still can't get over? You are warning me about my decisions, but what about yours?"

Naomi swallowed hard and walked away, her pain palpable. Esther's unexpected rage subsided in an instant. She regretted her disrespectful words, and the look they brought to Naomi's eyes. Her mother's ideas about Patrick were not new to Esther; they echoed her own fears, and the arguments only made her more nervous about her interest in him.

The tension between them persisted, and Esther continued to go out with Patrick, but she was as discreet as she could be. Naomi said no more about it, but her unsubtle grunts and groans marked the young woman's exits and entrances.

There was no sign of Bradley until a month later while Naomi was at church, and he sat awkwardly at the kitchen table watching Esther. After weeks of what she described as a break to clear her mind, she had asked him to come over. He sat looking serious and hopeful as she paced the floor, wringing her hands. "But, Esther, I don't see the problem. We can get married; just a quick and simple wedding; nobody have to know anything else."

"Married, Bradley? We broke up, remember? I'm with somebody else and—"

Frightened at the thought of what she might say, he watched her face intently and waited. "And?" The pause stretched out.

"No, Esther; tell mi yuh never sle—"

"Of course, I didn't! You believe I would go so far with somebody after you and me just broke up?"

"No, no ... mi wasn't thinking that; mi just wondering why ... anyway, this baby is mine. So why we shouldn't get married? The quicker the better. We can just tell Miss Naomi we decide, and we not waiting for any long planning."

It was not obvious to Esther they should get married. In fact, she hated the thought and dreaded a nasty outburst from Naomi. She berated herself for getting pregnant because a baby would upset all her plans to take more classes, get a diploma, and prepare herself for a proper job so she could afford a little room of her own. Her idea of moving to be on her own never included being married so early–certainly not to Bradley.

Nothing was wrong with him, but she was not sure what was so right. He was a good person and a caring man; neither tall, dark, and handsome, nor short, pale, and ugly, he was ... well, ordinary. At 5 ft. 11 inches tall, he stood two inches above Esther in low heels. If he were a swimmer, he would not exert himself doing butterfly or breaststroke. He would ease himself along in an unhurried backstroke, with intermittent glances at the sky. Esther was not sure why she yearned for more; she just did. But no alternative presented itself. Although Naomi had no right to take to high ground about a pregnant unmarried daughter, Esther felt certain she would never hear the end of that. Constant reminders would haunt her about the cryptic warnings and the opportunities wasted. What else was there to do, but promise Bradley they would talk again soon? He was on his way, much happier at the prospect of marriage than Esther would ever be.

Gasping through morning sickness, she spat out the unwelcome news, and leaned against the bath, equally stunned by repeated whiffs of Naomi's smelling salts and her calm reaction. With more than a little help from her mother, Esther convinced herself she could count on Bradley's heart. Marrying him would spare all three of them the shame of having the child with no ring on her finger. This was much worse in Kingston than in the rural areas; her job, as well as being tied up with the church and the sisters, would only make it worse.

There was still another reason she never mentioned to anyone. The voice of a father was unknown in the lives of all the women she'd been around, and she harbored a secret longing to speak like girls at her Kingston school who blithely inserted *Daddy* in all their sentences. Her envy of the girls shaped her promise to herself in one of many pivotal sixteen-year-old moments. *No baby for me without a father in the house.*

CHAPTER 28
ONE DAY AT HELLSHIRE BEACH

Kingston, 1990s

Esther had long ago broken the promise she made at sixteen, and now it was back to haunt her. She cringed at the reality that her child was growing up in a fatherless house. Everybody knew who was to blame and who was suffering the brunt of the consequences of Zarah's troubling behavior. Their relationship was at its most brittle, and anxiety about the impact of Bradley's absence shadowed Esther's every move. Little did she know worse was still ahead.

True enough, an uneasy calm had settled over the Duhaney Park house as Zarah and Damien observed the new rules. Miss Lucretia watched and waited, constantly looking for evidence to prove she was right about the boy. But the young people seemed set to prove her wrong. They sat in Esther's living room most Saturday evenings watching TV or listening to music. Bradley dropped them to the movies at Carib or Sovereign once a month and took them for treats afterwards. He deposited them at a few select birthday parties, from which he always picked them up by midnight. The plan seemed to work, and they appeared to be keeping their side of the bargain, with Zarah maintaining her activities and her grades. Damien was still not the type of boy they wanted Zarah to be around for long, but they exhaled, figuring she would soon tire of him.

What they saw was the tip of the iceberg. As Miss Lucretia and Zarah herself had surmised, Damien was not one to follow rules indefinitely, and Zarah fell for the adventures he dangled before her. He trained her in the ways of camouflage and secret movements, so they came and went with no one knowing. Very often, the "Keep Out" sign was not just the typical teenager's room decoration, and when Zarah added words like "Big exam," Esther never questioned the real purpose. Although Zarah had lied in the early stage of her association with Damien, her mother felt it was okay to trust her up to a point.

They had not bargained on the boy's boldness. Damien found every way possible to sneak in and out, keeping Esther and Bradley completely fooled. Zarah bought into his idea that they had no choice because her unreasonable backward parents "locked her up like a bird in a cage." Knowing what some of her friends' parents allowed them to do before she was even interested in doing them, Zarah imbibed his line and convinced herself he was right. *Is not my fault the two of them still living in the Dark Ages! And even if Daddy is not the same, he never stands up to her.*

Damien stood up to his father, who was always warning him half-heartedly about getting girls into trouble. But he only saw the boy now and again, and his lifestyle was not one a father could hold up to his son as a shining example, so Damien never paid much attention. His mother had migrated years before, and his experience did not include girls who came from homes with rules. He tried standing up to his school authorities and the principal of one of Kingston's top high schools expelled him. Zarah kept this detail from her parents, but it was the first thing to set off an alarm in her head.

"What you going to do now? You know everybody is supposed to finish school."

"Babes, don't mi tell yuh from yuh know mi dat mi not into no book business?"

"So, how you going manage without even a high school diploma? What kind of job you think you can get?"

"Don't worry over dat; mi soon get the work mi want; car and bike and music is what mi interested in."

By this time, Zarah was sure Damien was the most important thing in her life, so she left it alone. But she was smart, and long before Damien, her mother had taught her all the facts, so she knew how to stay out of trouble.

Damien is fun, and I love him, but no way I'm forgetting my goals. I won't make stupid mistakes and mash up my life.

The summer holidays were coming up, and Esther worried about Zarah's long days out of school. Bradley got her a holiday job, and it gave them a little breathing space while opening up new interests for her. None of this was enough to dislodge Damien. Arguments raged about the parties and beach trips Zarah wanted to attend, and through sheer exhaustion, Esther gave in to some. At least Bradley was keeping an eye, as his driving them everywhere remained a condition of their going out. It was a condition Zarah could afford to accept because she knew how many other places she went to on the back of the forbidden motorbike.

After Zarah's summer job ended, Esther traveled to Trinidad for a training program to prepare her for promotion. Miss Lucretia was now in charge at Duhaney Park both night and day, and everything seemed in order. Bradley dropped Zarah at the studio for the fifth day of a dancing camp to prepare for the end-of-summer show. Little did her parents know the camp was to last for four days and Zarah had tampered with the letter so she could carry out her plans for the fifth day with no interference.

On that morning, Damien picked her up at the studio as soon as Bradley's car disappeared, and off they went on the motorbike to spend the day at Hellshire Beach as he had begged her to do for months. Zarah had questioned herself, made and unmade the decision, calling the outing off and on for weeks; but in the end, she knew she could not put him off any longer, and it seemed harmless enough. She would be back at the studio in time for her father to take her home, and no one would ever know.

Speeding out to the beach with her arms wrapped tightly around the waist of an overjoyed Damien, she chatted and laughed at his jokes. Deep inside, she knew what could take place before they got back home, but as always, she worked it through in her head and she would deal with it. *What difference this can make now, after all we do already? All this hypocrisy about waiting to have sex to keep boys interested is just foolishness. All my friends having sex already and they are just fine.* With no little help from Damien, she had been persuading herself that at some point soon, she would have to overrule the miles of words her parents and Grams used to convince her to resist early sexual involvement. From time to time, their voices rang in her ear, causing her to feel less certain it would be "no big thing" as her friends claimed.

Young people littered the seaside, and reggae music blared. After hours in and out of the water, they bought their "fish an' festival" lunch, left the crowded area and settled in the distant cove he picked out for them. The harmless games and chatter soon ran out of steam, and their attentions turned to one another. As they became more involved, the competing voices battled in her head.

"Wait, Damien, wait."

"What?"

"Just slow down a little." As she turned on her side and hugged her knees, Damien stalked away, kicking the sand into the air. Her mother's voice rang in her ears. *Zarah, promise me if something happens and you are not sure how to handle it, you will tell me, and we'll work it out together.* She remembered her grandmother's long stories about all those women and girls in the family and others in their districts who brought babies into the world and faced a long future at a standstill. Naomi's hints about being husbandless and pregnant with Esther came back to nag her. But under the summer sky at Hellshire, all the talk seemed a universe away; so why were their words flitting in and out of her mind, preventing her from doing what she was sure she wanted? A part of her dismissed what now seemed like old women ranting in her head. *Of course bad things happened to them, but I don't plan to live their lives. I'm not taking any chances; no baby for me before I reach my goals.*

Not yet over his tantrum, Damien stood above her, still glowering. "Yuh ready to go home now? Well, tek up yuh things and come!" She remained still. In her mind's eye, long months stretched out before her with no Damien to offset her loneliness and the emptiness of life with her mother and Miss Lucretia. He slid back down on the sandy towel next to her, his face turned away. The smell of his salty perspiration, mingled with the remnants of cologne left after hours in the sea and the sun, was too much. Wrenching themselves from any connection to her brain, her hands stretched out to gather him close to her. Without hesitation, Damien reciprocated.

"Yuh love me, Babes?"

"Of course," Zarah said, "you think I would be here if I didn't love you?"

"And yuh know is yuh I love, right? Yuh know yuh are my girl?"

"Yes, I know. But remember what you always promise when we talk about this?"

He knew, of course, and although reluctant to take it, he grabbed the tiny packet glistening in the sun.

Their bodies took over, skin against skin, sweat mingling with sweat. All the spaces between them narrowed, and they drifted away from the noise of the beach and the clamor of questions in her head. Afterwards, she wanted only to lie there in the stillness, savoring the rise and fall of their chests, but his chatter was unending.

A few hours later, her father drove into the parking lot at the studio, and she bounced into the seat next to him, just as she had always done. "Everybody else left? Am I late?" Bradley asked.

"No, Daddy; you are right on time. Sir said he could see our feet were abandoning us, so he let us off early, and everybody scrambled. I knew you would soon be here, so I just waited."

Bradley saw no sign his daughter had crossed the Rubicon.

CHAPTER 29
A BROKEN PYREX DISH

Three days after Hellshire, Esther returned from Trinidad, and Miss Lucretia's nights in the house ended. As soon as she stepped in, she noticed her daughter's unusual hovering around her. Words would start coming from Zarah's mouth, hang in the air, and then fade to silence. *Hopefully, she missed me a little; I should leave her more and make her feel the house without me.* Zarah herself could not figure out why she felt a need to be closer to her mother after the day with Damien. She had crossed a threshold, but there was no certainty about how to move forward.

School resumed, and her pre-university twelfth grade classes soon brought their own excitement and distraction, but none of it lasted long. Damien's hunger was sucking her into a routine of sex that brought its own confusion. Sometimes a kind of peaceful resignation to the new phase settled upon her; sometimes the sense of having lost something irretrievable overwhelmed her. It was as if an idea she had been certain about was no longer clear. As confusion replaced satisfaction, her brain went to work analyzing what it all meant.

Half of her wondered what all the hype was about. It was done; the decision was behind her, and it could never bother her again. She and Damien loved each other, and he had never pressured her to have sex, *right? The time came, and I was ready—and sensible. I've done it; the world is still spinning, and I'm still the same girl.* So, why did the needling inside continue? Why did she avoid looking those she loved in the eye? And what made her feelings about Damien swing so wildly from one extreme to the other?

Sometimes, her desire for him frightened her–the hunger for his body, the willingness to risk everything and deny what she knew, just to have him in her life. At other times, resentment toward him surged inside her, and all their lies and sneaking around felt sickening. The desire to slap him out of her room was often overwhelming, and it was for no other reason except his presence around her, and her knowledge that his life away from her remained an unopened book. She longed for the certainty of her mother's words, her calming voice, and her reassuring hugs. But they lived on the far edges of the relationship they once had, and it was too late to turn to Esther.

Standing at the kitchen sink washing up after dinner, Zarah tried three times to stick her handful of knives and forks into the cutlery drainer; three times, they all fell back into the sink, the clatter breaking into the steady slosh of soapy water. Her elbows propped on the rim of the countertop, her left foot tapped against the floor, and every few minutes a mysterious sigh escaped. Her mother sensed something unusual, but afraid to ask what was going on, she left it alone. Without warning, the crash and the shattering of glass brought Esther back from the garbage bin outside.

"Mummy, quick, a paper towel, please."

"What is it?"

The cut was not huge, but the blood dripped over the side of the sink and onto the floor, running in and out of the huge shards of glass strewn everywhere.

"Sorry. Is your good Pyrex dish and the cover. The soapy water ... they slipped; sorry, I'll buy them back." The tears streamed down her face.

"You couldn't be crying about a dish, so what's going on?"

"I'm not crying; the soap—" Zarah said, disappearing from the kitchen. Believing at least one of her worst fears had come to pass, Esther hurried after her.

"You know this is not about a dish and a cover; so, tell me what it is about." In that moment, Zarah was on the edge of telling Esther everything; the pressure in her chest was getting worse every day–like the confusion she felt every time she looked at herself in the mirror, every time her mother's face superimposed itself on Damien's as they shared her bed. But Esther's nearness was too much; Zarah needed to resist the urge to be a little girl again. And she could not burst her mother's bubble about who she had become, so her mind conjured up the picture of the mother who had caused all the trouble. Zarah yanked the shutter down on any temptation to open up to her.

"Sorry about the dish; I'll buy it back."

"Zarah, please; don't leave things like this. Tell me why you are in this state."

"There's a big exam tomorrow. I have to sleep and wake up to study."

The opening had come without warning, and in the same moment, it was gone.

CHAPTER 30
A SHOWDOWN IN DUHANEY PARK

Zarah and Damien carried on, their quarrels interspersed with their secrets. But Zarah forgot about the hawk eyes of Miss Lucretia, who had always known what Damien was capable of and never trusted Zarah's apparent compliance. With three grown daughters of her own, the woman knew the signs of every landmark, including the day when each of them "fell." Familiar with the road they had traveled, she spotted the new boldness of the eyes, the unmistakable thrust of the hips, the freedom of knowing there was nothing more to lose. And so it was with Zarah, whom she had suspected for about two weeks.

The search was underway, and the evidence soon showed up in the washing. Just once, Zarah forgot to take care of her garbage. A concerned mother and one who cared deeply for Zarah although she despised her dishonesty, Miss Lucretia could not hide the truth from Esther, who had entrusted her with the care of her daughter for so many years. Her head hanging and her face fit to announce a death, Miss Lucretia handed the evidence to Esther and watched hope drain from her employer's eyes.

By the time Zarah reached home, both parents were pacing the living room floor.

"Evening, Mummy; hi, Daddy."

"Evening, Zarah," Esther said, standing at the window with her arms tight across her bosom. Heavy and threatening, her formal greeting hung over the room.

"Hi, Zarah," Bradley's voice was shaking.

"Daddy, how come you didn't say you were coming over today?"

"No reason."

"Something happened?" Zarah asked, looking from one parent to the other, certain of the answer before the question was out.

"Yes ... this." Esther said, waving the offending condom wrapper as if scorning something filthy and disgusting. Zarah's ears and neck fevered with shame, not so much for what she had done, but for what it was clearly doing to her parents; for letting every moment pass, when she could have told her mother what had happened. All the images of who she had been, and wanted to be, dissolved in the disillusionment in their eyes. *I promised myself I would never deny it; now at least, nothing can get worse.* A daunting silence prevailed, the scarcity of words from her mother and father stunning her more than her discovery that the secret was no longer a secret.

The disappointment echoing in their silence was as brutal as it was deafening. The depth of her parents' reaction hit her harder than if they had ranted and raved; a slap across her face would have been easier to endure. *This is it; you might as well just curse me and throw me out; get it over with! Say I'm not your daughter anymore. Please, just say it.*

"What yuh have to say, young lady?" Bradley asked, with hope slipping away. Her father had never used that tone with her before, and her murmur was close to inaudible.

"Nothing, Daddy."

"Right here in the house, Zarah?" It was the first time she saw such suffering in her mother's face, suffering that made her choose fewer rather than more words, framing a question without relevance or meaning. It stunned Zarah, and she did not know what to say. *How anybody can answer that? What difference does it make where it happened?*

"We trusted yuh," her father said, "yuh promise me; I promise yuh mother yuh would never do this, not before talking to one of us."

Then came the rush of more useless words. "Sorry. Honestly ... I don't really know what I'm sorry for. More lying doesn't help anybody. What we did may not be something anybody can be sorry about, but your disappointment and anger make me sad. This may not count, but I didn't rush into this for the fun of it. Damien knew we had to wait until I was sure, and that came a long time before we did anything serious. We love each other. You told me that when the time came, I should consider all those things, and I did."

"What about all our talks?" Esther asked, defeat in her tone of voice.

"I did remember everything you said, and I never handled it like some stupid irresponsible girl."

Some of what Zarah said was so candid, and so unembellished, neither parent could deal with it; so Esther picked at the one sentence to which she could manage a response.

"You remembered? Really? So, how you could think he was the right person? How could you believe lying and hiding would be the right way? No wonder you've been so edgy of late." Her hands flailing, her voice carried a tone of defeat neither Bradley nor Zarah ever heard.

"I know I let you down. Seeing you disappointed always hurts; but you think I didn't want to tell you? Over and over, I started and just couldn't go on. It was just too hard. But what you would do if I said we wanted more? That the occasional movie and a party was not enough? You know what a freak everybody would consider me if that was all I did with my boyfriend? How long you think he would be around?"

"When did you turn into the girl who does what everybody else is doing–the girl who does what a boy wants just so she can keep him around her?" Esther asked as Bradley joined her in staring at their child.

"Why the two of you don't answer my question?"

"What question?" Bradley asked.

"Yes, what question?" Esther echoed. She got up and sat right back down as if to stop herself from falling. *Where is the daughter I thought I prepared so well?*

"What you would do if I said we were going to ... we were getting more involved? What you would say if I asked permission to have him in my room? I am seventeen and I'm responsible like you taught me, but just because Damien is not the boy you would pick for me, you never once gave me the chance to show it."

It was Bradley who took charge this time, grabbing his daughter by the wrists and looking her straight in the eye.

"Stop it; just stop it, Miss."

"You're hurting me, Daddy." No one was sure if it was the grip, or the coldness in his "Miss" that cut her to the quick.

"Just don't shift the blame to yuh mother for what yuh did. Yuh just said yuh never rush into it. That mean yuh consider the whole situation, and yuh still mek the same choice yuh know we wouldn't want for you."

"Exactly! She knew she was doing the wrong thing, and that didn't prevent her; she didn't care what we would think."

"I did care; I did the best I could to—"

"To hide and lie and do what you knew was wrong?" Esther asked, frustration and disappointment spilling from her words.

Zarah fumbled for an answer, wiped her tears, slid down the wall, and covered her face. At her feet, Esther saw images of a woman and a girl merged in a pocket of familiar pain. *My God, what more should I have done to prevent her from taking this turn that can only bring hurt? I thought I was raising this bright modern girl, and it made no difference; she's just as helpless as I ever was.*

As Zarah stood up to answer, Naomi's face dangled before Esther; and from across the years, her words flew out of Esther's mouth, her forefinger shaking before Zarah's face.

"Well, you might think you're a grown woman now, so I hope you are ready for the trouble and the pain your stubbornness and lying will bring. And if this doesn't tell you how bad that low-life drop-out is for you, I don't know what will!" The words and the tone sent Zarah fleeing; she slammed her door, but it could not lock out her heart-rending cries echoing throughout the house. Esther and Bradley glanced at each other in silent acknowledgement of the ice-cold truths before them.

Without conviction, they grounded Zarah and forbade Damien to come near her. She fled to Naomi, who listened; but she too was disappointed and frightened by what her granddaughter had done, and she called Bradley to take her home. They had lost the war and knew it would be almost impossible to enforce the new rules. The daughter whose intelligence and maturity they could have appealed to before was no longer in the house. The stranger who lurked in her shadow was distant, wounded, and already on a path from which there was no turning back. Bradley's visits decreased to the bare necessities of transporting Zarah. Esther and Zarah measured out their words in tablespoons, timing their movements, scarcely breathing the same air.

CHAPTER 31
ZARAH FINDS A REFUGE

Zarah had only a few more months in Grade 13, and after talking to a close family friend, Bradley shared with Esther one last-ditch idea to remove their daughter from the danger they still saw in Damien. They calculated their savings, checked out scholarships to overseas universities and contacted his relatives in Queens, who would be happy to have Zarah with them. They took all her school records to an organization helping outstanding Jamaican students get into good universities in America. The director pored through the papers and stood up, removing her glasses, "Congratulations! This is an excellent record. You both did a great job with your daughter! But where is Zarah? We need to fast track the entire process."

"That's the problem," Esther said. They gave the woman the background, leaving out the most embarrassing details.

"I'm sorry; I see situations like this all the time. Your daughter is a bright girl, and I understand you want to get her out of this nasty situation. But we can't do anything without her. Encourage your girl to study abroad; show her the importance of going after one of the many opportunities available. It would be so easy, and so good for her."

Full of excitement and hope, Bradley and Esther headed for Duhaney Park. They spread out all the paperwork on the dining table and called Zarah from her room. Both agreed Bradley would start off the discussion, but Zarah's angry interruption came the moment she grasped what he was saying.

"Daddy, what all this is about now? Look how long I show Mummy and you my provisional acceptance letter from our own university. Why the two of you come up with this scheme now?" The anger below Zarah's facade broke through more easily every day. This time it seemed to have been waiting, and her sharp words cut through everything her parents said.

Esther followed the advice of the woman at the scholarship office and joined the discussion with a much softer tone than she had been using. "Zarah, please just listen for a minute. You've never wavered about wanting to get a good degree and go as far as you can in school. We know what you can do, and we want to give you the best opportunity."

Bradley followed her lead, "These people can set you up with some of the best schools. You will probably be able to choose between three or four top-notch colleges; in six months the process could be over. It's too late for this August, but in America you don't have to wait another academic year; you can start in January."

Zarah's response was clinical. "All that suits your perfect scheme, right? But I'm starting in August after my 'A-level' exams. Natural Sciences Faculty, University of the West Indies, Jamaica, just like we agreed one year ago. We have scholarships here too, you know. Both of you trying again to break up Damien and me, but look how long you've been trying. You say we can't be together in your house, and since I don't have anywhere else to go, I have to hear you, but soon I'll be living on campus, and we can spend time together. I can't believe the two of you hate us so much you would do this to take away the one little happiness in our life."

"Do what?" They asked together.

"Send me to live with people I've never seen and waste your money sending me to one of those American colleges that give people credit for square dancing and flute." Bradley countered by naming the outstanding colleges the woman had mentioned, but Esther was so angry at her daughter's arrogance, she stopped him, scraped up the documents, and walked away.

The discussion about college in America was over, and Esther longed for the weeks to pass, so Zarah would be on campus. What was the use of fighting? She no longer had her daughter. They went through the motions, signing documents and showing interest in the reams of paper Zarah hurled at them with details about what was ahead. Her hard work and her confidence in getting a scholarship to the university bore fruit, and despite their disappointment in her decision not to give herself the chance to do even better by going overseas, they celebrated with her.

***

On campus, Zarah flowered. Free from the tension at home, and certain her new environment would allow her relationship with Damien to thrive and prove itself, she enjoyed her classes, and nurtured a small selection of friendships. Apart from her studies as a natural sciences student, she took part in several extracurricular activities, developing her dancing skills and discovering a variety of clubs and societies that she found engaging and fulfilling. Drawn like bees to her blossoms, bright young men tried to get close to her, but she dismissed them all, making everyone aware she was unavailable. Damien inserted himself into her campus life, never conscious of how out of place he was. In Zarah's estimation, his commitment to her was only growing stronger. *They will see; we will prove them wrong!*

During the semesters, her visits home diminished, but she also found every reason to remain on campus during breaks—summer jobs in the chemistry lab, rehearsals for dance recitals, preparation for final exams. Esther felt the threads of their relationship severing, but Zarah's absence from the house brought her relief as well, and she agreed when Bradley said, "but remember we almost sent her to America; if she went, we would have even less contact with her. We just have to leave it alone now and hope she will grow out the boy."

CHAPTER 32
SNIPPETS OF JOY

Just past her twentieth birthday, Zarah earned first class honors and right away a top company recruited her to join the research team at their nutrition lab. As she walked into the living room, dressed for the elegant graduation ceremony, Esther covered her mouth at the vision of her only child. And when she walked off the stage with her certificate and prizes in hand, her radiance filled her mother with pride and joy, tarnished only by a scruffy Damien in the row across the aisle. Her heart yearned for their lives before the boy's arrival–for the days when she could reach out and hold her daughter without the stiffening in her back, without the tension lodged like a stone between them.

Back at Duhaney Park, Zarah opted for a routine to keep her away as much as possible although the strictness of the house rules had eased a little. Despite her objections to Damien, who seemed as wayward and idle as ever, a grudging Esther accepted there might be some substance to the relationship since it weathered so much time and opposition. Relieved he had not derailed Zarah from her path, and pleased her daughter landed a good job with opportunities for exposure to other bright young people, she resolved to do her best to repair the bridge between them. But the foundation had become brittle, and the same old conflicts soon gnawed at it again. Plans for Zarah's 21st birthday brought the worst one.

"Excuse me, Mummy; what is this? No... this couldn't be right; you couldn't seriously have a list of people coming to this ... what you call it ...

21st birthday dinner? And my boyfriend's name is not on it?" Esther had left the list where Zarah would see it, so she was ready for the outburst, and her response was almost casual. "It's a family event; you didn't really believe I would have him there, did you?"

"So, even though I am twenty-one, you still want to control who is around me? I've been with Damien for years; when will you realize you are not breaking us up?"

"Too many years; but don't start with me today, Zarah; I'm the one having this function, and I can decide who will be there." She moved to the other side of the counter and laid out the cucumber, callaloo, and celery for her smoothie.

"And I can decide I won't be there; in fact, I soon won't even be living here." Zarah stood across the space from her mother, her arms akimbo and her feet apart. Like a tennis player, she had fired the ball across the net and stood ready for the return. But Esther had long abandoned the match. Her only response was the sudden roar of the high-speed juicer. Zarah never bargained on that, but she was not about to give up so easily.

"You are my mother, but you are the most unfair person I know! Just because Damien don't come from a family like this one, you hated him from the first time you saw him." Esther paused the juicer and Zarah waited, thinking her volley would bait her mother into a response; but the new whirring was the only sound to be heard. "And by the way, what's so great about this family?"

"It's not a great family; but I'm willing to bet it's a damn sight better than the one that produced that good-for-nothing boy inveigling you to mash up ours."

"Seriously?" Zarah burst into a cynical laugh. "Me and Damien mashing up this family? Why we would have to mash it up when you did such a great job yourself?" Zarah was in high gear now; she had decided long before she saw the list that if her mother left off Damien, it would be the perfect setup for her to have a showdown and threaten to move out. A friend of hers needed a roommate to help with expenses, and Zarah knew she could get that opportunity. Esther grabbed her by the hand and dragged her through the kitchen into the living room. No effort to pull away could stand up to her mother's determination. Esther had not expected the threat to move out, and her panic sparked her decision to let Zarah have it this time.

"No, you come. Look around you."

"I don't want to look at anything," Zarah protested.

"Well, this evening you have to look." She dragged Zarah from room to room showing her the modest but tasteful furnishings and conveniences. "You know how much struggle and sacrifice provide you with all this? You would prefer being in this family before we had any of this?" By then, they were in Zarah's room, decked out with her favorite possessions. "I suppose you are ready to give up all this and rent half a room with him while you pay all the bills?"

"Who knows? I might be." Her hand free of Esther's grip, she said, "You never once gave him a chance, just because he didn't finish school or plan to become some middle-class professional that you want everybody to be. But it's not just about school, right? We both know it's bigger than that: he's too low class, and he doesn't speak the English you always harping on to make you feel better about yourself. I bet if he came from a Hope Pastures or Norbrook family, you could forget the way he talks and forgive him for dropping out of school, right?"

"Don't talk rubbish, girl! When did any of us ever talk about Damien's class, or where he lives? In fact, you even know where he lives?"

"Face the facts, Mummy! Everybody in Jamaica know there is black and there is black; we have Jamaica above Cross Roads and a separate one below." Zarah had joined a student group committed to delve into problems of race and class relations in Jamaica, and their debates and beliefs provided new fuel for her argument. "I never forget what Grams said about color and what it caused in this same fine family of ours. You think everybody can't see that your constant talk about acting right and speaking perfect English is all about getting into the right class?"

"Just listen to yourself, Zarah. How can you allow yourself to believe all that university claptrap means anything to us? What you're saying about Jamaica is true, but you couldn't think our worries over you and Damien all these years were about that. You believe color and class made us work hard to provide the best foundation for you? Look at me and your father; you think we could be concerned about that, when we both came from nothing?"

"Is not about me; and you can never convince me that if Damien was high brown, with curly hair, and from a so-called good family, you'd be against him like you were from day one. I know you'll never approve of him."

"You're right; and for the hundredth time, let me tell you why. He will add nothing to your life, Zarah; he's a worthless bum, and you will spend every cent you earn on him. And by the way, if he was white as snow and came from Jack's Hill, he would be a snow-white upper-class bum! You more than anybody else know it. Why else you gave up so many of your other good friends? Why do you speak properly with everybody except him? You thought I wouldn't know?"

"Of course you know; the entire world can see that you know everything. You are sure about what's going on with me, what I want, what I should be, and what is good for me."

"I'm sure about one thing: You were the girl who promised never to give up who you were for any boy; you would always be too secure within yourself to make anyone dictate who you would be and what your life would be like."

"Yes, well, guess what? I changed my mind; and by the way, it's not because of any boy; I changed my mind because I hate the thought of turning out like you!" Grabbing her bag, she slammed the door, and headed down the street. The curtains closed on the 21st birthday plans, and when the time came, Zarah announced she would spend the weekend out of town.

Lonelier and more disconnected than ever, she lived in parentheses between being with Damien and losing her family. Every move she made felt like dancing on the thinnest ice, knowing her mother watched from a distance waiting for her to fall through. Desperate not to lose his daughter, Bradley was driven to the middle, trying his best to encourage Damien to do something with his life, for Zarah's sake.

Naomi maintained Damien was no good and Zarah would find out for herself; but in the meantime, she did all she could to prevent a rift between herself and her granddaughter. She kept Zarah's secrets, dried her tears, allowed her to stay at Ulster Road as often as the conflict with Esther boiled over; and she eventually let Damien visit, thinking they were safer there than on the streets where crime was rampant. She prayed she was doing the right thing, and she hoped some of her gentle persuasion and harsh warnings would have some effect on the boy. This was no good for her tepid relationship with Esther. "I thought I could count on your support in this; Bradley is already making it easy for them, so they think I'm the monster; now you—"

"Esther, don't talk like dat."

"But is how I feel, Mama. Look from when we have this problem with Zarah and this boy, and is like it can never end, but all the time, I'm the one who gets the wrong end of it."

"Yuh hear what mi say?" Even with a daughter of 21, Esther fell silent when her mother used that firm tone, and Naomi grabbed the opening. "The Lord Himself know mi support yuh in every way. But sometimes yuh can be just as hard ears as Zarah. All the while, mi ask miself if every mother get the curse my mother always tell mi about. Must be dat prevent us from talking to our children about hard things. Or prob'ly every mother pass it on to her child."

"I didn't believe in any curse, but I agree it is hard, and apparently I will never get it right."

"Yuh get plenty things right, but yuh could ask yuhself if is time to change how yuh deal wid Zarah. Look how long this problem going on, and yuh still dealing wid it same way. Yuh think mi want to see yuh and Zarah lose one another?"

"How she can lose me? I'm her mother."

"Esther, Zarah is a woman now; she have her own money. Yuh think yuh can prevent her from moving out to live with the boy? At least if she stay in yuh house, yuh have the chance to save her from him controlling her completely. Dat is why mi mek dem stay right on this couch sometimes. At least mi can hear some of what dem talk about. Esther, yuh don't see we near to losing her?"

Like many mothers, Esther's images of the future never varied from the one in which her daughter would live with her until the day she stepped out the front door in her wedding dress on her father's arm. Most of her other dreams had withered along the way, but despite the long struggle, she was not quite ready to give up on this one.

A month after the birthday explosion, Esther stood by the kitchen door and watched Zarah eating in the usual silence. She waited for her to stand, and without a word, she pulled her daughter toward her in a gesture shared a thousand times in what now seemed like a vanishing world. Zarah stayed in the spot, but she held her back straight, not tucking her head into her mother's neck as she used to. Left standing as Zarah walked away, Esther took out her frustration on the kitchen, reorganizing every shelf, drawer, and countertop, before falling into bed as dawn peeped through the window.

CHAPTER 33
ZARAH'S SOLUTION

For over a month, Zarah was home right after work in the evenings; even weekends found her there, not a rumble or ringtone on the bedside table. Across the hall, hope stirred Esther to prayer. *Lord, please make this mean a serious quarrel, something that can open her eyes; help us end this long war before it's too late.* She whispered her hope to Naomi and Bradley, and new prayers went up, asking God to make it a long separation and bring Zarah to her senses. But Damien had left for New York to visit his long-lost mother, and his absence only made Zarah's world more desolate.

In the eighth week of his absence, as her taxi wound its way through the dense traffic, a weary Zarah came upon a road repair crew causing a huge traffic jam just below the American embassy. A robust woman, with a voice to match, stood in the middle of the chaos in a blood-red T-shirt stretched to its limits, her belly button peeping out between folds of shining fat skin. Her left and right hands alternated, each holding up branches of hibiscus in a primitive routine. Wilted red flowers halted the traffic; sweaty leaves, once green, but now sun-burned and limp, waved in the sun, letting the other lane go.

The dancehall music on the taxi driver's radio clashed with the sounds from the other taxis, parked crisscrossed facing all directions in the lot across from the embassy. The absurdity of the scene mirrored her life, urging her to laugh loudly; but the soreness inside, coupled with the heat and the dust and the noise gave her a stronger desire to vomit. *How am I ever going to find my way out of this chaos?* The minibuses edged up against her taxi, and a conductor leaned out the door of a red one, with his ragged dollar bills laced between his fingers. "Hey bwoy, come out the effing road, so good car can pass yuh pop-down Lada!"

Sinking down into the seat, she shut her eyes. *I'm so sick and tired of this ramshackle place! And all I'm going home to is a silent house, cold like a deep freeze. Everything dragging me down and I can't see a change coming!* Every day she passed the embassy and watched black people sweating in a serpentine line to get into the building that could make the difference between struggling in Jamaica and making a life in America. In the months since her lifeline left, a day had not passed without her thinking of joining the line so she could get a visa and go to him. In one move, she would put an end to his nagging and to the unbreakable tension in the house with her mother. *But I hate the thought of New York; and joining Damien would be the last nail in the coffin of my relationship with everybody.*

It was a struggle with no pause, bringing a tautness in her stomach. Without consciously deciding what to do, a part of her set about freeing herself. Staying at work late a few evenings provided long hours on the Internet, scrolling through information about short work-related courses and U.S. visas of every kind. Her mother's filing cabinet produced the confirmation for which she had hoped. The passport with her seventeen-year-old face would not expire until she was twenty-seven. And then came the shocker: The visitors' visas she and Esther got for their only overseas trip would last the same time—*no need for the long line at the passport office or the embassy! No need for paperwork my mother can interfere with. Someone is on my side.*

Not even the purchase of her ticket and the dollars she would need brought home the reality of the decision she seemed to have made. Only one action made it completely real.

"Mummy, remember not to expect me home Friday evening. We made all the arrangements; it's a birthday party in Ocho Rios, so after work, we're heading out."

"Well, it's nice it all worked out; so, you're coming back Saturday, you said?"

"Saturday or Sunday."

"Enjoy the break from Kingston." More hopes were eager to fly out of Esther's mouth, but she swallowed them. *I guess if I sound too approving, she may change her mind.*

On Tuesday, Zarah packed a suitcase and left it at her friend Shari's house. At 7:15 on Friday morning, her usual taxi idled at the gate, waiting to take her to work. She stood at the bedroom door with a small piece of luggage. She glanced at the bed–scene of countless talks with her parents, secret escapades with Damien, too many moments when her tears spilled onto her pillow as she wept for the lost simplicity of her childhood. A wave of sadness engulfed her.

Her hurriedly drained coffee cup sat alone in the sink. She was halfway to the taxi. Esther rushed into the kitchen for her own quick cup. Zarah looked back at her and waved. Without a thought, she ran back inside, pulled her bewildered mother to her and said, "Bye ... Mummy."

Time robbed the moment of the answer leaping into Esther's mouth.

***

On Saturday night, the check-in area at Norman Manley Airport buzzed with travelers. A mix of anticipation and anxiety warmed Zarah's face. Her feet felt unsteady as passengers rushed in, sweeping her into the check-in line. Documents redeemed, suitcase weighed for loading, and nothing else to delay the reality before her, she turned to Shari.

"This is it, girl. Come give me a hug; and listen, I'm sorry you had to bring me out here so late. You are a genuine pal, and I couldn't appreciate you more. Get home safe, my friend, and don't worry."

They stood apart, hands resting on each other's shoulders, eyes locked. "Zarah, I tell you a hundred times I don't feel good at all about this. Just let me phone your mother or your grandmother tomorrow and say something. I will make up a story just to give them a little cushioning."

"I know you want to help, but I have to deal with this my way. You don't know how bad things are with them. Even if it doesn't work out with me and Damien, I have to get away."

"That might be true, but why leave without telling them? Why not forget this madness and talk to your grandmother? She's always keeping secrets for you. And this whole situation scares the hell out of me. Suppose something goes wrong? What if Damien doesn't show up to meet you? The two of us know how he can go crazy sometimes."

"Shari, trust me. All the terrible possibilities went through my mind already. But I have to go. I will call you; I promise." Zarah hurried away, not looking back at her friend who she knew was probably right. But she could not afford to consider what Shari was thinking; she was already on the brink of abandoning her plan and heading home. Shari walked sideways toward the exit, half of her body resigned to leaving by herself and half leaning back to watch the friend she feared was heading for certain trouble.

CHAPTER 34
ONE DRY TOOTHBRUSH

Kingston, 1990s

Like every other Monday morning, Esther's alarm woke her at 5:45, but she struggled to get up. Half-expecting to hear Zarah come in, she had not slept well. The first of her three morning cups of coffee was due, so she headed toward the kitchen. Her daughter was always first to the bathroom for her long routine, so she expected her bedroom door to be open. There was no light, no sound along the passage, no hint of activity anywhere. Esther tapped and turned the knob; still nothing. Zarah had not slept in her bed. Her cell phone went straight to voice mail. Esther's nervous fingers automatically found another number. "Bradley, it's me; sorry to call so early."

"What's up? Yuh okay?"

"Yes; well, I'm not sure; you heard from Zarah?"

"No, I thought she went to Ocho Rios."

"She did. I fell asleep waiting up for her, so I assumed she came in late and slipped in, but she's not here. She didn't come home at all. And no matter how bad the situation may be, she always keeps her word about when she'll be home."

Bradley was fully awake now. "Yuh call her?"

"She's not picking up; suppose something happened ... an accident, or .... I didn't meet the friends she went with. They're from work."

"Yuh think they ran late and they might head straight to the office?"

"Doubt it; and you don't think she would have called one of us?"

"Yuh guys had an—"

"No. We didn't quarrel. I was glad she was going out with friends for a change. I'll keep trying her phone. Call me back if you hear from her. I have to get ready for work."

On Wednesday, Detective Cynthia Fraser's team was all over the Duhaney Park house. They searched Zarah's room from top to bottom. "What do you hope to find in there?" Esther asked.

"Mrs. Thomas, we checked the hospitals and there's no admission record with your daughter's name. We have no police report of an incident in Ocho Rios. We are looking for any clue we can find–phone numbers, diary, friends' names, anything. You need to tell us what is missing from her room." But there were no obvious signs–not until they emerged one by one–more than the usual spare hangers, a couple of missing shoes, and on the dressing table, curious blobs of dust between clean circles and squares where bottles and jars of cosmetics should have been.

"Some of those would have gone with her for the weekend trip," Esther said.

Notifications of missed calls from "Auntie Es," littered Shari's phone and her messages cluttered her mailbox. Shari swayed between wanting to help the woman who'd been like her second mother, and keeping the confidence of her best friend since prep school. With all the messages signaling Esther's desperation, Shari had no choice but to give Esther a little relief by telling her what she knew. "I'm sorry, Auntie, I should have called you before." Esther shushed her, sparing both of them the agony of details.

Esther had to face the fact her daughter had deceived her once again. Made without a word to her family, this decision of Zarah's seemed irreversible, and Esther said as much. Naomi was sure if they ever found Zarah, the only appropriate actions would be overtures of peace. Bradley asked for more time to contact Damien's father. But Esther knew it was time to end the deception of herself and everybody else. Disagreements had been weakening the bond with her daughter too long, and now it had given way. All she could do was leave it alone. "I know you mean well, Mama, and you too, Bradley, but obviously Zarah finally made her choice. Apparently, we don't have to be in her life. We just have to accept—" Voice breaking, she fell against Bradley, and with Naomi at their side, he closed Zarah's door, and they saw Esther to hers.

Hour after sleepless hour, her footfalls echoed through the emptiness of a house that had scarcely been without Zarah. For as long as she had a child, this woman had defined herself, her purpose, and her vision of life based on her identity as Zarah's mother. That premise was now gone, and so had her moorings.

At midnight, her eyes remained fixed on the ceiling. The house was so quiet, she imagined hearing the water turning into ice in the freezing compartment of the fridge. Pausing at Zarah's door as she so often did before turning in for the night, her eyes surveyed the empty bed up against the wall; they landed on the inches between the bedspread and the floor–right there, where Zarah's slippers waited, aching for the warmth of her slender dancer's feet. The mute television and boom box admonished the stunned mother, but they were nothing like the purple toothbrush standing bone dry beside hers, in the alabaster toothbrush holder.

A spotless kitchen stretched out around her, and she longed to see an unwashed plate, an uneaten dinner stuck in the back of the fridge, a half-finished soda gone flat on the counter. The few times Shari came to assure her Zarah had sent a quick email, and she was okay, Esther took comfort from their shared moments, but the visits diminished after the exchanges between the two friends ended abruptly because Shari could no longer deny telling Esther what she knew.

Esther settled into a routine without her old dependence on gleaming tiles, polished furniture, rows of glasses, or sparkling crystal curios uniformly laid out in straight lines across the shelves. Without the daughter for whom she had been desperate to set the best example, there was no need for perfection in trivia.

PART TWO

CHAPTER 35
REUNITED

New York, 1998

In the baggage hall at JFK airport, a long line stretched ahead of Zarah while she examined the luggage spinning on the carousel. Having traveled only once before, and with her mother in charge, she was not sure what to do, so she just followed everyone else progressing toward the customs area, now swarming with officials as fierce looking as the dogs that sniffed random pieces of luggage and the body parts of their owners.

Relieved to get past the stern-looking customs officer, Zarah hurried to the pickup area, where a steady stream of cars slowed down and after picking up their passengers, sped off into a New York night with anything possible ahead. Zarah watched keenly for a familiar grin through the windscreen of a car she had never seen. After an hour, she rested her back against a concrete column and searched everywhere for her phone. *No! The washroom at the airport. There better be a pay phone and quarters in my wallet.*

"Damien, where are you? I've been out here almost two hours."

"Babes? Lawd, yuh voice sound like a hot Jamaica patty! Don't worry yuhself. Some business come up. Mi soon reach; and, girl, mi dying to see yuh!"

Why did I even believe he would be on time?

Another half an hour had passed, when a red car with a bright yellow stripe on the side shot out of the tunnel, swerving and screeching as loud rap music blared. No need for Zarah to wonder; that would be her Damien. Shaking her head and smiling despite her annoyance, she stood with her arms akimbo and frowned as he pulled up dangerously close to the curb, opening the door and leaping through it, all in one move. As he swaggered toward her, the expensive army-print shorts way below his underwear, and the tracksuit top with the hoodie, drew the glances of several onlookers. A huge gold chain and pendant, a baseball cap with the bill pointing backwards, and high-top Nike sneakers hugging his ankles completed his outfit. He lifted Zarah into the air, belting out Freddie McGregor's hit song "You're my Jamaican girl."

"Keep quiet, man," she said, glancing all around to see how much attention he was drawing to them. As he stepped back frowning, she gave his outfit the once over, and giggled.

"What is all this? You're American now?"

"This is the look, girl. Yuh soon get with the program. Is not Jamaica this, yuh know; so what, not even a little chups? Yuh never miss me?"

Planting a quick kiss on his lips, she said, "It's late. I had a long hard day and night; let's just go."

Damien picked up her bags and led her to the car, other drivers honking their horns as he spun around and wagged his finger in her face, shouting, "Awright, Babes, but look here: this is the Big Apple. Just chill; and don't bother bring yuh Jamaican nagging up here." Zarah gave him a questioning look. He kept trying to hug and kiss her, but she was too concerned about the stares. "Hey! What yuh so jumpy about? People mind dem own business over here yuh know, Star. We can do what we want. Anyway, how long?"

"How long what?" Zarah asked, handing him a bag. "Here, put this in the back, please."

"Is what going on wid yuh, girl? Mi asking how long dem give yuh to stay up here?"

"Oh, six months."

"Not much. Anyway, no problem. My contacts work out a plan wid mi arready. This is the life, Babes. Yuh going wish yuh did follow what mi say and come wid mi up here. By the way, how much money yuh bring?"

"Just what I had."

Damien pressed the gas pedal and shot into the maze of streets and traffic outside the airport. A little calmer now the trip was over, Zarah stretched across the seat and gave him a peck on the cheek. He swerved and grabbed her face, attempting a serious kiss. "Stop it man. You don't see how the street busy and the cars switching from lane to lane?"

"Screw the street! And look here: Yuh going stop picking on mi over foolishness?" Damien was happy to see his girl, but serious unfinished business was in progress at his friend's house, and he was in no mood for Zarah's gravity.

"And what about you? I came all the way here to be with you, and you leave me waiting forever; and since you pick me up, it's been one dig after another. You think that shows you're glad to see me?"

Damien straightened up and pulled away from her, dipping into his pocket and fussing with something before lighting up and taking a hard draw.

Zarah watched the scenes unfolding as he sped past. Although he had turned the windows down, the smell was inescapable.

"You can't get in big trouble driving and smoking weed over here?"

"Yuh don't think mi know what mi doing by now?" He kissed his teeth and shrank against his door, jammed the gas pedal, and sped away. Zarah leaned on her side and stared into New York's grim face.

Chapter 36
A Dingy Green Wall

Forty feet of dingy graffiti-smeared green wall emptied into fractured gray tiles, and steps chipped at the edges. One rusty light fixture in the ceiling was missing its bulb, and the other dangled from its socket, leaving the third to shed a quivering light across the faded QUEENSBURY COURT sign. Damien crossed the foyer, leading Zarah straight to the elevator, glancing away from the startled look on her face. "This ... this is your mother's place?" Zarah asked trying to cover her hope for him to say, "No."

"Mother? Babes, yuh mad or what? Yuh believe mi leave Jamaica to come to the Big Apple and suffer under the same oppression?"

"So, who are you staying with here?"

"I'm my own man now; well halfway there; I'm sharing with the guys."

"I'm staying with a bunch of guys?" Zarah asked, no longer trying to hide her displeasure.

"Shit, woman; what wrong with yuh? I don't hear yuh say one good thing since you reach."

"What good word you said since I came? Let's just get to wherever we're staying. The two of us are tired, and this place is creepy."

"Well, I hope is not anything more than dat. But remember we not at Duhaney Park now, and mi don't want no misery and quarreling." They got out of the elevator and Zarah was close to tears, so he drew her close. "Babes, just chill. Everything criss. Talk the truth: Yuh not glad yuh free now? Come, come this way." He fumbled with the key to Apt. 326. Feeling her eyes on him, he glanced away from her obvious dismay. Every detail was different from the picture he had painted all the months of pestering her to join him. His clothes were different, his speech and his tone unrecognizable, and unlike the apartment he had described as his mother's, this place was a dump.

A mess of videos, boom boxes, clothes, and Styrofoam containers with scraps of food of various ages welcomed them inside. She secured her luggage in a far corner behind a door, leaning against it as she gave the room a once over. Damien hustled to clear the bed.

"I need to use the—"

"Right behind the door," he said, a mix of embarrassment and nervousness creeping into his voice. Zarah stepped gingerly into the bathroom. Damien flipped through a few items in her bag. As soon as he spied the notebook computer he shouted,

"This look nice; where yuh get it?"

"What are you—Damien! come in here!"

"What?"

"They are everywhere. You can't get rid of them?"

"The effing cockroach dead, woman, Damien shrieked, stomping on the roach. What's the big deal? Jamaica don't full a roach?"

"Excuse me! When you ever saw a roach where I live?" Stomping all around the bathroom, he killed one roach after another.

"They must be out here too," Zarah said, still frantic. "And where I'm supposed to sleep?"

It was just what Damien needed to hear, so he grabbed after her. "Now yuh talking; come, clear off this bed; is not like we getting much sleep tonight, though." He saw the wanting in Zarah's face, felt her body shudder when he reached for her. Another rapid shift in his mood and tone. She pulled back from him. *One minute he's calm and the next minute he's irritable; I bet he's smoking too much of that weed again.*

"What? Clear off one for us? You mean somebody else is coming to sleep in here and is almost two o'clock in the morning?" By this time, she was cleaning up around the bed.

"Babes, relax yuhself. Is just how things roll. Mi cousin sleep here sometimes; but him might not come because it late arready. In the morning, Ghost will come by." He stretched himself out on the bed, shoving stuff onto the floor and taking off his shirt.

"Ghost? Who is Ghost?"

"Ghost is my key spar from the rock. We go Windward Road Primary School back in the day, but we lose touch when him leave and come up here long time. As mi reach up here, mi check for him and him help mi out all the while. Him will soon be a key man for us, Babes."

"How?" Zarah asked, from the other side of the room, where she was trying to find somewhere to put a few things.

"Plenty ways. Him know all the runnings and how to get around the system. Just a good man to know."

"What a name, though."

"Him nearly drown one time on a school trip and, from dat, him name Ghost. But yuh don't have to run from him." His old belly laugh broke the tension and made Zarah feel a little more at home. She sat next to him on the bed and started twirling his hair, running her fingers over his face and all over his chest, where she rested her head. He settled in, happy she was acting more like herself at last.

"Damien, who else live here?"

"Yuh turn detective? I tell yuh this is where everybody hang out. Everybody in my circle who come up from yard can stay here first if dem need a place. We have to hang together and help one another." He pulled her head back to him and kissed her all over, but Zarah had seen another glimpse of his quick mood change and she was on her feet.

"I must ask about the place where I'm staying. I don't understand why you acting so ignorant."

"Me not ignorant, but we not in Jamaica where yuh accustom to yuh family house and having what yuh want. Everything different over here. Is just so the runnings go; no Miss Lucretia to wash an' clean an' spy. But it soon work out; trust me." He stood close behind her and pulled her to him. His warm breath brushed her eyebrow.

"Okay, but it sounds like so many people come around here, and the place is small. You must know a woman can't just hang about with guys indefinitely."

"Look here, don't yuh father have relatives up here? Yuh want mi carry you there tomorrow?"

"You heard me say I was going anywhere? Just forget I said anything."

The next afternoon, they went out to buy food, and Zarah saw her surroundings for the first time in daylight. Young people—mostly black teenagers—were hanging all about; some leaned on their bikes, some darted around on skateboards, and younger ones played with all kinds of toys. Unshaven, bushy-haired old men wearing pitchy-patchy merinos slammed dominoes as they hunched around a low table, beer bottles everywhere. From the beginning, Damien's attitude was enough to make it clear he expected her to keep her feelings to herself. The prospect of living in this place made her shudder, and as the weeks passed, the enormity of her mistake became overwhelming.

A surly short-tempered boy had displaced the frivolous best friend who had made her laugh so much at home. Bereft without him, and with her relationship with her parents at its worst, an emptiness had settled upon her. Joining him was supposed to set it right, yet here she was after leaving home out of desperation—an aching for a kind of peace and relief—and questions nagged her all the time about who he was becoming. She learned to fear his shifting countenance, keeping as much distance as she could when his eyes threatened to go dark, or his lips twitched, or his knees shook uncontrollably.

Those were the signs whenever a tempest brewed—signs of a nasty side he had hidden all along. What had brought these changes? Was this how he had always been when they were not together? She looked all around her for the other Damien for whom she had given up so much, the one whose absence had deadened her inside. She rummaged for evidence the situation might turn out better than everything suggested.

CHAPTER 37
THE BLUE LINEN SUIT

It was a shivery Friday in the last week of September, about three months since Zarah arrived. Make-up and tears mingling to form a smudgy mess, she pondered her dilemma for hours. On the bed lay the plain blue linen suit she bought for $12.97 at the thrift shop; on the floor, the shabby white sandals she wore from Jamaica waited. They no longer suited the weather, but her money was dwindling, and Damien's sketchy activities brought in unpredictable earnings. Zarah did not know where he got his money from, but based on the steady stream of hustlers through the apartment, she guessed he was one too.

Bounding in through the door, his eyes shining with excitement, he stopped short as he saw her pacing the floor, still wearing her robe. "Come on girl, the big day come at last! Wait, why yuh not ready?"

"Because ..." She slipped down onto the bed and buried her face in her hands.

His eyes narrowed, and he spoke through clenched teeth, "Because what?"

"Sorry, Damien. I can't go through with this crazy plan."

"Oh yeah? Yuh not going through with it? So, what yuh plan to do: swim home to Mummy and Daddy?"

"No, and don't make fun of serious business."

"Oh, so yuh sending home for money to buy a ticket back to J. A. before yuh visa run out; or yuh forget yuh cash in the one yuh come with?"

Wrenching her purse from her hand, he hauled her to him and held it up before her. "Or yuh must be have more money and you can buy a ticket."

"Let me go; I can smell the disgusting weed on you, and beer too; you're always carrying on like this of late; no wonder you can't even hear what I've been trying to tell you."

"What yuh talking about?"

"I keep telling you I'm afraid to go through with it, Damien. Why you can't understand?"

"Fraid for what? Ghost is mi good friend and him always around us. What wrong wid him? Him have citizenship, and him know how dis business work. Mi not legal, and mi mother not legal, so we have to stay underground. But yuh can be legal and later on when we get past all this, we can work out other problems."

As suddenly as his rage had escalated, his voice became consoling. "Mi not asking yuh to do anything to hurt yuh. Girls from home–guys too–do it every day to stay in America. Is not like yuh going really married. It will be easy, Babes."

"Easy? You call it easy to get married to a stranger just to stay in America? And especially somebody like Ghost? I don't even like him around me."

"But him willing to help us out, Babes. And mi don't want yuh leaving mi to go back home to all the problem dem."

"You say you love me, and you want me to marry Ghost? That makes sense to you?"

"Then how yuh love me, and yuh won't do this, so we can relax and don't fret over visa problem, and money problem, and going back home?"

"Can't you see this is different? You can come home too, and we can make a life there; up here, we will always be in this dump, or another one just like it. My family—"

"Family? The people dem yuh run from to come up here? Who believe mi not good enough for dem because mi don' come from uptown? Well, yuh can go back home anytime yuh ready, but don't bother look for mi down there."

"What you mean by that?"

"Just what mi say!" He was stomping about now, his fists clenching and unclenching.

"I thought we were arguing about me marrying Ghost, but what you are saying right now is worse; it's about whether we will even be together."

"Worse than the misery and the pressure since yuh come up in here complaining every day? Since yuh come finding fault with everything mi do and mashing up mi plan to make a situation better? How much time mi tell yuh dat yuh have to be legal to get good work so we can pay the bills?"

At last. His words confirmed what her mind had been telling her for weeks. Damien was not up to the responsibility of having her with him. His work was sporadic, the bills were constant, and her money was running out. The novelty had passed, and her presence limited his movements.

"But I'm working," she protested, "What more do you want from me?"

Damien knew this reference to her work would hit a nerve. With a visitor's visa, she had few options where jobs were concerned, and her frustration was mounting about being stuck in the one alley drugstore whose owner risked employing her "off the books" as he called it. Selling cheap cosmetics and over-the-counter drugs to girls and women who looked her up and down, she wanted to explode at their whispers about where she came from, talking like she was better than they were.

"Yuh call one half-ass job selling lipstick in a drugstore working? Is only school dropout do dem kinda work! Yuh know how much money yuh can get with yuh degree when yuh legal?" She got up from the bed and walked toward the closet. Damien watched and waited. *Yuh just put back yuh clothes in dat closet; do it and see what happen!*

Zarah's frustration boiled over, "Why you don't tell me about school dropouts? Don't you know much more about them than me?"

Her unexpected outburst stunned him, landing his right hand across her mouth.

"Who yuh calling dropout? Yuh want to leave this place right now and find yuh way to people yuh father know? In fact, yuh know what? This foolishness going finish today. Is one thing or the other; put on yuh clothes or pack up what yuh have!" He glanced at her huddled in the corner, blood dripping from her mouth.

Zarah sidled along the wall past him, into the bathroom. His heavy breathing broke the silence, backed up with his footsteps pacing the floor. Fearful of what he might do, she locked herself in, sat on the toilet, and wiped her face, her hands and knees shaking. She tried hard not to admit what Damien had done, but the throbbing in her head and the blood on the crumpled toilet paper insisted. *It's my fault. I shouldn't call him a dropout, but I was so mad, and now this.*

"Zarah, yuh make up yuh mind? Yuh don't see time going?" His rage seeped under the door.

"I'm just ... I'm coming."

As she turned the lock, he pulled the door open and shoved the blue suit inside. "I hope yuh know what yuh coming out to do–either put on this or collect yuh belongings!"

"So, you're coming to hit me again? How many times I tell you that's one thing I won't take from any man? And just because I have to depend on you for the first time, this is what you do?" With the reminder of the slap, his rage disappeared like a light turned off.

"No, Babes. Yuh know mi never mean to do dat. Is the first an' last time, promise. But yuh should respect a man for trying. Yuh know mi wouldn't mek anything bad happen to yuh. Mi can manage, Zarah, but yuh can't manage long if yuh turn illegal like me. This is the easiest and cheapest way yuh can be straight."

Her visa had time on it, but he was right; established employers offering suitable job opportunities would not risk employing her; it was against the law, and they could face serious trouble. Despite how easy some of Damien's friends made it sound, being illegal terrified her. Ghost had arranged all the paperwork; the rest of his solution sounded quick and easy, and although the thought was terrifying and the process would use up a huge chunk of her money, Damien peppered her with stories of young Jamaicans who arranged marriages to remain in the U.S. past their allotted time.

Dressed in her blue suit, she walked hand in hand with Damien onto the subway heading from Parsons Boulevard to City Hall Park, New York, NY, an address she would not forget for a long time. Ghost slouched outside the building smiling in his brown shirt and beige tie, the neatest trousers

Zarah had ever seen him wear, and clean white high-top sneakers. Her husband-to-be was a laughable sight, a symbol of a life she would never escape. The trap loomed, and as they came within touching distance of Ghost, Zarah wrested her hand from Damien's and sprinted past the entrance and her almost husband. The men were so shocked, they stood still. Only the appearance of the first bus stop slowed her, and her breathing came close to normal as the doors opened into the first bus that would take her close to Parsons Boulevard.

Damien stayed away from the apartment for the next week. A plastic bag from the supermarket swallowed the blue suit, and she buried it behind the suitcase at the back of the closet. Between her stomach walls, her despondency took root.

The bruise from Damien's blow soon disappeared, but the ache inside was unrelenting. Her late-night walks from the third shift at the low-level drug store were nerve-wracking and home was a cheerless, oppressive apartment. Still, without Damien and his hangers-on, the peace brought a surprising clarity to Zarah's mind. He came home when necessary but only during her hours at work. She did not want to clutter her mind with arguments, so brief text messages became her norm and they brought only cold, abrupt answers, suggesting he was commuting between his cousin's place and his mother's apartment in Brooklyn, while working on one of his usual nameless projects.

Free of the tension and arguments, Zarah used the time to gather herself and reflect on what was ahead. Home was not an option; the time had been too short for her to prove anything, except that her decision to join Damien had been ill considered and doomed to failure. The countless spoken or unspoken "I-told-you-so" reminders would be too much to bear. *At least a diploma or certificate must be in my suitcase before I go back.*

Determined to make school her new priority, she arranged to meet the one person she had communicated with outside of Damien's circle. Mavis was an older Jamaican woman who lived in another block of the same project, and she had befriended the lonely-looking Zarah while grocery shopping. It was easy to see how bright Zarah was, and Mavis surmised she was from a good Jamaican home, but her experience suggested the girl's situation was not what it should be. At every opportunity, she inveigled Zarah to focus on her plans for school. That was the one thing that kept her own daughters out of trouble.

Mavis worked as a nursing assistant at a nearby facility for the elderly. Recently widowed, she had seen her two daughters off to college years before, so she was happy for Zarah's call and readily agreed to meet her at the coffee shop, where she shared all she knew about student visas and college applications. It was just in time. Only weeks remained before it would be too late to apply to convert her visitor's visa to one for students, so she could go to school and work part-time at jobs better than the drugstore stop-gap.

Between working overtime and scouring school websites and regulations, there was less time to worry about Damien. A month had passed when they exchanged quick words as the elevator clunked to a stop. Her apparent indifference, along with a shortage of cash, and the inconvenience of commuting conspired to bring him home.

The tension eased after a while, and both did what they could to subdue their anger. Relieved but cornered, Zarah tried to make the best of the situation, especially since she had her own new plan. There was a chance Damien would act like a normal person now she had shared her ideas about school, and he realized marrying Ghost was not the only way to become legal. But the condition of their lives—the cards and dominoes, the boxes of half-eaten fast food, half-smoked spliffs, beer bottles, and other remnants of aimless people leading aimless lives—made the situation intolerable for her. Every morning her stomach turned when the dismal surroundings greeted her.

Clusters of young people hanging about the building mirrored many little ghetto communities even in better parts of Kingston. Images of the tiny but well-kept gardens in Duhaney Park drifted in and out of her mind. Before leaving home, she never thought about the meaning of living there. It was a housing scheme where most people were probably poorer than those here in Queensbury; but back there, almost every family seemed to strive for better. *At home, at least I knew what I was about, and I was on the way to being somebody!*

When November and December came, the ugliness of leafless trees and dried-out flowers made her yearn for the warm sun and the Christmas breeze she remembered from home. Her thin clothes left her shivering, and as she trekked to the bus stop in the slush after rain or snow soaked everywhere, her bones ached for the Duhaney Park bed where comfort had been hers all her life.

The cold increased her temptation to call Jamaica if only to hear a sound bearing a vague resemblance to the old tenderness of her father's voice. And, yes, though it was hard to admit, even if it had a tone as icy and bitter as it had remained during her last months at home, her mother's voice would have been like a balm. But every time the thought crossed her mind, her fear of rejection mounted, and Damien's fist loomed close to her jawbone. At night, he sprawled next to her, drugged beyond consciousness. More and more, the sheet on his side of the bed remained unwrinkled.

CHAPTER 38
A GIFT GOES WRONG

Zarah clung to the job at the drugstore, but her search for a suitable study option went into high gear. Without telling Damien, she had transferred money from home to cover all the costs ahead of her, but she was tired of administrators who questioned her Jamaican school records, or why her BSc. took three instead of four years. Though they were beyond belief, some questions brought a smile to her face: *Where in India is the University of the West Indies? Did you take the test for speakers of a foreign language? Did you do any real experiments during your studies?*

Sometimes Damien was his old self. He pressed Zarah to keep on searching for a better job, but he was patient and he showered her with praise for organizing the apartment and cooking all the Jamaican food he craved. It was still hard to tolerate guys dropping in at all hours, sometimes sleeping over, and always borrowing from the little money she and Damien earned. Ghost came and went with the others, and though he always reminded them of how much he could help them out "with his great old plan," there was no real trouble. His presence unnerved her, but she realized there was no chance of getting rid of him. Fragments of his hushed conversations with Damien often drifted into the kitchen or to the little porch where she sat with her notebook, seeking refuge from it all. These gave clues suggesting their run-ins with the police were increasing, but her comments or questions about their activities often pushed Damien to the edge of his patience, and her fear of his eruptions kept her quiet. *Let them carry on with whatever they want; it's only a matter of time.*

She could never be sure what mood would come home with him, and she worried whenever Damien showed up with a sullen face, or on a high.

"Hey, Babes, come quick; mi have something to show yuh."

"Soon come, just getting out the shower."

He usually came in late, so his arrival before nightfall was a surprise. She wrapped the towel around her and stepped out to where he stood, the old Damien grin lighting up his face.

"Hmm; yuh smell good, Babes. Come give mi a nice long kiss." Keeping him on an even keel had become important to her peace of mind, so she had learned to respond to every little overture like this one.

"You're early; what's going on?"

"Yuh think we wouldn't celebrate the good news?"

Her search for a class had taken her to a nearby college to register for a food technology program she knew would come in handy no matter what was ahead. The process had been nerve-wracking, but the student visa had come through a few days before. She would start her course in January and look for part-time work on campus as long as she kept to the number of hours allowed. Knowing she was no longer in danger of becoming illegal and that this was the first opportunity to take a constructive step toward a real future for them, Zarah was ecstatic. Damien wanting to celebrate brought even more pleasure.

"Put on nice clothes; we going somewhere special. But hold on ... I bring something for yuh."

"Like what?"

"Turn around and shut yuh eye tight." Zarah could feel his breath against her neck. His body was up against hers, and his excitement and desire were palpable. But the weed and liquor on his breath turned her stomach. His hands were around her neck now. "Awright, turn around and look in the mirror. Quick, Babes," he said, fingering his crotch. "Your boy down here in a hurry." The exquisite gold chain with her birthstone pendant worsened the nausea.

"Where you ... we can't afford—"

"Only dat yuh can say?"

"No, I mean ... thanks. I love it, and of course I'm happy you want to give me a nice present, but you have to take it back. We don't have money to spend on this."

"Yuh see it? Yuh see how yuh can mash up a man vibe? All day long yuh complain, and now mi try do something good—"

"We need to keep our money for what is important." How could she tell him she had a pretty good idea how he came by that expensive necklace? That she had just figured out the meaning of the urgent whispers between himself and Ghost a week before, about the "cool opportunity" they had to go after?

"Shut yuh mout' and gimme back the effing chain!" His slap was like a clap of thunder, and she folded against the bed.

How could he believe I would wear this when it's obvious how he got it? Her eyes had remained closed to the truth for too long, and now, shame stabbed at the back of them.

Damien wandered into the chilly night and a taste of freedom from the pressure that had invaded him ever since Zarah's arrival. He sensed that as expected all along, she would leave him, sooner than later. Shortly after meeting her at Devon House, his mind had told him he would never truly have her for himself; she would always be on loan from a world where he would never belong, and it would constantly call her back. He had no pass of his own to take him across that threshold, and even if he had one, he would forever be a trespasser. But neither did he plan to stay in that filthy world from which he came.

Even as a little boy, he railed against the confines of poverty all around the ramshackle tenement yard he and his mother Audrey shared with twenty tenants in one of the worst areas in East Kingston. Early on, his fear of beatings at the hands of his on-again-off-again father tempered his attraction to the wildness surrounding him. To keep him away from trouble, his mother Audrey pestered God and her boy in equal measure. Only her presence stayed his impulse to explore the gullies and the derelict buildings where little boys found shelter after robbing and fleeing. They relished sharing the hideout where powerful gang members raped young girls at dusk, and seasoned criminals executed deals and killings at any hour; there in its shadows, they learned from the masters.

Damien's primary school teacher said he was a bright boy, and for a few dollars a week, she would give him extra lessons to help him get into high school. His mother stopped praying and pestering; instead, she walked up and down past the big pretty houses, knocking at high wrought-iron gates until she found three women who needed a day's worker to wash, iron, and clean while they went out to work at more important jobs. She saved what she could, and after Damien passed his exam and started high school, she gathered up every penny she had and paid for her passport and visa to visit America.

Like her friend, a seasoned hustler who had been encouraging her to try her lifestyle, Audrey planned to bring back a barrel of cheapness and sell it all to improve her situation. Life would be better when she returned, Audrey had promised, convincing the boy her trip would help him. "Yuh will have good sneakers and clothes, and if mi sell all what mi bring back, prob'ly yuh can get a Nintendo." On a scorching summer day in Brooklyn, she woke to the stack of crisp dollar bills in the hand of the American man who turned up before 7 o'clock to collect the marijuana Marlene had sent. *If mi can mek money like this, is better mi stay up here and work through her to mek a better life for mi and Damien.* She lost herself in the shadows of New York's hustle.

Back in Jamaica, Damien's grand-aunt saw less and less of him. His face receded from his mother's nightmares, and with only occasional contact, there was no way of knowing about the angry scowl etched on it as the years passed. Nor did their scattered phone conversations betray the voice of his premature manhood and the seething resentment of a boy abandoned by his father as well. He knew he stood on a precipice overlooking a dismal future, and he begged his mother to come home. But Audrey had lost herself in a network of hustlers who dared not show up at any U.S. airport. It was easier and easier to explain how scarce money was, why his visa and passport would have to wait, and why she could not keep sending remittances and barrels back home.

With no more credit on the cell phone his father had given him for emergencies only, the boy could contact no one for lunch money and bus fare. He refused to answer when his teacher asked why his parents had not attended previous conferences mentioned in their letters. Then, the principal told him "for the last time," his attendance and his grades were getting worse, and if his mother or father failed to show up for the next appointment, the school would send him home for good. What was he supposed to do about parents who did not care?

As he stepped through the broken-down gate to the room he occupied alone, the scrawny black neighborhood cat slithered up against his pants, mewing and sniffing at the plastic bag of food items stuffed into his shirt at various little shops on his way home from school. He placed the bag at the root of the lime tree and grabbed the cat. His grip tightened around the animal's throat, and he never stopped squeezing until its yellow eyes bulged, and its body stretched out in his shaking hands. Into the gully the cat sailed as Damien turned around, only to walk into the scowl of Lurch, the gang leader of the Ironman Posse, whose sick grandmother doted on the animal.

He punched the stunned Damien all over his face until he landed on the ground, the chilling metal of the 9 mm Glock above his left ear.

"Do a thing like dat again, and yuh will know how it feel when a bullet go right through yuh head." The prospect of regular confrontations loomed before Damien, and he set about cozying up to this new enemy he knew he could never stand up to. Forgiven for the black cat transgression, he hung around the areas Lurch frequented, making use of every opportunity to show how useful he could be to the gang. Though disgusted at first, Lurch had seen potential in the boy's clinical disposal of the nuisance cat, and he was soon accepting his help with getting key information about rival gangs and opportunities for increasing his reach in the area. Rewards followed, including brand-name sneakers, along with the bike and the Walkman Damien had talked about non-stop, after he sauntered up to Zarah when they met the first day at Devon House.

To the extent he was capable, he had loved her from the very beginning. Her world had drawn him in—actual houses in Duhaney Park, her bedroom with its fresh sheets, the clean tiles between her furniture, restaurants in uptown plazas, and the cinema in the posh Liguanea shopping center. Unlike the girls he was used to lying with, Zarah bathed twice a day with

Castile soap and rubbed her skin with perfumed lotions that made him think of fresh flowers he only glimpsed in uptown shops. His mind conjured up a vision of a changed life with her at his side, and he sheltered her from the crude reality of where he came from and who he was.

For more years than he ever thought possible, he put all he had into fitting into Zarah's life. Despite her parents' fierce opposition, he sometimes convinced himself it would work out in the end. But when Lurch was injured in a drive-by shooting, and things threatened to get too dangerous for Damien, he convinced his mother it was urgent for her to send him money for passport, visa, and ticket, so he could join the New York contingent of Jamaican hustlers.

His second chance had come when Zarah gave in and agreed to join him. Far from Duhaney Park and her family, he was free of the pull between her world and his, but her complaints about how they lived were driving him crazy. It reminded him every day she might finally opt for where she belonged. Being trapped in a situation that made him responsible for someone else was overwhelming. Zarah had never been whiny and dependent, and the more he saw this unknown side of her, the more his impatience turned into a blinding rage, planting his hand across her face. Now he had done it again, what chance was there of her staying?

CHAPTER 39
A MOVE TO MONA HEIGHTS

Kingston, 1990s

Waking in a cold sweat, Esther rushed to Zarah's room to see why she had cried out, but once again the emptiness swallowed her. For the fourth time in a week the same cry had dragged her to her daughter's abandoned bed. The pillows still held onto the lemony smell of her shampoo and conditioner, her light body lotion, and her mild perfume. Esther huddled on the bed as a thousand "what ifs," "should haves," and unanswerable questions assailed her. The images of how it had all started plagued her– the blandness of her life with Bradley, Patrick's hotel bed, the hurricane, her lost baby, the empty corner in the living room after Bradley moved out ... the space that had never stopped growing between her one child and herself.

Nights like this one made her feel it was urgent to leave the house at Duhaney Park. She had to move out to move on. Half of her agonized about leaving the house Zarah would head for if the day of her return should ever come. When she broached the subject with Bradley, he encouraged her to do what was right for herself and not for Zarah.

"She move on, Esther. We have to do the same."

"But she won't know where to find us; you moved from the one other place she knew," Esther argued.

"She know where we work, and she know where Naomi is."

"But if I move, hopefully Mama will go with me; she's getting older, and I'm not comfortable with her by herself at Ulster Road."

"If she want to find us, she will do it." His voice said he had no hope of such a time.

For weeks, Esther practiced writing her new address, 117 Gardenia Avenue, Mona. The house was old and unimpressive, but the refurbishing and extension kindled a new fire in her. She remodeled the entire kitchen, added two bedrooms and bathrooms, including a self-contained area where Naomi could be on her own. French windows replaced all the aluminum louvers to give her wide spaces with fresh air streaming through.

Preparing for the move was exhilarating, but disposing of Zarah's possessions would make her feel she was clearing her daughter out of her life.

"Carry what yuh can manage, Miss Esther; nobody know what the future can bring." The comforting voice of Miss Lucretia had seen Esther through the darkest of moments with Zarah, and it helped her prepare for the move. But the distance to Mona would be too far for Miss Lucretia to travel, and her health had been deteriorating. The long-time relationship that had helped Esther through years of challenges would be gone soon, along with so much more.

The movers packed box after box marked "Zarah" and stacked them in the walk-in closet in the modern room Esther reserved for her. Friends warned against too much hope, reinforcing her own doubts Zarah would ever live in the same house with her again. But she turned them away and pressed on.

Naomi moved in, relieved to be away from the increasing dangers of crime in the Ulster Road area. But there was trepidation for both, because they had not lived together for many years, and their relationship had suffered during the strife over Zarah. Though her disappearance had brought them closer, Esther was still unpredictable; she and Naomi did not see eye to eye on many issues. *I have to be here but thank God we won't be in each other's way.*

Naomi threw herself into creating a garden from the tangle in the backyard, and Esther left her to do whatever she wanted with it. On her hands and knees, she planted an assortment of fruit trees, vegetables, and flowers, transforming the space into a haven where she fashioned her own renewal, giving Esther one more small pleasure. It was a clean start, but everyone worried about the days when traces of the past would invade.

CHAPTER 40
A CHILLING NEW YEAR'S EVE

New York 1999

Swaddled in layers of clothing and their one threadbare blanket, Zarah curled up alone, sipping hot chocolate. She watched without seeing, as the major channels carried images "Live from Rockefeller Center, the New Year's Eve spectacular" featuring thousands of people hugging one another, singing and swaying to "One Love, one heart; let's get together and feel all right." But not even the words of Bob Marley could rouse her spirits from the deepening hole of regret. Underneath the cheap scratchy blanket with the pillow over her head, she tried in vain to shut out every thought about the mess she had made of her life. A loud insistent knock sent her to the door. Looking through the peephole, she released the chain.

"What you doing here, Ghost? Where Damien is?"

"Keep quiet and open the door. Yuh expect mi to talk while mi ass freezing out here?"

"Just tell me where—"

"Shut up and open the door. Serious business going on, and this not the time for foolishness." Flecks of snow flew from his jacket and sneakers as he barged in past her.

"What serious matters? And why are you here when it's coming up to midnight?"

"Oh really? 'It's coming up to midnight,' Miss Right and Proper Jamaican girl?" he said, imitating and taunting Zarah because her speech had always been a stinging reminder of how he might have sounded if he had not dropped out of high school at home. "Yuh don't think mi know the time? Yuh believe this is how mi want to spend a big holiday night? If it wasn't for yuh blasted mad man, mi would be somewhere else. How much money yuh have?"

"Not much. Damien got into trouble?"

"Yuh have to ask? Blasted idiot always getting in trouble with him loud mout' and bad man style; now we have to pay off people. Him say yuh must send all the money yuh have."

"What kind of trouble?" she asked, handing him the money she had after concealing one last $100 bill. Ghost flicked through the ragged bills.

"What difference it make what it is; trouble is trouble. You sure is only this money you have?"

"Yes, I'm sure; just give me a few minutes; I'm coming with you."

"Coming? Girl, yuh outta yuh mind?"

"But if Damien is in trouble—"

"Yuh argue too much. Yuh know the trouble yuh can get into if yuh know too much? Him will call when him get the chance. Lock the door behind me, and don't answer unless yuh hear three quick knock, and then two more." Her head was swimming. "And girl, yuh better get tough or go back to Jamaica. As long as yuh stay here, this will be yuh life, not some bedtime story 'bout some proper little island girl making it in the Big Apple!" He looked around the apartment and then stared at her. "What a girl like yuh doing here, though?" He was gone.

With still no word from Damien, Zarah had no clue what to do or where to turn for help. All her calls to his cell phone went to voice mail, and he returned none. The guys who had always passed through the apartment had not given her their phone numbers, and none showed up. Darkness brought her home from the drugstore, shivering from fear and cold. Once inside, she locked herself in and kept the television volume low.

Packing up her clothes to go down to the washing area, she jumped up at the sudden sound; her heart galloped as her cell phone pierced the Sunday morning quiet.

"Hello?"

"Who is this? Who do you want to speak to?"

"Is Audrey–Damien mother. Is yuh name Zarah?"

"Yes, Miss Audrey. I'm glad you called; do you know where Damien is? When last you talked to him?"

"Damien say yuh talk nice, and is true."

"Thank you, Miss Audrey," Zarah said, impatient with the woman's useless comment. "But have you spoken to Damien?"

"No, I don't talk to him, but the police come over here looking for him. Damien in big trouble. I just get yuh number and the story from him cousin."

"He sent Ghost for money from New Year's Eve night, and since that, I haven't heard from them."

"If yuh know what good for yuh, go back to Jamaica, or if yuh have family up here, go to them. Police soon come there and ask for him, and yuh might put yuhself in trouble. Dem might send Damien home, an' dangerous people might be looking for him too." Zarah could hear the woman's breath as each waited for the other to speak.

"Me only call to warn yuh. Leave and go somewhere before trouble tek yuh over there. Mi not in no position to help yuh or Damien, for mi not even legal miself."

"Miss Audrey, Damien begged me to come over here and make our relationship work, and now I don't even know where he is."

"Find yuhself home to yuh family." *Click*. The phone slipped to the ground. *Go home? With what? What a fool I was to listen to all his big talk and cash in my return ticket!*

It was another week of loneliness and worry before the three sharp knocks startled her. She waited, counting; and just as Ghost had said, after about a minute, two sharp knocks followed.

"What are you doing here again?"

"Open up!" Ghost shouted. Letting him in was the last thing she wanted to do, but a commotion would make somebody call the police and she could not risk it. *At least he might have news of Damien*. A beer was in his hand and hard liquor on his breath.

"Yuh have food?" Ghost asked, his speech slurred.

"No, and how you said you would come back to tell me what's going on with Damien? Where is the money I gave you to carry to him? You better give me back."

"Or else what? Girl, yuh think dem few dollars yuh give mi is money? That is just a pittance." He yanked the fridge door open. "Yuh don't have food? Yuh stop eat because lover boy gone?"

He had never sounded so cold and menacing. She kept the conversation with Damien's mother to herself. His demeanor made her wince at his nearness, and the lie shot through her lips.

"I don't have any food," she said, "but my friend Mavis is bringing some soon; she's just about five minutes up the road. You can take home some if you like. Please just tell me what's happening with Damien. Why won't he call me back, or even send a text message?"

"Call or text wid what, this?" His eyes were red and unfocused as he dangled Damien's phone before her, "Where dat boy is right now, phone don't have no use to him."

Thoughts of Damien without his phone brought more panic. "Give it to me; I'm begging you, and tell me where he is, please."

"Where him blasted big mout' should send him ass long time." He was back on his feet, making his way toward her.

"Where?"

"Awright, since yuh want to know ... is County Jail dem have him. And yuh want to know more? Him soon be on a plane straight back to J.A. wid some more deportee! Serve him right; ears too hard!"

The last shred of hope dissolved. Most of her money had gone to the college application, the fee to change her visa, and the tuition for the upcoming course. She had less than $100 to her name.

"And good riddance," Ghost said. "Dat asshole just won't hear what people with experience tell him. Tell mi the truth—no friend not coming with food, right?"

Like a lizard changing color, his features altered before her eyes; his voice became soft and sleazy, and she stepped away.

"Guess what? Yuh don't have to fret over food, or friend, or Damien; mi always promise to help yuh, remember? Do what mi tell yuh, and yuh won't have to worry no more." He was right up against her now, backing her into the kitchen sink.

"What are you doing? Just get away from me, or—"

"Or what? Scream if yuh bad. And mek somebody call the cops in here, for them well want a connection to Damien and anybody who know him."

He grabbed Zarah, her feet kicking against him, her arms flailing across his back, as they stumbled toward the bed. "Is time mi get back something for all the problem yuh man cause me."

"No; he's your friend. Don't do this, please; I'm begging you ... no, Ghost, please—"

His hands covered her mouth. He smothered her face with the blanket, ripped away her skirt, grabbed at her underwear, and tore his belt off as he fell on her, beads of sweat gathering across his forehead, his eyes bursting with the hunger of a wild animal. The darkness and the pain engulfed her.

CHAPTER 41
BY THE LIGHT OF DAY

A sliver of a sunbeam landed across Zarah's face. Her eyes followed it to a gap in the blinds. Faint sounds floated all over the apartment: Someone called her name; someone else called Damien's name; Ghost shouted her name, battering the door with his fists, and from under her pillow her faint whimpering persisted. Had the voices been from the nightmares that had wrested her from every moment of fitful sleep?

A slight movement on the floor near to the door drew her attention, and she dragged herself over to see what was there. It was a note from Mavis.

Zarah, you need to call me; I waited for you Tuesday for our lunchtime snack, and you didn't show up. You have me worried; please call. She crumpled the paper into a tight ball and threw it in the bin.

The next day Mavis was in the corridor harassing the superintendent. "I'm telling you she might be sick, or in some kind of trouble; she's not answering her phone, or the door, and after New Year's Eve, she stayed away from work."

"Yow; What me must do about it, lady? Break down da doh? She live with a Jamaican boy, so if anything gone wrong, he must look after it, and don't put me in no problem!"

"But none of his friends around here have seen him," Mavis said, her patience on the wane.

"Well prob'ly they gone away!"

"No, she should be at work; this is not right."

"Okay, come, lady, come."

Zarah panicked as she made out the sound of the key in the door. She tried to rush into the bathroom, but Mavis was already inside, trying to get rid of the janitor.

"See? I told you something wasn't right; anyway, I will take it from here. Thank you." Mavis handed him a few dollars and shut the door.

"Zarah, what happened?"

"Thanks for checking; sorry I didn't get in touch, but please just leave; I have to be by myself."

"Your boyfriend and you had a fight? He hurt you?"

"No ... but please go ... I'm okay." She pulled back into the corner of the bed, pressing herself into the wall.

"Look at you ... how I can believe you're okay? When last you ate? And look at the place!" Mavis said, glancing at the disarray.

"Come, get up and tell me. Your manager said you abandoned the job."

"I guess I did. But it doesn't matter. I just want to stay right here." It was a mere whisper from a throat still raw and sore from groaning and crying. Mavis was too alarmed to give up. Her panic emboldened her. As if in one move, she hauled her stunned friend from the bed, shoved her in the shower and washed her from head to toe, wrapped her in a warm blanket, and plopped her in a chair. As if possessed, she grabbed sheets and used tissues off the bed, rolled them into one heap, and put everything in its place. The smell of coffee soon filled the air, and she was getting set to force-feed Zarah with thick oat bran cereal. It was an hour before she finally got it all done, and Zarah still sat in her trance.

"You can tell me what's going on, or not ... you decide. But you better believe I'm not going anywhere and leaving you like this."

Through sheer inability to stand up to Mavis, Zarah started, and once it began, the story had no pause for breath.

"We have to go to the police now."

"No, no police."

"Why the hell not? The man raped you!"

"You don't understand. The situation is complicated–Damien, his friends, the police. I don't even know the details myself, but just take my word: Staying away from the police is a must. But that piece of garbage who did this knows too much about Damien and me. Damien is always acting like a bad boy and getting into scrapes with police even though he is not even legal. His mother and Ghost must know what they were saying about the deportation. I don't even know how that works or how long it takes."

"That stuff is foreign to us; but you are the important thing now. What you plan to do for yourself? Staying in this apartment is a bad idea; what if that devil come back? What if police come snooping around? And what about money?"

"Is just too much; that's why I wanted to lock myself in here until I can think straight." One look from Mavis reminded her that was not an option. "We pay for this month, and they have one month's security. But you're right, I can't be around here if the police might come looking—"

"Listen, a girl like you should never be in this situation, but we are here, and we have to deal with it." Mavis had put on her Jamaican mother's voice—the voice of control and firmness—the one that suffered no argument. "Both of us know you have every reason not to stay here. Plus, you need to see a doctor to make sure that nasty dog didn't give you any disease."

"I didn't even think about that ... You mean God could really make me face that too ... after everything?"

"Sit down and gather yuhself; only one step we can take right now; come, say it with me: 'The Lord is my Shepherd ...'" It was the first time in years Zarah had uttered a prayer, but their voices blended, and the words flowed without hesitation.

"Remember, God help those who help themself, Zarah. If Ghost can do this one time, him can do it again. Who can tell if him might do worse? You can't take chances with people like him. Find somebody connected to your family."

"No way! Nobody from home can know about this. They—"

"They what?" Mavis got the entire story then, without so much as a comma.

"Almighty God, girl, what a hell you went through for this boy! You think him could care about you and make you give up so much? Well, you might be rid of him now, but there's still the other one; we only have one solution. Go home."

"I don't have money to buy a ticket, and I could never go home like this ... not without getting at least one positive outcome from this disaster. That's why I needed to get the student visa and do the course we talked about. Now, I don't even think I'm up to taking any course, and it's starting next week."

"You don't have a choice; to keep a student visa and get work, you need to maintain your attendance."

Another layer of hopelessness fell over Zarah's face. "Right ... I'm trapped. Plus who could blame my family if they moved on without me?"

"I'm a mother; I can tell you this: No parent ever move on from losing a child. No matter what you did, they will take you back, especially after knowing all you went through."

Going home was not possible–not then. Most of her savings from home were gone, and she had no job. She lacked the will or the energy to move an inch. Only the thought of Ghost's face through the peephole made her gather her belongings and go with Mavis.

The manager at the drugstore said Zarah was a good worker, but he could not let go the girl who had filled in when she disappeared. "And I can't afford to take a chance on somebody who might go missing again." *No hope of a reference from him.*

Zarah shared the bad news with Mavis, assuring her she would not stop trying until she found a job, and she would pay her back every dollar. "I have to start the course in a week, and I can get part-time stints on campus as long as I'm in school."

CHAPTER 42
"IF I CAN HELP SOMEBODY"

The gray chill of February and early March soon lifted, and new baby leaves brought a semblance of color to the dismal bone-dry winter trees. Zarah no longer had to force herself to go out. Though her mind was not on food technology, the diploma would be part of her preparation to go home, and studying distracted her from her worries. Although a job had not yet become available on campus, there were prospects. Still, nothing Mavis tried could nudge her. Neither words, nor activity, nor stillness could bring her solace: not the encouragement of a friend who tried every available remedy, not the food she coaxed down Zarah's throat, not her singing of psalms and choruses, or the prayers she prayed, urging Zarah to join her.

Mavis gave up on the idea of getting help from the police, but she drew on her experience at shelters and nursing homes, laying on gory details about rape victims infected with dangerous sexually transmitted diseases. Zarah dragged herself to the clinic on the campus. The doctor confirmed there was no sign of infection, but as her sore listless patient sat up on the examination table and tried to look away, the woman stepped to the same side, and their eyes locked.

"Apart from those heavy periods, is there any other problem you want to tell me about, Miss Thomas?"

"No, I'm just run down. Do you recommend vitamins or some kind of tonic?"

"I noticed you were tender and tense during the examination; are you okay otherwise?"

"Apart from what I told you, I'm fine." She hauled her skirt on as the tears brimmed.

"Well, be careful; sometimes too much rough intercourse can cause problems." Zarah jumped from the examination table.

"Do you think that's prying a little?" The woman put her hand on her shoulder and spoke with an urgency that needed no volume.

"Please, I'm just trying to help; if there's more going on, and if anyone harmed you—"

"Are you finished? I have to go." By now the tears were about to fall, and her hand was already on the doorknob.

"Okay, well, just give me a minute while I write you a prescription, and I want you to come back and see me in a month." *Yeah, right.*

Zarah figured the woman was stalling to make her change her mind, but she knew how close her breaking-point was, so she clutched the doorknob, ready to run.

***

Mavis was relieved to hear the results of the doctor's visit, but she worried still about her friend's mental state.

"Well, thank God that brute didn't leave any disease behind, but is a pity you didn't feel comfortable enough to tell her what happened."

"She can't help me with that, so what's the point of telling her? Next thing she will add my name to some kind of social service report, and they come prying into my business. I know what America is like. I just have to get a job because once I get busier with this coursework, searching may get harder."

"You may be right; but it's not good to stay alone in here all day; until you get work, you can volunteer at my place. People say volunteering can lead to a job, and Miss Beck is always glad to have people help us because we can't spend enough time with the older residents." Mavis had already checked out the situation and discovered that her employer collaborated with Zarah's new school, and students from there worked with her before. Miss Beck could get permission to employ Zarah for a set number of hours.

"So, what you think?" Mavis asked, "You think is worth a try?"

"Of course, if it can lead to work, I'll try."

"It could be for the best. When you see how all those people suffer, you might realize even though your situation is awful, you have a long way to go before you reach rock bottom." Her words made little impression on Zarah, but work was essential, and she would try whatever opportunity came. Miss Beck was happy to have a volunteer as qualified as Zarah and they hit it off right away. Keeping busy made a tremendous difference and soon the words from Mavis made sense. Helping old people was not something she had ever contemplated, but then, nothing about life in New York had been.

They were clearing up one evening, when Mavis interrupted Zarah's stories about her day at the center.

"You dropped that?" Mavis asked, reaching for something on the floor. It was the prescription and the business card Zarah had dumped in her bag after leaving the doctor's office. Mavis read from the card, *Crisis Center for Victims of Abuse and Rape;* the doctor gave you this?"

"She gave me a prescription, and I didn't even look at it, so I didn't see the card. It must have dropped out when I was looking for the key."

"Smart lady ... and at least she cared; you should try it; you can't go on like this."

"I know; I'm trying my best; please give me some more time. I promise I will pay you back every cent."

"That's not what I mean; a job will come, and I know you will pay me back. You need to get better, and I can't help with that. The people at these places know what they're doing, and this one is free."

Zarah doubted there was anyone who could ever help her. The card remained in the little book of prayers Mavis had left on the bedside table.

At the nursing home, Miss Beck had been observing how the new volunteer operated. It was obvious there was much more to Zarah than most people her age. It puzzled Miss Beck that someone so young and so obviously well brought up and educated had so much time to volunteer in a place like hers. Why was getting more hours so important to her? Rules prevented the woman from asking personal questions, and Zarah had passed the required background checks, so she would keep a close eye on the young woman. By the time the part-time job in administration came up, Miss Beck was even more impressed with her, and she had no hesitation in making the arrangements for the college to approve the hours Zarah could work there while studying.

The prospect of a little relief was as real to Zarah as it had been on the night she sat on her suitcase at JFK airport waiting for Damien. At last, she could pay Mavis a small amount, buy a few more necessities, and start saving toward going home.

"Miss Beck, I'm just wondering about this new patient, Greg; how come he's here, and he's—"

"Not old?"

The edge in her manager's voice did not escape Zarah, so right away, she added, "Sorry; I didn't mean that the way it might sound."

"It's okay; his situation just makes me angry. This is not the right place for him, and the social workers know that." The man was in his early fifties and Miss Beck explained that although his stroke had been serious, with the right therapy, he could do much better.

"Why can't he get what he needs here?"

"We don't have the facilities or staff. He needs more strenuous and varied therapy, but also constant mental stimulation beyond what we do."

"Why did they bring him here?" Greg's family had insisted. They could not manage him at home, and with limited insurance support, the care he needed was too expensive. Above all, they wanted a facility close to home.

"So, can we help him?"

"I'm glad you asked; you aren't trained to work with patients in any way involving treatment, and you're supposed to be in administration only, but you still have volunteer hours, and with those, you could take on a special assignment. We could treat it like a project if you're willing to try something different."

Zarah tried to conceal her excitement. "Thanks a lot, Miss Beck; I'm willing to work at whatever you need me to do; but what would I be doing?"

"For a while, spend all your hours with Greg. We all know he was ... is an intelligent well-trained man, and he had worked in scientific research at a local college. We can get material from the library for you to read to him and talk to him about activities he engaged in; encouraging him to talk will be good."

"You think I can help him?"

"It's an experiment, but from your paperwork, I know you are the only volunteer I have who can do what I'm talking about. He needs to use his brain to the greatest extent possible." Happy for the opening, Zarah shared more details about her studies at home.

"Well, there you go; you can do this. You can help him connect with who he was before all this took place."

Greg's eyes soon came alive, and even his limbs were more responsive; it gave Zarah ideas about other useful approaches, and Miss Beck gave her permission to do more. It was not everything she needed, but it was a start, and it was even more important that the project was helping her. *I'm on a college campus, so my brain works again; I have a job and something extra to do.* At last, a reminder of an almost forgotten time when she had a life worth living.

CHAPTER 43
"WHAT IF I DON'T GET ANOTHER CHANCE?"

Mavis relished the changes she saw in her friend. Periods of despair and depression haunted her, but many more days of lightness and hope broke into the darkness in which Zarah had been living. A few such days had passed, when Mavis bounced in from work, full of excitement.

"Girl, everybody at work was talking today about how you helping Greg."

"I feel so bad for him; I'm just glad I can make a little difference."

"Shame on you; you're making a big difference. I feel so proud of you, I brought us a treat!" she said, as she set the ice cream and Jamaican potato pudding on the counter.

"Yes, Miss Excitement! Joking aside, Mavis, I can never say thanks enough, but you're the best cheerleader, and a genuine friend—"

"I have daughters, Zarah and I hope if one got into trouble, somebody would help her. This is the only way I can help," Mavis said, fiddling with yet another brown bag.

"And what you have there?"

"How we can celebrate without wine?"

The clinking of the bottle against the glasses followed, and the women savored the sliver of happiness.

"Good point, so let's drink to you, Mavis; I can't imagine what these months would have been like without you. I can never thank you enough."

"All the thanks I need is seeing you on your way out of the dark time and knowing you feel better about what you are doing."

Zarah did feel better about her classes and her interactions with Greg, and the days meant a little more. But as soon as Mavis was out of sight in the late hours, the same impenetrable gloom overtook her. There was no word from Damien's mother, and there was only one conclusion—the man who had encouraged her to join him was back in Jamaica and perhaps he had not given her a second thought. On her brief visit to the dingy apartment with the ugly green walls, the superintendent said he had not seen him or any of his friends. He handed her the final security refund and the documents concerning the apartment. After transferring the money to Mavis's account, she hurled everything else into the back of Mavis's cupboard, trying to block out her memories of the most desolate time in her life.

Between two sips of wine, Mavis capitalized on the thoughtful look she saw on her friend's face. "But what about you, Zarah? What's happening inside?"

Sensing where the conversation was heading, Zarah busied herself clearing away the clutter and preparing for the washing up. "What are you talking about?"

"You can't hide the pain and sadness in your eyes. Maybe you believe you might be over what happened, or if you don't think about it—"

"I never said I was over it. But what's the use of talking? I can't change what happened. I'm just trying to get to a stage where I feel like some pieces of my life might come together again."

With clashing plates and cutlery banging into pots and pans, Zarah created as much distraction as possible.

Intent on making the best use of the small window she glimpsed, Mavis shouted over the racket, "Well, they are coming together, but you might not feel genuine relief until you get some help. And even if you get to go home, both of us know you won't be looking for help there. Remember the center the doctor gave you the card for? Well, I know you might get mad with me for this, but I checked it out."

The noise ceased, and Mavis could almost touch the eruption ahead.

"Wait ... before you answer, let me explain: You can go in a group session with other people who had the same experience; or you can see somebody by yourself. I can go with you the first time." The water was still running, and the sink was filling up, giving Zarah the time to collect her thoughts. Her annoyance with herself surged, encompassing her rage at Damien. *None of this and no support group was supposed to be part of my life.*

"Sorry. You give me some wonderful advice, and I could never ask for more support from you. But this is one time your suggestion is too much. My parents didn't bring me up telling my private business to strangers."

"Girl, you think is you alone? I can still hear my grandmother when we were growing up: 'Always keep yuh business to yuhself and never wash yuh dirty clothes where other people can see.'"

They both knew Zarah would never seek help unless she was truly ready, so once again, they abandoned the discussion and focused on the good things.

A week later, Zarah bounced into work for her extra hours with Greg.

"Good afternoon, Miss Beck."

"Hi, Zarah, give me a minute in here." Miss Beck hustled her favorite volunteer into the conference room, and Zarah knew the news was bad.

"What happened? Is it Greg?"

"The nurse found him this morning; he was unresponsive; another stroke. They took him to the hospital."

"Can I go over to see him? I have to talk to him."

"Sorry, my dear, only family; they don't think he'll make it. You can go home."

The evening after they buried Greg, Mavis found Zarah pressed into the corner of the bed almost as distressed as she was on the dark day at Damien's old apartment. Nurse and mother took charge again, but it was once too often. Loss of the only promising experience since the confounding months with Damien brought Zarah to her knees again. Her tears flowed at the loss of Greg; but they were for much more–the terrible turn her life had taken, the futility of her efforts to help him, the dark shadow falling so rudely across the little rainbow her time with him had brought. Those weeks had stirred a vision of who she might become again, and now, even that was gone.

Face to face with the loss of Greg, who was about the same age as her parents, Zarah panicked. *Suppose Mummy or Daddy get sick like Greg? And what about Grams? What if I don't get the chance to make up for all the awful pain I caused them? Is one thing to play with fire and burn myself, but how could I do this to the people who gave me all they had? I can't even believe all the awful lying and hiding I did to be with Damien although I knew it hurt them.* The sharp edges of regret cut through her long years of denial, and her heart found its voice.

"Mavis, what if I never get my old life back; suppose I can't get back my family and make it up to them?" Before Mavis could respond, a flood of emotions pushed their way through the walls Zarah had erected around them for too long.

"Thank you, Lord," Mavis said, as the room teemed with Zarah's sorrow, shame, and regret, sprinkled with her friend's efforts at consolation. "Girl, this opening up is new to me, but what you doing right now can only bring good, so don't mind me; if more of this will help you, I will be right here, so carry on." Zarah did just that, and the stories poured out–about growing up in Duhaney Park with the best parents, Hurricane Gilbert and the start of all the trouble, the firm but caring Miss Lucretia, Naomi's stories, dancing recitals, campus, and yes, the disaster named Damien.

"Probably everything happened to remind you what kind of family you walked away from for this damn worthless boy; excuse me for saying so, but—"

"That was Mummy's favorite description of him, and you are both right. I can't explain what made me think he was anything else."

"Girl, you believe you was in love, that's all. My grandfather tell us all the time–love can turn the wisest man into a damn fool. God alone know how far you would reach by now if you didn't leave Jamaica! But whatever happen is for a reason, and you coming to your senses now, so this may be the turning point."

"You think somebody can recover from all this though? And what about them? How can I ask them to give me another chance? I doubt if I can ever make myself into somebody they would want to have around them again."

"You can do it; with all you going through, I know you not giving up. You doing good in the course, you have a job, and you helping us at work. This is the beginning, and it will take time."

"Mavis, I can't count the times I let them down; how many lies I made up. I'm so ashamed."

"Shame is hard, but it serve a purpose; you will never behave like that again. All of us go through times when we tell lies and don't listen to what our parents tell us. Is just the way life work. My grandfather always say if God made a mistake, it was giving us bodies that grow faster than our brains."

Zarah lay on the floor of her friend's third room, wrapped in a calmness and an icy clarity she had not felt for as long as she could remember.

When she got up, she bore the full weight of her errors, the gravity of her condition, and the recognition that she could not fix it alone. To bend her mind toward forgiveness of herself, reconciliation with her family, and a chance at wholeness, she had to get help. Acceptance of this truth brought comfort–or so she felt in the moment; it was a heavy burden too–as she expected, but it would make her stronger–or so she hoped.

CHAPTER 44
A LITTLE COUNTRY ACCENT

The room was bare and its furnishings basic. Fifteen metal chairs formed a circle around the middle. About seven people remained seated, all grappling with whatever had traveled with them. Men and women huddled in pairs and other small clusters, a few clutching mugs or paper cups.

"Excuse me, it's Zarah, right?" The voice was strange but familiar in ways she could not define. "Good evening again; please don't be annoyed at me for saying this: You always seem to listen keenly to the discussions, but I haven't heard you speak since your few words of introduction." Zarah put the coffee down and looked up into the deep eyes of a tall chocolate-colored man who seemed a few years older than most of the people in the room. *How this stranger mean to come up and confront me about not talking?*

"I believe somebody said we could take part in any way we can." The edge in her voice was unmistakable. "So, I'm doing what I can, and besides, I haven't heard you say much either."

"Of course, you're right. I just wondered. And about me not saying much, remember I'm a kind of assistant to the facilitator, so part of my job is to observe how the group is working." Recalling some sort of introduction he gave at the first meeting, Zarah softened a little. Still, she had attended only three times, so what did he expect? She had sat in every one without saying much, intent on making herself invisible, her arms tight across her chest, her foot tapping on the floor, hoping nobody would ask her any question. Every time the idea of sharing her thoughts presented itself, she struggled for breath, her hands became clammy, and the words she wanted to say vanished to wherever they were trying to emerge from. It seemed like a huge mistake to be there. The room was oppressive. To avoid eye contact with anyone, she glanced around at the faces. *Will they think I brought it on myself? That I was drunk, or a loose girl looking for trouble?*

"So, my job is to encourage you to share, Zarah."

"Sorry, what did you say your name—?"

"McIntosh, Donovan; you left me for a moment there, right?"

"Mr. McIntosh, sorry; to be honest, I did drift away; plenty on my mind."

"I get it; but please, not *Mister*. Don't make me sound like an old man."

"Okay, Donovan, no offense but I come from Jamaica, and we don't play with this stuff–what you people call it? This self-disclosure business. I'm just trying to see if I can learn how to do it."

"You don't have to tell me; I know all about keeping our business to ourselves," Donovan said with a laugh that made her loosen her grip on the cup.

"'Ourselves?' You are Jamaican?"

"Born and bred. St. Elizabeth ... but you want to know why I don't sound more like you, right?"

"I picked up a little trace, but I was not sure. Now I can hear the Jamaican clearly, though to tell you the truth, it's a little—"

"Like a country bumpkin?" Donovan asked.

"Yes, you could say that."

The tension eased a little as the coffee break ended, and they returned to their seats, feeling easier after the initial awkwardness. Zarah wondered what had brought a man like him to America to work in a place like this. *All the same, I hope he doesn't think because one more Jamaican is here, I will spill my life story before these people. Even if all of them went through what I went through, I don't want strangers in my business.*

When the session ended, the country accent was in her ear again.

"So, you have some time to spare? I'd like to help you get the most out of the group. Don't worry, you're not the only one; I do this with anyone who needs a nudge or two." A hint of steadiness in his demeanor, and a calmness in everything about him, made her think twice about walking away. His voice was like the Quincy Jones music they used at the dancing studio back home. *Definitely too serious and intense. This one will try to drag every thought and every feeling out of me.*

But there was work. "No, sorry, not tonight," she said, glancing at her watch. "Late shift for me this week."

"Oh, well; sorry. Could you come in a bit early on Thursday? We could chat a little before the group starts."

"I'll try. What time do you get here?"

"I work just across the street, so I can come over anytime. Just ask the receptionist to buzz me."

On Thursday, she arrived at the center an hour before the group session and spoke to the receptionist. In a few minutes, he came striding in.

"Hi, Zarah! Glad you made it," he said with a grin that made him seem younger than the last time they spoke.

"Sorry, I hope she didn't interrupt your class—"

"My class?"

"I saw the school across the street, and I figured—"

"What! You think I'm a teacher?" His laughter echoed through the room.

"What's so funny?"

"If you knew me better, you'd never think I could be a teacher. I work with the church next to the school. We help with activities over here. Come on, let's talk."

He walked over to the window and pulled out a chair for her. Zarah had forgotten what it was like to be with a gentleman. In fact, Damien had been around so long, there had been few opportunities to experience any other man. They spoke easily, exchanging harmless information about his work at the church and hers at the old people's home. Everything else, they kept to themselves. Her side-eye studied him from the crown of his head to–his eyes stopped her. In a communications course at university, the lecturer had spoken about the power of eye contact and as natural science students, most of her class had giggled at the woman's intensity about an idea they had never thought about much. But this was ridiculous. This man's eye contact felt like a laser beam into a person's soul.

I wonder why he doesn't say much about himself. I should be the cagey one. Having explained the fear of opening up in the group, Zarah tried her best to skirt the issue of her reason for being there, but Donovan's tone was so gentle and his manner so comforting, he soon got the bare bones of her story.

"Remember, every person here has experienced some kind of sexual assault; everybody hurts and each one struggles, one step at a time, to find a way forward. The process won't work for you unless you share. I know how hard it is for us from our part of the world to get into this business. People here are more used to it."

"You can say that again. It feels like there's a counselor, or counseling center, or support group on every corner. For me though, it's hard—"

"The fact you came here even so long after the assault or the rape—"

Zarah stepped away, but he reached out and gently helped her to the chair.

"No, please don't walk away. I know I stunned you by using the word, but you have to start by calling the name of whatever a despicable creep did to you. As long as you can't start there, it keeps you in denial, and trust me, denial is the biggest drawback when you are trying to recover."

Zarah felt he was cornering her with his stare and his directness, and the rattling inside her came out with more than a hint of anger. "Yes, Mr. Expert; but tell me something; how would you know? How could you even guess what it is like to be—"

"Come on, say the word."

"Raped." The word freed a rush of feelings she wanted to gulp back down. Donovan was quiet, allowing it to pass. "I guess like most people, you think only women get raped."

She had not thought about it, but as soon as he spoke and his face darkened, it was clear this man had his own story.

Donovan had just finished a course in group counseling, and he was monitoring the group as part of his practical training to prepare him to lead a group of young boys. Minute by minute, this man was becoming more engaging. But the others would soon file in, and he wanted to try a couple phrases she could practice saying to the group to help her share her own story. His determination to help her benefit from the experience was palpable, but he could not have guessed how challenging the process would be. Zarah had no plans to put her trust in anyone, not even a compassionate man from home.

Donovan was single-minded, though, and he would not sit aside and let Zarah lose out in the group. For the next few weeks, they met ahead of every session, and he urged her along the path to uttering the uncomfortable words of a rape victim–rape survivor, as he insisted. The weeks flew by, and soon he seemed like someone who had been around her for much longer. The group heard her story in bits and pieces, and she understood some of his ideas about how to get the real benefits through participation. Ounce by ounce, the weight she lived with was becoming lighter.

CHAPTER 45
EVERYBODY HURTS

No man or woman close to her age group was as sincere, as caring, or as profound as Donovan. But how many men had she known? As their communication extended beyond the group, he shocked her with the way he could get her to talk, deflecting every effort to shift the focus to him. Wariness was not all on her side though. By tacit agreement, they danced the dance of avoidance–dodging each other's efforts at probing into the unmentionable personal stuff. During a session of mutual dodging, Donovan was hovering on the fence between burying his story and sharing it, so she nudged him from his perch: "So what was it?" she asked without warning.

"What?" Donovan said, a nervous look across his face.

"Whatever happened to you." It was all he needed for him to retrace the moments of his own devastation. With few words of her own, Zarah gave him her full attention.

"I was eleven, and I'd learned to tease my sisters and their friends for being terrified of every kind of lizard. But when the awful croak stunned me from sleep, my eyes were riveted on the three croaking lizards slithering between the dark rafters at the retreat center in Mandeville. When the biggest one turned the corner and lumbered down the wall, I understood at last why every Jamaican–man, woman, and child, regardless of how many denials–hated their slithering ugliness.

"It was my first time at altar boys' retreat, and I was excited to be big enough to leave home for a weekend, so I had to conceal how the croakers scared me; plus, everybody else was fast asleep. I slid off the cot and tiptoed out to the back door. It was easy to release the bolt without a sound, freeing me to sit on the step and calm myself. To make me feel better, I tried to think of scrimmage at school and my mother's bread pudding with ice cream.

"Father said we should keep our minds on important spiritual ideas while on retreat, so I conjured images of church: bright shafts of sunlight falling on the altar through the stained-glass window, the thrill of serving as an altar boy, how it felt when I squared my shoulders to carry the scepter. My mother's proud eyes flashed before me, as she watched me hold up the massive book of readings for Father and ring the bell at communion time. 'Young man, what brought you out here so late?' The voice was indistinct, but it startled me for I'd heard neither the door nor the footsteps. I spun around and faced the bulky outline of the priest."

Zarah's hand was on his shoulder. "Did you get in trouble?"

"I said it was hot inside and I came to get air. The man could never know croakers terrified me; I was no girl. Thinking he would send me inside, I braced myself, but the priest sat beside me. Unaccustomed to anyone but family members being so close, I inched away and Father kept talking about all kinds of topics–family, school, what I wanted to be; what life was like to grow up in America, what he had done before the seminary.

"Father's interest in me felt good; Mama would be happy to hear of the priest paying attention to her son. We lived in a poor remote district; my mother had her children, her work, and the church; and we had school, netball or basketball; first communion or confirmation class, and Mass. Everyone looked up to the priests; this new one was all over the community doing church work, and everybody treated him like someone special. My mother made Sunday dinner for him all the time, especially macaroni and cheese, roast chicken, fry plantain, and baked bananas with coconut cream for dessert. I was always the one at the rectory door with the basket of goodies.

"Every altar boy believed priests were perfect–just one step down from Jesus Himself. Every word they said was like gospel. Sitting there listening and answering this one's questions made me forget about the croaking lizards."

Donovan drew close to the woman beside him, and her rapt attention encouraged him to go on. Zarah sensed the hardest part of his story was imminent, so her fingers found his.

"Between the words, a hand had slipped around my shoulder; another one was soon at my waist, then on my leg, inching their way to my thighs. At first, I was not sure what it meant, but everything inside told me none of it was right. I bolted into the darkness and kept running, certain Father would head for the house.

"I galloped away until I was out of breath and had to slow down, falling onto the dirt road under the moonlight. As I recovered my strength and shuffled my way back, Father stepped out from behind a tree near the house. I opened my mouth to scream, but the priest pressed his hand hard against it, pinning me to the tree with his other hand. His husky whispers told me all was well; but regardless of what the man said, I knew it could not be; I writhed in protest, beating my fists against Father's chest; but this was a big heavy man, and he was fastening my body against his.

"Something was much worse than croaking lizards! I vomited into black space. My cries had made no sound, but my throat ached. Time passed with me tossing and turning under the tree until sheer exhaustion hauled me into a restless sleep. At sunrise, his disgusting hulk cowered on the ground. His voice was insipid, a poor attempt at consolation. His words were supposed to convince me it was okay: 'I've been watching you, and I knew you were special,' he said. 'What happened will give us an important bond now; we will serve the church together. I'm depending on you to keep our special experience between us. Other people will never understand the meaning of what we shared. Not even your family can know.'"

The story silenced Zarah. It was not just the alarming story that had captivated her. It was how he told it, as though he knew her love for words; as if he had somehow come upon the miles of words along her walls at Duhaney Park.

Drained by the telling, Donovan had no more words. For the first time, his eye contact was nowhere to be found. What was there to say? How could she ask him what it felt like, or how he had recovered? Her own experience told her there were no answers. For an instant, she rested her hands on his arm and left him with the space he needed. She took her time, fetched two paper cups, and strode across the room to the water cooler.

Donovan sipped, his movements slow and deliberate. In time, their breathing approached normal.

"I can't explain how awful I feel knowing you suffered through that. What Ghost did to me was unbearable; but at least he was not a responsible man taking advantage of a little boy who trusted him."

"It's no point comparing stories. Rape is rape, and it's never less than a nasty violation." His voice was soft, but firm, and he gazed at the tips of his brown loafers.

"How could you even move on to this kind of work? I mean I still feel dirty all the time, no matter what I do or how much time passes."

"I felt just the same—much worse as I got older; and you know how we react to the gay business back home. At the time, I knew nothing about that, but I was certain what had taken place was terrible, and my life would never be the same. Staying away from all my church activity was my only way to deal with it. I had to stay silent about it, no other solution presented itself to fix what I was grappling with. When I got older, shame made me frantic and desperate as I convinced myself I was the one to blame—something about me must have made the priest pick me."

Later in the group meeting, Zarah watched Donovan from across the room with fresh eyes and, with emotions beyond admiration, listened to his contribution to the group. How could he have come through so much and remained so focused on what he was about? She shared what she could with Mavis, without divulging the private matters Donovan had opened up about.

"All I can say is Thank God for the doctor and the card she gave you. Obviously, you're getting help, even more than I was hoping for. At last, you may find out what a decent man is like!"

CHAPTER 46
A SLANTING LIGHT

The more Zarah learned about this man who'd found her in an unimaginable space, the more she wished their circumstances had been different. On their long Sunday afternoon walks, and brisk morning runs in Baisley Park, she rediscovered how good it felt to be outside in warm sunshine. Conversations with him made her wonder at all the time she had wasted on Damien.

Once Donovan's story was out, their interaction proceeded at its own pace and in its own way. Not once did the question arise in her mind about whose pain had been worse, or whose struggle more taxing. Their suffering was enough, and this new bond was a way to help each other get past the ache, which for Donovan had eaten away at him almost his entire life. "I blamed the church; my mother got her share for leaving me to them. Even God must have heard my rage. When I stopped going to church, my mother figured it was the usual teenage rebellion, and she prayed every day I would go back."

How thankful the woman beside him now was that he had done so, after his journey toward and away from the priesthood! For here he was—an unhoped for partner in a process she had never foreseen. Her compassion for him deepened as he spoke about the realization he could not be a part of a priesthood in which so many covered up what people like him had endured.

"You think you'll stick with this kind of work and stay in America?" she asked. Her nervousness about his answer astonished her.

"Yes, for a time anyway. I have to tell my mother I'm out of the priesthood. I've hated hiding it from her, but I have to go home and hold her hand as she hears all that."

"So, the two of us have to go home."

If the splinters from their wounds had not remained lodged in their hearts, Zarah and Donovan might have felt the looming chemistry, the stirring of affection, the hints of more to explore. But their gashes were still too raw, the bleeding still too fresh. Both clung to the walls they had erected to secure themselves against any rekindling that could lead to new anguish. They listened, consoled, held up each other—learned one another's songs by heart. Still, with no words exchanged, they withheld permission to show themselves as man and woman. Their hearts congealed around the shared hope of finding enough inside themselves to move on—to go home to a safe harbor.

A slanting sliver of light fell through a small window into Zarah's diminished life. Patches of green and yellow hope insinuated themselves against the bleak grayness that had enveloped her for too long. She continued her work at the center, impressing Miss Beck even more as the months passed. At school, she stepped up the pace, getting permission to complete her diploma on a fast track, fully supported by the faculty who had seen from the beginning that she was way ahead of her class. A vague outline was taking shape—a world in which she could reclaim some of what she had thrown away. She was grateful for Donovan, for he was helping to shape those images. He was the first to come upon an obstacle to the path on which they had set their eyes. His mother was dangerously ill, so he prepared for the journey to Jamaica, sharing the trepidation he felt for more reasons than his anxiety about his mother's condition.

The day before he was due to leave, they met at the park and before they even did their warm-up, his unexpected words tumbled out.

"Listen, I have an idea; it came to me as I sat in the travel agency."

"What?"

"As bad as my situation is–heading home to I don't even know what–both of us can get something from my trip home. I'll be able to explain everything to my mother at last. And I can help you reconnect with your family."

"Slow down and explain; I don't get it."

"What if you write a letter to your parents? We can assume your mother still works at the ministry, and I can go there. Even if she's not there, somebody will know where to find her. I will take the letter to her and prepare the ground. That will be more personal; a buffer, that's what I'll be."

Besides all he had been for her, Donovan would now be Zarah's mail man and buffer.

The news brought laughter to Mavis. "Thank you, Jesus! Girl, I tell you Donovan come into your life for a reason? So wait, why you face drop down so, after coming so close to something that can take you home?"

"It felt like a good idea, but I'm nervous. What if they don't react the way we hope? Suppose they tell him I can't come back to them?"

"Come on; I tell you all the time you're not a mother, so you don't understand; but I'm one, and I can tell you there's no way a mother will say her child can't come home, no way! Zarah, when the time is right, all the pieces of this puzzle will come together. The situation might not be easy at the beginning, but time and work will make it better, and look how hard you been working already. Plus—"

Another hopeful look popped into her eyes as it did every time she wanted to spin stories about Zarah and Donovan.

"Mavis, don't start again about me and—"

"No, seriously; today I heard some news, and it seem like one more sign you can put this awful part of your life behind you."

"What?"

"Somebody shot Ghost last night, right outside the supermarket! His own gang people kill him!"

"You're sure?" Shock, anger, doubt, and relief vied for a place inside Zarah, but it was fear that came out in her next words. "Wait, what if it's a mistake? What if he may still be around?" Even after Mavis confirmed the news more than once, Zarah feared her torment would continue.

"Suppose he's dead, and I still don't get relief from this haunting inside me?"

"We can't be sure, but it should help; at least you don't have to worry about running into that brute again.

Donovan's absence left a yawning gap. How Zarah would have loved to talk to him about the feelings she had after Ghost's death! His compassionate attitude, attentive ear, and calm voice had become her weekly doses of reassurance, which made all the difference between stepping forward to grab the promise of home and retreating to the belief it would never be possible. She forced herself to stay with the group, but it was Donovan's empty chair that held her attention. Their profound conversations echoed in her thoughts, and as she returned to the trails they had walked, memories of his calming words and rich laughter allowed her to imagine what it would be like if, at some other time, they could find their own trails at home.

Four weeks after Donovan's email arrived with the news of his visit to her mother, and after Esther and Bradley had broken through their confusion to reach out to Zarah, the envelope arrived bearing Esther's neat handwriting. Inside, a brief note enclosed the ticket for Flight JM 16 to Kingston.

Visions of the Caribbean Sea clouded the small room at the back of Mavis's apartment, bringing back the aromas of Bradley's aftershave lotion, Limacol steeped in the pillow at Grams, Pine-Sol in the air at Duhaney Park, Sunsilk shampoo in Esther's bathroom. Zarah breathed them in, allowing them to fuel hope for her return home.

CHAPTER 47
A DEAD GIRL'S ROOM

Kingston, 2002

Zarah was still shaking after the disappointment and anger that had destroyed her first night in Esther's house in Mona. The voices from the kitchen had diminished, and now a heavy silence prevailed. Slowing her breaths, she took in the crisp cool air of the room where Bradley had left her luggage earlier. *After Duhaney Park and those little apartments in Queensbury, this place is like a palace!* She turned the key to the four-drawer jewelry box Esther had given her on perhaps the last birthday free of tension. It seemed like a relic from someone else's past. "Waltz of the Flowers" filled the room as the little ballerina in her turquoise costume rotated, tears brimming in Zarah's eyes as she watched. *Look how many times I danced to that, my first leading role, and in the same color costume.*

Arms outstretched and fingers poised in the soft curve mastered in another life, a shaking body rose on its toes and tried to turn. Light but unbalanced, she felt as if she had three feet, each one in the way of the other. The arch of her left foot twitched, warning her to take her weight off. Her fingers inched to the cover of the music box and lowered it. As she moved away from the dresser and glanced up to the wall, her eye caught the little nutcracker statue standing close to the mirror, and there it rested.

Running her thumb over the elegant brush script letters of her name, Zarah took down her framed certificates, including the one that brought her most pride, "First Class Honors, Bachelor of Science, Chemistry." After a small gasp, she tucked it behind the dresser and glimpsed her entire body in the long mirror on the closet door. *Look at me; I'm out of place in this spotless room–haggard and beaten down like an old woman.* She reached for Socket, the eye-less old teddy bear on the unfamiliar bed. Socket felt all his owner's frustration as her fists battered him just as they had done so many times as a child.

She paused before Naomi's wall hanging, starched and ironed with its flawless embroidered lettering, beside it a picture of herself in cap and gown for her high school graduation. The young girl smiling back at her was almost unrecognizable, her narrow face framed with the stiff tendrils every girl styled her hair with that year. Perched at the end of the unfamiliar bed, Zarah passed her hand over the yellow flowers raising their heads on the classy comforter. It was a long way from the Barbie covers and chenille bedspreads at Duhaney Park, not to mention the cheap scratchy blanket a different version of her had been so relieved to throw out at the Queensbury dump along with other remnants of her New York disaster.

The freshness of the pillow gloved in her mother's crisp ironed case brought a moment of comfort as Zarah's disoriented fingers traced the letters of her name stretched out in elegant satin stitching. Her mother had thought of every detail–every stark reminder of who her daughter used to be. Zarah fought hard to remember the dead girl to whom this room belonged–the one her mother would have been much more comfortable to welcome home.

***

The storm behind them, Bradley helped Naomi calm Esther, and before he left, the older woman led them in fervent prayers for the readiness to accept the version of Zarah that had come home to them. It was not their old Zarah, but a broken woman–someone damaged by battles for which nothing had prepared her. Naomi thanked God for whatever had brought Zarah back into their lives, vicious scars and all. Bradley left them, and after too many hours, both found relief in brief episodes of sleep between tossing and turning, staring at the ceiling or the floor, or pacing from corner to corner of each room. But for their prayer, Zarah's night was no different.

The next morning, Esther tiptoed from the dresser where she had rested the breakfast tray. She stole a quick glance at the shape in the bed and turned to go.

"Morning, Mummy, please stay. I'm sorry things got so hard last night."

"I know. You don't have to get up. I heard you walking up and down."

"You got any sleep?"

"Not much."

"You think we can talk a little now?"

"If you are up to it, I'm up to listening."

Esther's tone reflected the commitment she made the previous night, and she waited.

"I have to be. Everything I did was horrible, and storming out last night just made it worse. I got some help and it should have prepared me ... but I don't know what I'm doing. God knows how long it will take me to tell you and Daddy all that happened– or if I can ever do it. But last night was all I could manage, and I still made a mess of everything. I know you did your best but it was a lot for everybody; but it doesn't change the fact that I couldn't be more grateful to be home; at least I hope it can be home because running doesn't suit me."

"You may not need to run anymore."

"I had to go through hell to see that ... and so much other stuff. My priorities are different now. But one thing I'm begging you is to tell me the truth: You think ... I mean ... I don't deserve it, and it might be impossible, but if I try to explain where my head was ... and everything I'm learning ... you believe you and Daddy could forgive me?" It had taken all her courage to frame the question, and once it was out, she froze. Like a cloud about to burst, her words hovered in the air, and the moment stretched out, waiting for the answer that would make all the difference.

"Parents forgive their children, Zarah. It's what parents do." The words fell with a thud. Less than the answer her daughter needed, and much less than what her mother had buried in her heart, it was all Esther could manage.

"What about you though? Can you do it?" Again, Zarah held her breath. Daughter and mother watched each other across the stillness. Esther wracked her brain and heart for words she could say and mean. Zarah sighed, staring at the floor. "Never mind; I think I got the answer."

Perplexed and embarrassed, Esther filled the space. "You found everything you needed last night? How about trying to eat a little breakfast? Grams made your favorite: ackee and salt fish with fry dumplings."

Zarah continued the charade. "Of course; and that breakfast sounds like old times; thanks for bringing it." But she picked at the food as her mother walked over to the dressing table and started re-organizing items that were already out of place. Esther finally broke the silence.

"Zarah, I can see you've had an awful time, and believe me when I tell you only God knows how glad I am it's over."

"I didn't mean to let you down. At first, I thought I could clear my brain, straighten things out, get a job and even go back to school; I figured I could persuade D—persuade him to take some constructive steps to improve himself. But it was a different world, and he was not the person I expected. My life was out of control and after a while, I figured I could never make it right with you. I'm telling you the truth."

"I believe you; It's hard for me to understand, but ...." This time, she would not let the bitterness turn her back. After the previous night's false start, Zarah's parents and Grams had agreed to encourage Zarah to share her story in small doses. So now she bit her lips and chose trivia, urging Zarah to make plans to call up her friends, go out with Shari, and think about what she would do next. Zarah knew what her mother said was important, but right now, the words sounded as if they were for a different person–the one who owned this lovely new room.

Esther's gaze settled on the splinters of her broken child huddled on the bed. How she wished she had the strength to switch on the light in another room from another time and draw her little girl to her breast again. Parts of her wanted to do nothing but that; to make the situation right. But she still ached from what Zarah had put them through. And what about all the struggles the unfamiliar woman in the bed had endured for that worthless boy? Would they ever know all of it? Would he be back in her life? *Where will I get the strength to keep those promises I made last night?*

Each day, they got up and put one foot before the other, searching for new ground, determined to live above the details of the missing years. Three weeks went by with no confrontations, but the atmosphere was cool, and between Zarah and her parents, the passages were as slippery as a dozen eggs shattered across the kitchen tiles. Naomi said everybody needed time, and everybody wondered how much.

CHAPTER 48
WHAT DO TEA LEAVES KNOW?

Esther told no one about the trip she made a few miles out of Kingston one month after Zarah's arrival. In fact, when she had left for work that morning, she did not know she would end up in St. Thomas. How could she explain her decision to seek advice from the unlikely Ol' Higue, one of the island's best-known tea-leaf readers–the guide, mentor, and oracle consulted by corporate moguls, husbands and their wives, mistresses who were other men's wives, lawyers embroiled in wrangles, and even leaders eager to know the best time to call an election?

Inside the woman's grubby room, everything was a shade darker than reality. Through the small window, Esther could make out the stunning blossoms of the Otaheite apple tree that took her back to the days of Oracabessa. How she wished to rest under its shade!

"Time going, Miss Lady! Yuh going tek whole day to drink the tea? Who send yuh here?" The woman's voice was like a whip, and Esther was so nervous, she almost missed her own answer.

"A co-worker."

"Then what yuh co-worker tell yuh dat mek yuh so jumpy?"

"Nothing, but I've only done this once before, and ..."

The woman looked down her nose and dispensed a dose of bitter sarcasm, "An' people like yuh don't need help wid yuh troubles; yuh go to university, and yuh go to church, and stocious people like yuh don't believe in my old-fashioned foolishness. Right? Mi know is dat yuh want to say, but yuh too 'fraid."

Esther avoided the slightest movement. *Marva didn't say she was sending me to Madam Lashy; boy, her mouth is as sharp as a butcher knife.* A heavy silence hung over the unlikely pair as the woman challenged Esther with a stern stare. The usually confident self-possessed supervisor looked down at the unfamiliar hands that fidgeted in her lap.

"Is not true what mi saying?"

"I suppose so."

"Yuh suppose so? Lady, yuh would be awright if it was dat alone worrying yuh head—"

"How you know what I have to worry about? I didn't even finish drinking the tea." Esther had shoved her cup aside and risen above Ol' Higue.

"Yuh think mi only know things from tea dregs?"

"I don't care; just tell me what you know. Is it about Za—?"

"No! Don't call anybody name to me. Drink and settle yuhself."

Esther gulped the tea, grimaced, and placed the cup on the table. *What am I doing here locked up in this smelly hole with this crumungin old wretch?*

Across from her, the scrawny tea-leaf reader waited. As bad as being there was, Esther needed to stay put. The first weeks of Zarah's presence proved almost impossible to manage. Though the serious talks came in spells, a dull knife could sometimes cut the tension and anxiety in the air. Bradley's presence brought some relief, and he visited often so they could all follow through on their commitment to work with the reality that had come home with Zarah. Still, other evenings and nights stretched out with mother and daughter eyeing each other across loaded questions and vague answers that heightened their discomfort.

Hijacked from her journey to work, Esther now sat amid the grime and the darkness of the room because she hoped the shriveled up old woman and her caustic tea could somehow tell her something to help her deal with what was ahead. Ol' Higue drew the curtain and sank into the chair across from her reluctant visitor. Her eyes rolled over, settling on the dark cobwebbed ceiling, turning the cup around and around. Esther looked behind, above, and beside her, every minute glancing at her watch.

"Hmm, yuh watching clock? Yuh think things going happen as fast as yuh gulp down the tea?"

"What? No; but you were hurrying me, and to tell the truth, I'm not the most patient person."

Ol' Higue chuckled. "Yuh don't have to tell mi dat."

"What are you? A tea-leaf reader or a mind reader?"

"Mi never tell a soul mi was one or the other. Yuh and mi know why yuh come here."

"I'm wondering why I'm here; in fact, I think I'll go." She fidgeted with her bag as if to get up. The woman was undaunted; she shoved the cup away from her and slumped in her chair, glaring at her visitor.

"Listen, Miss High and Mighty, yuh know why yuh come here, so why yuh don't just mek up yuh mind and listen? People like yuh believe dem can solve every problem because dem go to big school and study big book. But not one soul set foot in this place unless dem need help to figure out some important business. Yuh not no different."

Esther sank into her own chair, her bag slumping to the cracked linoleum flooring next to her matching brown pumps. Ol' Higue started in a slow flat voice. On and on, she droned, revealing details about Esther's life no one outside the smallest circle of people could know. Between her witch's cackles, she dispensed advice on how the family should manage "the prodigal dat might soon come home."

The hair on Esther's arms stood at attention.

CHAPTER 49
A VISIT TO OLD PLACES

The cooling morning air caressed Zarah's face as she leaned against the Julie mango tree watching her grandmother. Naomi walked from plant to plant, trimming, cutting, and watering. With a little smile, Zarah listened as Grams approached each patch of gerberas, roses, and begonias, giving her consolation speech to these and other babies all over the garden.

"Morning, little one; I didn't even know you was out here. How yuh do? Glad to see yuh up and about; the nice bright sun will make yuh feel much better."

"Morning, Grams; I'm okay. I'm going to take a walk around the campus; soon come back."

"Glad to see yuh want to get out. But tek care; everybody say the campus is not how it was."

"Don't worry, Grams; it will be okay; I soon come back."

"Awright; but be careful; and what about my suggestion? Yuh think about going to Mass wid mi?"

"Yes, I will go; but not right now; to tell you the truth, I'm not ready to see all those people."

"On a weekday morning, only a few people come. It will do yuh good to get Mass back in yuh routine."

If only you knew what my routine became, Grams.

***

The wide-open spaces of the university campus stretched out against the backdrop of the Blue Mountains. An array of emotions churned as the young woman who had been misplaced for so long stood face to face with the surroundings that had brought her so much peace, joy, and self-discovery.

What if I'd taken the scholarship and stayed right here on campus? What would my life be like now? Why hadn't she been truthful to herself? Why had she closed her ears to the small voice whispering in them as she turned away from her family and herself, on an inexorable plunge into the murk of life with Damien? Regret felt like the unraveling of delicate threads in her dancing tights; it only got worse.

Peeping inside the chapel, she stared at the immaculate, gleaming tiles, the luster of the polished wood, the sun streaming through the stained-glass window behind the altar, leaving multi-colored sunbeams across the floor. The sadness and hopelessness welling up inside her would pin her to the floor if she stayed another moment. She rushed out, leaning on the wall to steady herself.

The ten-minute transition period between lectures had just started; groups of animated students poured out of lecture halls, hurrying in every direction to their next activity. Some gesticulated and broke into laughter at their own secrets; others draped their bodies across benches and each other, under the shade of coolie plum, Ficus, and poinciana trees. *My favorite lignum vitae bench; we used to spend Sunday afternoons there, making all those plans.*

Her heart pounded as she slipped under the covered walkway and stood across Ring Road facing the Philip Sherlock Center for the Creative Arts, the place where she had danced her way to peace and joy. As the young dancers practiced their parts in the early morning rehearsal, the same joy filled their smiles and movements. The scene brought to mind all her performances over the years. Time paused as she watched them, losing the will and the energy to drag herself away.

"Excuse me, Miss." Even the cleaning woman's soft voice was startling.

"What? What is it?"

"Don't worry; is nutt'n; mi was locking up and notice yuh here by yuhself like yuh feel sick or drop asleep."

"No, sorry, thanks; I was watching the rehearsal and honestly, I dozed off; what time is it?"

"Nearly ten o'clock. Morning rehearsal finish, but yuh can come back in the evening."

"Thank you," Zarah said, passing close to the woman.

"Wait, yuh never use to dance here one time? Mi sure mi remember yuh face," she said.

"Yes, I used to dance here," Zarah said, her eyes fixed on the floor.

"Then something happen to yuh, Miss? How yuh look so different?" It was too much. She ran from the building and kept running until her breath abandoned her.

***

Naomi sipped her coffee as she sewed. Strident talk show hosts and cantankerous callers assailed the airwaves. *What, 10:20 arready? Where Zarah gone so long?* She picked up the phone and put it back down. Her sewing thrown on the veranda chair, she rushed out to the gate as Zarah walked in.

"Yuh okay?"

"Yes, I'm fine; you didn't have to worry. I went just where I said, for a walk on campus."

"Don't be so touchy; I didn't think yuh went anywhere else. But remember what mi tell yuh. Thieves holding up people at all hours; nowhere not safe."

"I know, Grams; but everybody have to stop worrying; I will not disappear." She hurried into the house, leaving Naomi shaking her head and retrieving her sewing.

"A little breakfast for yuh in the kitchen," she shouted, as Zarah walked away.

"Thanks, I will eat it later; not hungry right now."

Adrift once again in the unfamiliar room, Zarah threw herself across the bed, walked back and forth, and yanked open the door to the clothes closet. Under the lowest shelf, a neat line of boxes stood against the wall. A stack of old cartridge paper fell open, displaying the painstaking lettering in vocabulary words a young girl had used to adorn her walls. A flimsy giggle escaped as she recalled the girls in her class laughing at her in Duhaney Park as they examined the lists. *If only those days could come back again—those days before life went crazy.* Boxes were soon everywhere, as sheets, towels, and old clothes littered the floor—all the stuff her mother had packed away neatly for the move to the new house. Finally, a box with just her old dancing gear! She dragged out a faded leotard and matching tights, hauled them on, and made a sharp turn away from the view of herself in the mirror.

Another box caught her eye, this one labeled with a red magic marker, **"Zarah–This One."** Sensing a special moment, she slid to the floor, pulled the box between her legs and leaned her back against the bed, fingering items too delicate to ruffle. Brand-new underwear, fancy lingerie, pillowcases, and sheets lay crumpled in a pile of her mother's old hopes. Esther had wrapped every item in soft tissue paper lined with lavender sheets. With personal and household items all around her, she came to a large parcel—tiny baby clothes: pink, blue, yellow diaper shirts, warm sleepers, the tiniest socks she had ever seen. "No, no, nooooo!" she cried, burying her head in the comfort of the sweet-smelling fabrics.

"Zarah? Yuh okay in there? What is dat noise?" Naomi said, banging on the door.

"In the bathroom, Grams; I soon come. Please don't open the door; the room is a mess." It was too late. Naomi gaped at the disarray.

"What is all this?"

Zarah was a bizarre sight in the confusion. She wore one foot of her jazz shoes, the other one strewn across the room. Her pointe shoes had landed on another box. Turning away from her granddaughter's bony frame, Naomi gathered up the stuff lying all over the floor, trying to put it back in the right boxes. Zarah was sobbing without control.

"Since I was little, I did all I was supposed to do; I never gave trouble—not until I wanted what nobody else considered right for me; and for that I destroyed my life and family; now I can never be the person I was supposed to be. Look at all this beautiful house stuff and the special things Mummy saved for me; I can never use them. Baby clothes, Grams—when will I ever have a life that can include a baby?"

"Stop dat right now," Naomi said in her sternest voice. "Yuh flying in God face when yuh talk like dat; yuh are alive and healthy; and yuh come home to where yuh can get help to deal with whatever happen to yuh. I know yuh mek plenty mistake, but we don't choose the people we love; it just happen; and if it don't work out, we have to tek every day till we can do better."

"But why I had to love Damien, though? He turned out to be worse than Mummy predicted; but right now, I don't even want to call his name, or hear it."

"All in good time," Naomi said, "yuh don't have to know all the answers right now. If yuh want to talk about any of it, I have all day; I will listen."

It was the opening Zarah needed; in moments, she was re-living with her grandmother the string of events that had tossed her into a ring with Damien, setting off the journey that almost turned her into someone else.

CHAPTER 50
A CHILLING TELEPHONE MESSAGE

Kingston, 2003

The ugly details of the New York story had taken their time leaking into the family's conversations, but it was Naomi who picked up most pieces of the puzzle and guided Zarah as she shared the worst of it with Bradley. Then, he did most of the hard work of bringing Esther up to date with some of what Zarah could not reveal herself.

Several diners came and went while waiters cleared and set tables. Bradley sipped his drink and kept his eyes on the door. As he watched his elegant ex-wife striding into the restaurant, the pulsing in his temple increased and he peeled tiny shreds of skin from the side of his thumb. Zarah's return had once again given them a challenge on which to work together; it was almost like the old times—always discussing what they needed to do for her; how they could make sure she would be okay. They did not always want to discuss everything with Zarah and Naomi around, so they had met a few times for dinner, drinks, and lunches like this one.

At last, Bradley had felt he could restore his friendship with the woman he had long lost but never stopped loving. As he rose to seat her across from his chair, he could feel the tightening in his chest. Knowing some details could drive the last nail into the coffin of Esther's hope, he had struggled with how much of the story to share.

"Sorry I'm late. I was on my way, handbag and everything, but the manager got on the phone, and she just wouldn't make me get away."

"No problem," Bradley said, "I haven't been here long, and it's much cooler in here than driving up and down in the sun. I ordered sweet and sour chicken for yuh; is still yuh favorite?"

"Definitely can't go wrong with that; thank you." Bradley watched with a dull ache rising somewhere inside as she smiled a smile from another era.

"Yuh look nice as usual; nice dress."

"What, this old thing?"

"You never wear 'this old thing'; what yuh want to drink?" The waiter had come over and Esther ordered lemonade.

"You look worried; anything new?" she asked.

"A lot; some of it I don't even know how to tell yuh. Zarah broke down again and told Miss Naomi some more about New York. She wasn't sure she could stand up to telling us that part herself."

Esther was always relieved to hear that their daughter was talking, and she no longer got upset that it was not to her. But Bradley's sketches of the worst parts made her cringe.

"I know we'll never know all the details, and maybe we couldn't even manage hearing them, but you were right; what she went through may change her forever."

"Is true," Bradley said, "but it look like some of the change will be for the better. I don't pick up that arrogance we use to see before she left. Remember how she use to behave like she could never be wrong about the things she was feeling and saying?"

"I see the same signs too; she admitted making serious mistakes, and she wants to change."

A few quiet moments passed as each shoveled food around on a plate.

"So, what did your policeman friend think about checking if they have deportation records that could lead them to the boy?" Esther asked.

"Actually, he's retired, and him warn mi about talking to anybody active in case it get out. This guy has no connection with the force anymore, and he said we should stay away from the police."

"He was in the force, and he said that?" Esther asked, "Why?"

"He feels we should help Zarah move on, but police involvement will demand Zarah's information and that might set her back. Plus any investigation might alert bad guys in the force who can leak information to the wrong people."

Bradley saw the shock and fear in her face.

"Apparently some guys in the force have connections with criminals and gangs, and sometimes deportees fall in with them once they reach home and decide to stay outside the law. I didn't think of all that, but the bottom line is getting the police involved would be too risky."

"Well, thank God you found out. We should just leave it alone."

Their respite was over, and after a few moments of easy chatter, Esther checked her watch.

"Sorry, I really have to get back to work."

"Tek care of yuhself," Bradley said, helping her to her feet.

***

Bradley inched the car around the University Ring Road and out the main gate. Next to him, Zarah wore the face that told her father to give her quiet time. Her afternoon seeking information at the careers office had demoralized her, especially when the placement officer had looked incredulous when she saw the gap in her employment record. Zarah had fumbled her explanation, and the interview went downhill from there. The woman painted a bleak picture of the employment situation, and Zarah put little hope in the woman's one weak attempt at reassurance.

"Anyway, November to January is not the best time for job hunting. Keep in touch with me; remember we have a few career workshops coming up, and you should try to attend."

Her despondency filled the car as soon as she stepped in. "She may not be a big help; the gap in my work history made her frown."

"She might not mean what you think. Times are hard, and jobs are scarce. We have to be patient." Zarah had already heard about graduates complaining how every job required experience, and nobody would give them a chance to gain any. Many who were employed and wanted to find their own way had to continue living with their parents because they could not afford to rent or buy even a one-bedroom apartment. On and on her friend had gone, painting a gloomy picture of the landscape Zarah was trying to re-enter.

They were approaching Mona, and the thought of going home with no good news was too much. "Daddy, can I stay over by you, and you carry me home tonight?"

"Sure, no problem," Bradley said.

"I just need some space to take in all the stuff I heard today and try to think about how to tell Mummy it didn't go well. Can we pick up some dinner?"

"Good idea. They don't expect me back at the office. What yuh feel to eat?"

"I'm fine with whatever you want."

Back at his place, they were about to eat, when his answering machine churned out a couple of messages. The vaguely familiar voice and the surprisingly penitent tone raised the hairs on Zarah's arms. "Evening, Missa Thomas, is me, Sir; is Damien. Mi come back to Jamaica; how yuh do, Sir? Yuh used to talk to mi good sometimes, so mi was wondering if mi can talk to yuh, Sir; mi hear Zarah come home and mi want—"

Bradley killed the message and hugged Zarah as she threw herself on the couch. This time, there were no uncontrollable sobs. The look on his daughter's face betrayed a kind of fury different from anything he had seen. Both agreed they would spare Esther and Naomi from hearing about Damien's lurking. Bradley planned his next move, but he kept it to himself.

CHAPTER 51
A MEETING WITH A STRANGER

Kingston, 2003

The tiled floor at the law offices of Garnett, Parchment & Associates reminded Zarah of the straight lines she hated at Duhaney Park, but it was no time to dwell on old things. She and her parents were intent on hearing every detail in the lawyer's lengthy explanation of the prospects they faced. Following Damien's unexpected phone message, Bradley had sought advice about ways to keep the boy away from Zarah, and after he updated her and Esther on the latest developments, they had discussed the family's legal options, and the big step was at hand.

"You're sure about this, Zarah?" Parchment asked for the third time.

"Yes, I'm sure; it's the only way—"

"I don't like this part at all," Bradley said, picking at his thumb.

"Mr. Parchment, I know the boy sounded penitent when we met him with his father, but we can't be sure if when he sees Zarah, he'll do what he promised. She need to be in here for us to talk to him?"

"Actually, it is unnecessary at this stage," Parchment said, "and Zarah, your father might be right; the boy might sound one way talking to two fathers and a lawyer, but he could easily get agitated when he sees you. I mean, you did say he was ... he can be erratic."

"Yes, Zarah, it might be best for you to stay out of it," Esther said, "Mr. Parchment has all the information to do what is best. If the boy comes in here and shows any sign that he won't stay away from you, we go to court and take it from there."

"Stay out of it? Out of what I caused?" Zarah sat erect in her chair, her voice controlled and without equivocation about her part in the problems still facing her family. Her eyes shone with the determination Esther had not seen since the 21st birthday confrontation. No one dared interrupt. "I'm the one who brought Damien into our lives, and if he's a danger or even just a nuisance to everybody, I am the one to get him out. Mr. Parchment, Mummy, Daddy, I came because it's my job to clean up this mess, and I'm staying."

"Enough blame now," Esther said. "We all made mistakes."

"Yes, but we know whose biggest mistake got us into this, and we can't wait until he goes too far again. We put everybody through hell and enough is enough; I must get us out. Nobody here knows him better than me, and if he won't stay away from us, I have enough information to put him in big trouble. I came home to get my life back, and Damien won't stop me!" As the lawyer handed Zarah the forms, Bradley saw, for the second time, the same dreadful look that had appeared on her face when Damien's voice invaded his living room.

Using the deliberate cursive flourish with which she had always written her favorite words, Zarah filled in and signed each page of the application for a restraining order. Handing them over to the lawyer, she threw her head back and sank into the chair. Her fierce look lingered, but her father's fear was turning into pride. A roiling bitterness teemed inside her, and Zarah could not wait to see what it would be like to face again, the man who had dictated so much of her life for so long. Ever since he disappeared and left her to Ghost, her mind had conjured images of what the moment would be like. *Now I know; all the feelings are gone. Today he will know he will never stand in my way again or interrupt the life I'm supposed to live.* It had never entered her mind that pursuing one of her most important goals would occur in a lawyer's office. But it was her chance to take away at least some of the pain her recklessness had caused her family, and she would exploit it all the way. With her collusion, Damien had turned her life upside down, and she would make him taste at least some of the suffering and loss she had lived with before being able to come home.

In a few moments, everyone's attention turned to the sound of tentative footsteps approaching the door, the hushed voices just outside, and the turning of the knob. Someone Zarah once knew stepped in, interrupting everyone's smooth breathing. Looking like a stranger facing his worst fear, the man-boy with the thick lips and protruding teeth waited for the clerk to seat him. Except for the lawyer, all averted their eyes, and no one exchanged any pleasantries.

The boastful swagger long gone, he lurched forward, still no sign of a real purpose in his eyes. His face still bore remnants of the boy at Devon House who had filled a young Zarah with a yearning for something she hardly remembered. Glancing fearfully in her direction, he could see she was not the girl he had enticed into his purposeless life and then deserted, but he was not sure what the difference was.

In under thirty minutes, the room overflowed with stern words from Mr. Parchment, almost incoherent apologies from Damien, and unconvincing testimonies about lessons he had learned and changes he had made after coming back home. The stuttering young man now saw the differences between the woman at the table and the girl from a few years before. They stood out in the straight line of her shoulders, the hardened cheekbones, the precise movements of her lips as she uttered her damning words and echoed the warnings of her parents and their lawyer. Everything about her telegraphed one message, "It's over." Bradley and Esther watched their daughter's determination and knew their presence was enough, so they left everything to her. Damien knew it was over, but a shred of hope made him deny it and try to reclaim a time long gone. "Missa Thomas, Sir, yuh could make mi and Zarah talk outside a minute? Mi have something mi want to tell her about our future—"

"Our future? There is no 'our.' I don't know you, and I don't want to. As to the future, that is a verb tense that will never apply to you in my life again. You are past tense." The ice had leaked from Zarah's eyes to her words.

"I will say it in front of everybody, then, Zarah. All what yuh say is right, an' mi sorry..."

Zarah spun her chair around, leaving him to face her back. He wilted.

The lawyer took control.

"Young man, you understand all that I outlined about court? You understand I will do whatever it takes to prevent you from approaching Zarah or pestering this family?" Damien nodded, and when the man insisted that he state his agreement for everyone to hear, he got out a grunt that could just pass for "yes, Sir."

"And you realize if you go near any of them after today, we will deal with a judge and not this family?"

"Yes, Sir."

"Mr. Parchment, I think we can leave the rest to you," Zarah said, already on her feet. "Mummy, Daddy, please, time to leave all this behind us."

CHAPTER 52
A BROKEN WING

Kingston, 2003

The sun peeped through the morning sky as Zarah stepped out the front door to find her grandmother. Even though Naomi knew they had taken care of the situation with Damien, she remained anxious and agitated, so they kept a close eye on her. Zarah heard the soft hum from the side of the yard, and as "Rock of Ages" drew her around the corner, she tiptoed to the spot where Naomi sat on her stool paying close attention to what she was doing.

"Shh," Grams said, a finger on her lips.

The bird huddled on the paper towel her grandmother had spread on her lap. The blues, greens, and yellows of its delicate wing pleated into each other across the frail frame of tiny bones. Stale blood had congealed in the hidden injury, spreading its incongruous color and texture. She cleaned off the feathers with a soft rag dipped in warm water and dressed the skin with cotton, stained with iodine. Laying the broken wing across a thin piece of ply board, her deft fingers tied the parts together and looped the string around. Zarah raised it with equal care, extending its other wing until the bird shifted on its own.

Naomi sighed as she watched the bird struggle to raise the injured limb. Zarah sank onto the grass and put her head in Naomi's lap, closing a gentle finger around the flutter of the fragile heart.

"What yuh have on yuh mind this morning, little one?"

"Not a thing, I just wanted to watch you at peace in your favorite place."

"Don't worry, yuh well on yuh way to yuh own peace; look how much happen in the last few weeks to show yuh the power of prayer and faith."

"Is true, Grams; I feel relieved about a lot of things, but—"

"But what?"

"I mean, I worry so much: What if I can't get over all this? Suppose I never find somebody to love me, or I can't love anybody after what I've been through? Remember what the lady in Idlewild said about Grandma Pearlie and how she lock up her heart?"

"Yes, I remember, but don't forget that near her time, Mama open her heart a little for Bertie. No heart can shut down forever." Naomi's eyes took on a faraway look that hinted at an untold story.

"What about you, Grams? You opened up your heart again after the bad times?"

"Hmm, somebody did come along; but sometimes, yuh have feelings for somebody, and yuh have to look from far, and keep it to yuhself." Zarah sensed the veil falling over her grandmother's eyes.

"So, what about the curses and stains?"

"I know a modern girl like yuh never believe a bit of it; yuh too smart. To tell the truth, it tek mi a long time to stop believing Mama story about a curse. But that day yuh come back to us, I know dat even if a thing like dat was there, it was fading arready. Prayer stronger than any evil–stain or curse."

***

Two nights later, satisfaction filled Naomi's heart as Esther and Zarah dressed to go out together.

"Mama, you sure you will be okay?"

"Don't worry over me; I will be awright."

"Remember, Bradley said he can come and stay with you, and you can chat some more old-time stories."

"No, listen: Seeing yuh and Zarah getting out to enjoy yuhself together, and hearing yuh call Bradley's name in that tone of voice mek mi better than awright."

"Grams, Daddy's number is right beside the phone in your room," Zarah chimed in. "Just call him if you change your mind."

Naomi turned in early, but sleep refused to come, and she felt exhausted and lightheaded. *Wonder if is one of the hunger headaches Esther always talking about.* Naomi ate very little these days and had left most of her dinner in the fridge. Throwing on her blue housecoat, she made her way to the kitchen and plugged in the kettle. The pain in her head was severe. Cold sweat poured over her as she headed for the bathroom and grabbed her inevitable smelling salts. *Mek mi rest right here until this bad feeling pass.*

Back in the kitchen, she propped herself against the counter, pouring the water over the two tea bags. *Mi don't understand why Esther won't buy fresh ginger. Dis powder one don't have one taste.* The hot drink brought relief as one burp followed another, and she shared out a little food to warm it. Ripping a page from an old newspaper, she twirled it into a tight torch and lit it with a stick from the box of extra-long safety matches Esther kept near the stove for just that purpose. But she did not smell the gas in the air, and she did not notice the knobs turned to "on." She inched the torch close to the burner, vaguely conscious of her shaking hand and the weakness spreading through her body.

Boom! The sound sent her stumbling toward the wall. Lights flickered, and scraps of paper and kitchen towels fluttered everywhere. Something felt hard and hot against her back. How had she reached the floor?

The flames danced around the curtains.

CHAPTER 53
EVERYTHING IS DIFFERENT NOW

Esther's gray Honda rumbled along Hope Road, its occupants hunched forward as if their bodies could make it go even faster.

"Please, Mummy, slow down."

"I'm trying, but what if—"

"We'll get there, and she'll be ok."

At the admissions section in the Accident and Emergency wing, Esther spoke before they even reached the desk, "Good night ... which ward is for ... my mother is ..."

Watching her wilt, Zarah stepped forward and took over. "Her name is Naomi Bloomfield; the police said we should come straight here."

Esther leaned on the desk, her insides churning.

"Did you say Bloomfield, Miss?" The gray-haired woman stood between the admissions clerk and Zarah.

"Yes, she's my grandmother—"

"And I'm Esther, her daughter; can you tell us what's happening?"

"Please, come with me; I'm Dr. Magnus. I admitted your mother."

"So, you can tell us how bad—"

"It's too early to say, Mrs.—"

"Thomas."

"She has serious burns, but they're not the major problem; we had to tackle the stroke first—"

"Stroke? I don't understand; you mean the fire, and then—"

"Actually, we think it might be the other way around; the stroke could have caused confusion and loss of control over whatever she was trying to do in the kitchen. It could explain what caused the fire. We can't be sure."

"We can see her?"

"Not yet; it may be some time before she's responsive."

Neither Esther nor Zarah knew how long they sat in the waiting room before Dr. Magnus persuaded them to go home and get some rest.

On the way home, each woman mulled over what was ahead. At the threshold, Zarah took her mother's hands. "Inside might be awful, but we'll get through this, and Grams will come home to us; I know it."

As if in a carefully choreographed mime, Zarah led a distracted Esther across the kitchen. They took it all in–from the mound of black rubble in the center, to the charred wallpaper, to the broken curtain rod over the sink, and the shreds of a frilly curtain dripping stale yellowing water. They circled the mound where someone had heaped the remnants of the kitchen, and sundry pots, pans, and utensils flung far from the neat places Esther had designed to keep them in order. Zarah drew closer to her, and their fingers locked.

"Sorry, Mummy; this must be awful for you; come and sit down."

"These are just things. We can always replace them or do without. I'm only worried about Grams now; the whole thing must have been so shocking. Imagine being alone with everything falling to pieces. And now who knows if she will—"

"She will recover. I know she will. She not finished with us yet." They smiled and exchanged a look they both understood; when they answered the doorbell, Bradley stood there.

As meetings with the contractor progressed, Esther's lack of interest stunned everyone. None of that mattered to her anymore. Her education, promotions, the new house, and their rise above circumstances had brought great pride; but her perfect kitchen in shambles was nothing to compare with her terror about what might be in store for Naomi.

An overwhelming sorrow took hold of her: It was nothing like her regret over destroying her marriage, or the struggles along the hard road they had traveled. And it was nothing like losing Zarah. This was an unfamiliar ache;

every day when she saw her mother's condition and reflected on the spaces that had so often separated them, it bore down and settled deep inside her. Every time she saw Naomi, helpless and almost unrecognizable in the hospital bed, a thousand words flew to her lips. What if she never got the chance to say them? What if they fell upon Naomi's ears and brought no response?

Alone in the house in the evenings while Zarah sat at Naomi's bedside, the walls turned on Esther. Remorse overcame her for the times she argued with her mother, accused her of being too difficult, nagged her for singing the "same old Rock of Ages" constantly. What would she give for just one more chance to shell dry peas with her amid the smell of onion and scallion, listening to one of her old-fashioned hymns? Only one thing brought her relief in those hours—a slow drive to Half-Way-Tree where she parked under the lignum vitae tree at Holy Cross Convent, moments in the empty side chapel where she and Naomi had dusted the candlesticks and changed altar cloths. Though the prayers were slow in coming, she absorbed the stillness and breathed in all the hope she could. She pieced together old scraps of herself and her life with Naomi that merged into a reassuring mosaic. And no matter how many pieces they had lost to misunderstanding and turmoil, they had stood against the world and come through. *We not finished yet, Mama; please come home.*

Eleven weeks passed before Naomi saw her garden.

Adjustment to being immobile and unable to communicate was difficult, but visits to her garden lifted her spirits, so Zarah took her outside as often as her condition allowed. Halfway down the long concrete path Esther's contractor had built, Zarah put the wheelchair brakes on and stepped down to the oleander tree as Naomi protested with her good hand. "Coming right back. I want to show you something."

Concealing her hand behind her skirt, Zarah soon returned. "Grams, look, this is your little bird; remember you saved him? The string you left on the foot is still there." Naomi raised one eyebrow and gesticulated with her left hand, but only garbled sounds came out. Her inability to express herself caused the most frustration, but Zarah had been learning to figure out the garbled sounds, and she downloaded copious notes from the Internet to add to techniques Miss Beck had shared as they worked with Greg. Everyone supported postponing her rigorous job search to be at home, where she and Esther took turns in the battle to keep Naomi from giving up her efforts. The spaces between the three narrowed.

CHAPTER 54
A GENTLEMAN AT THE DOOR

Kingston, 2003

Naomi had been home a little over eight weeks. A nurse visited most days, but Zarah spent hours taking care of her every need. "Come on, Grams, drink this lovely beef soup Miss Mildred made for you; look at all these nourishing crushed vegetables and the thyme leaves all over the top just the way you like it."

"Miss Zarah, a gentleman is here to yuh," Miss Mildred said.

"What happen," Zarah asked, laughing, "the gentleman don't have a name?" Zarah had grown close to Miss Mildred, the helper who replaced the fierce Miss Lucretia, the housekeeper at Duhaney Park.

"Yes, sorry, Miss Zarah," the bubbly young helper said, suppressing a giggle, "is Mr. McIntosh."

"Okay, thanks. Please let him sit down." *Lord, let him understand why I didn't answer his last few emails.* "Help Grams finish her soup for me please, Nurse."

Up from her usual position by the bedside, Zarah glanced in the narrow wall mirror, just long enough to tighten the scroongie around her ponytail, check her teeth for lettuce and tomato shreds, and quell the rattle in her chest. The two had stayed connected by email all along, so each knew how much the other was coping with, and how taxing the last few months had been. All the same, now they would be face to face for the first time since New York, both were uncertain what to expect.

On the huge suede couch, Donovan looked thinner than she remembered. Had his mother's death caused him to lose weight? His face seemed as composed as ever, but the shadows of grief darkened his eyes.

"Hey, New Yorker, thanks for coming by," she said, hoping lightness would hide her nerves, "How you doing?" A quick embrace shifted the uncertainty hanging between them.

"Keeping my balance," he said. "What about you? I was not sure about just dropping in, but I'm heading back, and your mother said it would be fine to come."

"You talked to Mummy?"

"I went to see the lawyers–the only thing I seem to do in Kingston. I was coming up past her office, so I popped in to say hi, and to be honest, to get an update on your grandmother ... and you." His smile was awkward, but it did not matter. Zarah was just happy to see for herself how he looked in Jamaica–to discover how she would feel seeing him after so much had happened.

"Let me get a drink for you; soda or guava juice?"

"I'm a country man, remember? Guava sounds perfect."

Eyeing each other, they sipped, clinking ice cubes to slow down the rush of words needing release.

"You think I could say hi to your Grams? I heard so much about her—"

"Of course; I want you to meet her. I just have to check with her first; you know how it is when—"

"I understand, and if she's not up to it, there's no problem. I feel like I know her because of you." Zarah hurried to Naomi's bedside, Donovan following at a safe distance.

"Grams, somebody is here to meet you; remember I told you about Donovan from New York?" Naomi turned her face toward the doorway, summoning her best crooked smile, and Zarah knew right away it would be fine, so she beckoned him to go in. Naomi had heard all about the friend from New York and how much he helped Zarah, so her heart was open. With all her energy, she struggled to sit up, and with her good hand, beckoned him to come closer.

"Grams, take it easy," Zarah said, with little hope of compliance.

"Relax, Zarah; I had a grannie too, so I know I have to obey."

He stooped closer, and Naomi's better eye twinkled as she squeezed out another smile. Zarah soon saw enough to know Donovan already earned the seal of approval. Two hours later, the nurse had given Naomi her medication, and they crept out of the room as she dozed. He and Zarah chatted at the kitchen table, eating Miss Mildred's oxtail and beans, topped off with Devon House ice cream.

Donovan's visits increased, and it became easy to transplant their friendship into the Mona house after the miles of words they covered in the group sessions, around Baisley Park, and at New York restaurants. He was comfortable with Bradley, whose visits had increased, and it was obvious Esther had a soft spot for the man who had prepared the ground for Zarah to return home.

As they updated one another on the developments since each had made it home, Zarah learned all about how he found peace after leveling with his mother about his real reason for his temporary exit from the church and his eventual decision to abandon his studies at the seminary.

"How hard was it to tell her?" she asked.

"Not as hard as I feared. I expected shock and distress. But strangely enough, she didn't seem all that surprised. She had suspected things were not going well because I wasn't keeping in touch as usual, but she waited until I was ready to share. That was her way," he said, pride and pain in his voice.

Zarah saw how badly his mother's death had jolted him. They compared notes about her own return home, and he eyed her with pride as they spoke of more frequent heart-to-heart talks with her mother, and the progress both were making as they tried to put some of the terrible times to rest. The best part was Donovan's special way with Naomi. Grams had rallied in the weeks since being home, but when her frustration mounted, she still veered between numbing depression and fights with herself and anyone around her. Her worse moments came when the words she wanted to speak would dangle before her eyes as if within reach, and then disappear before she could form them.

Donovan read to her, or listened while Zarah did the reading, but he filled spaces no one else could. He made Grams break into laughter as he trotted out old sayings, tales of haunted houses, ghosts throwing stones on zinc roofs, dead people waltzing around abandoned houses. And like nobody else in the house, it was Donovan who could find just the right Bible verse or chorus.

Naomi had cherished the independence her good health offered, and despite living with Esther, she had done most of what she could for herself, never having to feel like a burden. Most of her life, she had enjoyed a few unremarkable pleasures: plaiting straw, shelling peas; wielding a sharp kitchen knife across slabs of meat and bundles of scallion, onion, and thyme; crumbling damp earth against her fingers and urging it around the fragile roots of whatever seemed likely to grow. A shiny needle running three strands of embroidery thread through a square of calico or Irish linen brought her inestimable joy, the rise and fall of colorful shapes bringing life to the fabric. And the solid piano keys responding to her fingers had settled her in the most anxious moments.

All that was gone now, and her immobility and helplessness were infuriating. Lately, her big triumphs were learning to button her blouse with one hand, to lift the spoon from her plate without spilling food, and to mumble one word for every ten that eluded her. It was a challenge to manage the small machine Esther had bought for her to listen to her favorite music, or the tapes that were teaching her to speak again. But she longed for her old pastimes of reading aloud for hours or reciting the psalms and her Daily Word messages. And never once did Pastor Bloomfield's harsh lessons about "speaking properly" cross her mind.

Watching Donovan and Esther chat at the kitchen counter, or take turns reading for Grams, filled Zarah with the joy she longed for during all those years when Damien had been the center of her life. *No wonder Mummy couldn't stand him; if only I'd known she was right all along.* Hesitant to risk interference, Esther withheld her judgment of Donovan, but it was there for everyone to see, and Zarah took it all in. *Mavis was right when she said a mother knows when a man, at least a boy, is no good for her daughter.* Did she dare rest her hopes on her mother being so drawn to this one now tiptoeing around their lives?

CHAPTER 55
RETURN TO THE SEASIDE

Kingston, 2003

It took over eight weeks of Donovan's visits and more coaxing from Zarah to persuade Naomi she was up to a trip out of Kingston. Then, they had to convince Esther they could manage all the preparation needed to make Naomi comfortable on a two-hour journey each way.

"It will be okay," Zarah said, "and Daddy will be with us. He can help Donovan with the driving, and I will keep Grams steady in the back seat. We have it all worked out and Grams has everything she will need in case of emergency."

As they left the early morning Kingston traffic behind and made their way on the first part of the journey, Naomi sat forward, craning her neck between Bradley and Donovan as the younger man wheedled the little Suzuki Swift along. At intervals she rested her head on Zarah's shoulder and drifted off.

Just past eight o'clock, when Ocho Rios was miles behind them, Naomi's heartbeat quickened with the realization she was on the doorstep of places she had known and loved but had not seen in the second half of her life. Over the years, Boscobel had stretched out from the main road beyond the familiar plains into the low hills and she was eager to get past the developed areas to the parts she hoped to recognize. Soon, they saw the track from the main road and the landscape changed to one resembling the Boscobel of old. Being in walking distance to the little square leading down to Miss Myrtle's alley brought her a feeling of excitement and she gestured for Donovan to slow down. The car was almost at a standstill, and Naomi peered through the window, looking for the little shop they always passed on the way to Miss Myrtle. The eyes of Bradley and Zarah followed Naomi's as she scanned the small area from where Miles had spied on her from the corners of an old school room, to where he had taught her to love him, beside the green ice cream bucket under the ackee tree. "Over there." Naomi forced the warped words out, pointing with her good fingers.

The shop wore fresh paint, and a small extension jutted out into the dirt road, where old men sat in their merinos, playing dominoes, and boom boxes blasted out dancehall music. Naomi screwed up her face, struggling to laugh out at the small boys with their bare little bottoms and squiggly penises exposed as they played without a care. It could have been a photograph Miles would have taken if he had a camera the day he walked Naomi down the alley to meet Miss Myrtle, his one-of-a-kind Grannie. New colors, new men, and new children—but the smell of fish, the salty air, and the mess of lopsided shacks against the trees and shrubs at the top of the alley were unmistakable.

"You're sure we can go down there?" Zarah asked. Both Donovan and Bradley vetoed the idea, and Naomi agreed they should leave. The feeling had come in a split second: She had seen and felt enough. Boscobel was the playground she had shared with Miles and later with a very young Esther. But her joy had been short-lived. The dryness in her throat reminded her this was also where Miles had deserted her. And not far away stood Oracabessa, site of Pearlie's pain, Naomi's dashed hopes of happiness in Pastor Bloomfield's house, his church with its message of brimstone and hellfire, and Esther's close shave with his evil—all stark reminders of too much suffering. With few exceptions, the Boscobel years were awful, and she wanted to get away.

Heading toward Oracabessa, the vehicle moved at a slow pace, Naomi's head twisting one way and another. She struggled to answer their questions, pointing out the dilapidated market and the paths leading to the river. Happy to reminisce with the newcomers, older people along the road pointed out the path to the old shop with Eudora's postal agency, and another one up to the area where Naomi guessed Eudora's house might still be. It was one she had no interest in seeing or talking about. Old houses, new fancy villas, churches, and shops dotted the landscape and Naomi became quiet again, pondering a jigsaw of memories and longing to find the spot she knew would stir fewer conflicting emotions. As they approached the main road, all the talk was about Idlewild.

"I don't see it on the map," Bradley said, "but it should be around here."

"Grams always said it was just a small strip of road with a few houses." Naomi was battling to get her words out, so Zarah handed her the notepad and pencil. "Upstairs house, Grams? You sure you remember right?" Naomi's nod was emphatic.

"But the sign over there says Galina," Donovan said, and Naomi was beside herself, for they had missed tiny Idlewild, and no one had noticed the landmark upstairs house.

"I'll turn back when I can." They made their way back along the winding road, all eyes peeled on one side or the other, looking for the missing house to help them find the clue to the Idlewild house. The blue of the sea and the sky stretched out as the little shops and houses disappeared, and the minutes sped by.

"Wait, look, Bradley shouted. The upstairs house is right over there!"

"Yes, I see it; oh my gosh, I bet it was a sight in its day," Zarah said.

Donovan slowed the car and reversed onto the strip of dirt outside the gateway.

There was no gate and no fence; just a dirt driveway between two halves of an overgrown hedge adorned with outgrowths of hibiscus, bougainvillea and wild love bush. Far in from the road, the lonely house stretched up against a backdrop of hills and sky, nestled among trees that brushed their leaves lovingly against the worn wooden walls. With its tired, rusty zinc sheets interspersed with a few newer patches, the roof looked like an oversized patchwork bedspread made of metal. The old wooden railing stretched across the upstairs veranda with its imitation fretwork curlicues broken or missing, but still a conversation piece, as they had been ever since Naomi knew herself.

Now facing the house that had been her landmark, she was no longer interested in it. Instead, her attention lingered across the street, searching for the one spot she longed to set eyes on–the old house where Bertie had taken a weary shivering Pearlie to his mother, where Pearlie had given Naomi a chance at life, and where Mr. Scott had planted her own navel-string and hibiscus tree, promising her a home of her own forever.

The old man and his coconut cart stood where Mr. Scott and his boys had built the wall of sea stones to keep Naomi and her friends safe from the main road. It was the spot where all the children gathered under the moonlight, their spindly legs dangling over the side as they counted the occasional motorcar passing by. The wall was their story-telling platform, where Naomi jumped off, running and screaming inside to Pearlie when the big boys started telling stories about ghosts and rolling calves.

The coconut vendor watched, knowing he should respect the silence of the little knot of strangers. When he thought it appropriate, he spoke to them from across the street.

"Begging pardon; is the old house yuh looking for? Mi can show yuh where it was, but bush grow over everything."

"Yes, please," Bradley said.

The old man's khaki pants stopped at his knees, and his merino danced around his frame as if it belonged to a much bigger man. His words exuded a rustic warmth and generosity that would induce anyone to follow him. The old road had transformed into a thoroughfare for tourists, well-off Jamaicans with spanking SUVs, minibuses with sound systems, and hustlers plying every kind of trade. As the vehicles swished by, the old man held up his sweaty washrag in a gesture he used several times every day. The traffic paused and they wheeled Naomi across. Bradley lifted her, and they made their way through a bushy path to the empty overgrown lot. Not a trace remained of the old house that had stood a few yards in from the road–no breadfruit or navel-string tree, no wall where the children had sat to count the few cars that passed, no shed where Naomi had slept in her bureau drawer lined with old clothes.

A tangle of unruly bushes stood where Pearlie had made jam and coconut cake, where she lived and died loving her child. Naomi fished in her purse for a handkerchief. Donovan settled the wheelchair in the clearest spot he could find, and Bradley set her down under the old beach umbrella Zarah brought.

"You were right, Grams. This is a place to see. I wish we came here before."

"Aaah, chile," was all Naomi could manage.

A little way off, Donovan announced, "All I can say is, anybody who sees a view like this can never be without hope." Zarah drew closer to him and took his hand. With her other hand, she held her father's, just in time to stop him from peeling the struggling shred of skin from his thumb.

Naomi leaned down as far as she could and reached for a handful of seaside rosemary bush; she rolled them around in her fingers and handed them to Zarah. "Wash hair." Zarah crushed the leaves between her fingers, breathing in the fragrance. No trace of McCarthy Pool was visible, and although sea-grape bushes popped up all around, there was no sign of conch shells, no guava jam bottle, no trail of red ants. But, for Naomi, it made no difference; it was sufficient knowing she was where her beloved Pearlie had found rest.

In the silence everyone allowed her, she gripped one arm of her chair, cast her eyes across the world she had known with Pearlie and the faithful Scott family, inhaling all its meaning. In garbled words, she murmured sounds made out only by Donovan who finished them for her in a voice that touched Zarah deep down. "Be still my soul, the Lord is on thy side." The waves and the wind did the rest. As Bradley lifted her, and Donovan folded her chair, her thoughts fell into Zarah's ear in a confusion of words; but they were enough to tell Zarah the message was serious. She scribbled the words and showed them to Naomi.

"Yes," Grams declared in the clearest, most definitive voice she could manage, her head bobbing up and down, and her eyes gleaming, "keep ... safe."

CHAPTER 56
BLUE BEYOND BLUE

Donovan wrapped up his mother's affairs, and only his unfinished business in the U.S. forced him to take the trip out of Jamaica. He said his goodbyes and accepted Zarah's offer to drive him to the airport. As they walked away from each other, words too basic to have ever made it to her old word wall hung between them: *Possible* and *definitely* stretched out in the unspoken sentences of their hearts. In the following days, her excitement about the job she would start within the month spared her long hours wondering what might lie ahead for them. The treasured moments with Naomi, at whose bedside she spent most of her time, helped prepare Grams for the days ahead.

Zarah's presence soon decreased; the time had come for her to return to her beloved university campus–this time as a research officer in the chemistry department. But they need not have worried about what Naomi would do without Zarah at home in those days. Since her return from Idlewild, Naomi had settled herself in a quiet space, where she relished being left with her thoughts. Sometimes she dozed off, dreaming in colors: Green was the color of her hope that Esther, Zarah, and Bradley would grab whatever happiness they could, and find an enduring peace. Purple was for Donovan, the young man she never ceased praying into Zarah's future. Blue brought back the peaceful Idlewild sky that sheltered the best years with her mother Pearlie. More than any other, it was the stark bone white that held her captive—the color of a place beyond her power to describe but one to which she felt an insistent call.

Though Miss Mildred and the nurse still buzzed around to see to her necessities, she was happiest when fumbling with her audio Bible and her tracts, spending less and less time on exercises and activities to improve her condition. She doused her young doctor's excitement about a new drug he wanted her to try. Faced with protests all around her, she was adamant. "No new treatment and the bad feelings that come with it."

Long hours found her gazing into space. When evening gave way to night, her daughter and granddaughter sat at her side, their bonds strengthened by the simple conversations Naomi wanted. Over and over, she struggled to give them "one last reminder" about the curse of enduring banana stains, and about her own fear of them during the lowest moments of her life. The difference now was her constant reassurance they had all conquered whatever curse might have followed Pearlie from the dirt-poor banana field of Oracabessa into their lives. She garbled the words, but always, they meant the same, "See? No curse can stand up to God and Mr. Time—even the stubbornest banana stain have to fade one day."

Sometimes, they sat without speaking, enveloped in sounds they had not paid attention to before: the soft fall of raindrops on oleander leaves, night winds rustling through the East Indian mango tree, the uneven cadence of Naomi's diminishing breath. Like a timepiece set to alarm once a week, she pestered Zarah with one question: Had she put up the scrap of paper on which she scribbled Naomi's words before they left Idlewild?

For the Easter weekend, Esther stocked up on bun and cheese, and Zarah printed the schedule of Sunday services Naomi would watch on the Catholic TV station. Her Easter Sunday dress waited in the closet, her hat and shoes brushed clean. Naomi had insisted on dressing to watch the service.

Outside her window, golden dots smothered the anthers of the Easter lilies, their white petals deepening to yellow and pale green on the inside. It was the hour when the first peep of sunlight nudged the day's reluctant eyes open. The dew beads glistened in the grass, and the birdsongs filled the air. Esther shouted across the space between their rooms, "Morning, Zarah, you up?"

"Getting there," came a voice still filled with sleep.

They drifted into the corridor in the same moment. Together they sensed the unusual hush—the tape recorder was silent.

Naomi had awakened just past midnight, this time sensing the arrival of the visitor stealing through the night like Nicodemus. Dying, she understood in those moments, was a quiet drifting, fading notes of her favorite hymn—no thundering roar, but a feathery murmur, like the flutter of an infant's eyelids. A breathy recital of Psalm 61, and she had gathered herself into readiness, certain and unafraid.

Zarah cupped the wrinkle-free face between her palms, wincing at its coldness as a whimper escaped. Esther stretched out her mother's elegant keyboard fingers and folded them into her own.

"You're sure?" Esther asked, surprised at Zarah's insistence.

"Yes, definitely," she said, handing her mother the crumpled paper on which she had scribbled the words Naomi had framed with such urgency on their last trip to Idlewild.

***

On the Saturday after Easter, the congregation swelled through every church door and into the corners of the St. Benedict's Church yard. The women of the Altar Guild had outdone themselves with the floral arrangements, culling white gladiola, yellow ixora, and red ginger from Naomi's garden.

Both senior and junior choirs were resplendent in blue and gold, and neither Esther nor Zarah could hold back the tears when the descant of the 23rd Psalm resounded. Deacon Larry's voice did not crack once as he read the prayer of the people, calling for the repose of Naomi's soul, and when

Father Richards spoke, murmurs of approval punctuated his glowing tribute.

Eyes searching, Zarah made her way along the center aisle in front of her mother and father, her wrists sagging with the incredible weight of the small urn bearing her Grams. Donovan craned his neck through the heads at the back where he was stuck because his flight from New York arrived late. As he found her eyes, Zarah paused, reading the message in his. Their old fears subsided, if only for those moments.

Bradley and Esther followed their daughter's eyes and gazed at the young man who had engineered Zarah's return to their fold, and they hoped he would remain in their lives. Esther rested her hand on her daughter's shoulder, and Zarah acknowledged it in the way of long ago, leaning her neck against her mother's warm fingers. In them, was the assurance she had not squandered her second chance. In them, she felt the strength that had been there all along, and she knew for certain she too had inherited it, for she came from a line of women who had often flinched before life's stern glare, but had rarely lost sight of its meaning.

***

The coconut man wore the same cut-off pants and merino. He recognized Zarah and Donovan the moment they stepped from the Suzuki Swift. Their faces wore a look he knew well; it was there in the face of Bradley. Most of all, it was in the eyes of the woman beside him, who had not been with them on the previous trip. He noticed the absence of the old woman in the wheelchair, and he knew. After a few words with Zarah, his eyes shone with understanding, and he led them through the same rough path, across which they lifted the wheelchair last time. He tipped his hat and withdrew.

Zarah led the way, uprooting clumps of rosemary with their tiny purple blooms. Around a sharp bend, the blue water shimmered, drawing them to its edges. Zarah stood between her parents. Bradley held the urn out. First Esther, then Zarah, then Bradley and Donovan tossed a handful into the blue, drifting Naomi into the wind. A whimper from Zarah drew Donovan's fingers to her cheek as he said, "You came back to her in time, and you are leaving her just where she wants to be."

All four gazed into the rippling water, its blues and greens reflecting the rays of the afternoon sun. Needing no words, they absorbed the stillness of the Idlewild Blue where Bertie rescued Pearlie, where Naomi laid her mother to rest, and where Zarah kept her promise to set Grams free.

TO BOOK CLUB MEMBERS, TEACHERS, AND READERS DISCUSSING *WHEN BANANA STAINS FADE*

I am deeply grateful and very excited that you are reading and talking about my novel. Below are a few prompts/questions that will point to key themes, character portrayals, and other features of the story. I hope you find these helpful as discussion guides.

Questions and Topics for Discussion

1. Several episodes in the novel remind us about the integral role played by elements of nature in the lives of the characters. Discuss how these are integrated into life on the island and how they function as important symbols.

2. The author portrays women as the characters on whose personalities and actions major aspects of the story turn. What are the roles and characteristics of the women?

3. How do the roles played by women compare/contrast with the roles played by major male figures?

4. The novel suggests that the passing down of erroneous beliefs and errors of judgement from generation to generation is partly responsible for cycles of conflict, dysfunctional relationships and adversity. Identify such erroneous beliefs and errors, their origins, and their impact at different stages of the narrative.

5. Sometimes, a reader's views/attitudes about major characters change as a story evolves. Which characters did you see differently at different points in the novel? Why? Which ones remained the same from start to finish? Why?

6. Why did Agatha (Pearlie's mother) believe so deeply in banana stains? How did her views affect Pearlie? What evidence do we have that Naomi inherited some of these beliefs but later modified them?

7. What impact do specific cultural and religious beliefs have on the

attitudes and actions of authority figures in church settings?

8. Throughout the story, characters refer directly or indirectly to remnants of colonial domination that have never left the island or its people. Cite examples of such remnants and identify their ongoing impact.

9. At the end of the novel, Zarah seems to stand on the brink of becoming "the right person." Discuss the events and errors that put her at risk of becoming the wrong person. Who and what helped her to change her path?

10. What is the significance of the scene in which Damien faces Zarah and her family in the lawyer's office? What evidence is presented in this scene to suggest that both he and Zarah have experienced significant change?

11. Throughout the novel, characters vary widely in their use of Standard English and Jamaican Creole. Why is the presence of both languages important? What do we learn about characters, relationships, and socio-cultural realities from the wide variations in the use of standard English and Jamaican Creole?

12. Comment on the importance of the following scenes: Esther's visit to the tea-leaf reader; Zarahs' refusal to accept the necklace from Damien in New York; Greg's death in New York; Zarah's visit to the university campus and her discovery of her special box in her new bedroom; The bird with the broken wing, Naomi's visit to the country with Zarah, Donovan, and Bradley.

13. Some characters are referred to in stories as "minor," even though they play significant roles in scenes that become turning points. Comment on the important roles that the following "minor characters" played: Miss Lucretia Bodden; the tea leaf reader, Mavis, Damien's mother.

14. "A harrowing story" but one that ends with hope and "a glorious little island [that] prevails." How accurate are these descriptions of When Banana Stains Fade"?

About the Author

Frances-Marie Coke is a lifelong educator, born in Jamaica and living in Florida. She is a writing consultant with Keiser University. After a decade as a high school teacher, she worked in human resources at a large telecommunications firm in Jamaica and later entered academia as an administrator and lecturer at the University of the West Indies, Mona, Jamaica. For decades, creative writing has been a major part of her life. Her publications include two volumes of poetry: *Intersections* published by Peepal Tree Press, Leeds, UK, and *The Balm of Dusk Lilies* published by the Jamaica Observer Literary Publications. In January 2020, her memoir, *The Spirit of Clovelly Park: Learning and Teaching at Kingston College* was published with iUniverse.

NOTE FROM FRANCES-MARIE COKE

Word-of-mouth is crucial for any author to succeed. If you enjoyed *When Banana Stains Fade*, please leave a review online—anywhere you are able. Even if it's just a sentence or two, it would make all the difference and would be very much appreciated.

Thanks!
Frances-Marie Coke